A WITNESS TO
MURDER

BOOKS BY VERITY BRIGHT

A Very English Murder
Death at the Dance

A WITNESS TO MURDER

VERITY BRIGHT

Bookouture

Published by Bookouture in 2020

An imprint of Storyfire Ltd.
Carmelite House
50 Victoria Embankment
London EC4Y 0DZ

www.bookouture.com

ISBN: 978-1-83888-757-5
eBook ISBN: 978-1-83888-756-8

To the greatest friends for cheering Eleanor and Clifford through every adventure. Thank you.

'If you tell the truth, you don't have to remember anything.'
– Mark Twain

PROLOGUE

'Welcome to Farrington Manor for our bijou soirée this evening. First listed in the official records of the Domesday Book in 1086, the Farrington Estate has only been in the hands of two families since 1463, the Farringtons having inherited it in 1657.'

Lady Farrington, Countess of Winslow, descended the gilded staircase with well-practised poise, the train of her silk gown slinking down each of the red-carpeted steps, her diamond earrings sparkling as brightly as the chandeliers that illuminated the domed ceiling above.

'Now, Clements will show you to the dining room where the fundraising evening is being held.' Her clipped voice floated down to the group milling about in the grand entrance hall, each holding a champagne flute.

'Ladies and gentlemen, this way, please.' A tall, slim-shouldered butler in an immaculate evening suit gestured for the small group to follow him. 'If you would care to leave your glasses on the tray here.'

Once the guests had left the hall, Lady Farrington scowled. 'Anna!' Her lady's maid appeared immediately. 'Bring me a cocktail. A large one!'

The butler led the group along the corridor, his highly polished shoes making no sound on the thick Wilton carpet. The party straggled along, mouths gaping open as they stared at the floor-to-ceiling portraits of the Farringtons that lined both sides of the passageway. The butler sniffed but said nothing.

As the party was too small for the main dining room, the butler ushered them into a cosier, but no less magnificent affair. Crimson and gold drapes framed a series of arched windows that ran the length of the room with classical statues set in the alcoves in between. The butler held up a hand and announced, 'May I present Mr Arnold Aris,' he looked down at a card he had pulled from his waistcoat pocket, 'Mr Ernest Carlton, Mr Vernon Peel, Mr Oswald Greaves, Mr Duncan Blewitt, Mr Stanley Morris and,' he peered hard at the card, 'Miss Dorothy Mann.'

'Finally!' Lord Farrington, Earl of Winslow, roared from the far end of the room where he'd been waiting alone with a cigar and brandy. 'I was going to start without you.' He strode over and briefly shook the first man's hand. 'Aris, you'll kick off the speeches? Lord Fenwick-Langham and his wife cancelled at the last minute.' The man nodded. Lord Farrington turned to the rest of the group. 'Take your seats, gentlemen and ladies, and don't dally on the munching, we've got a lot to get through.' Lady Farrington stepped in from one of the arched doorways and caught his eye. 'Oh yes, and it's cars and carriages on the dot of eleven. Sit!'

The canapés, duck confit and array of alcohol-drenched desserts were served and mostly cleared in a matter of forty-five minutes. Lord Farrington dinged his glass with his knife. 'Right, if anyone wants to stretch their legs or anything more pressing – the footman will show you where it is – we'll take five minutes and then have the toasts and speeches.'

There was a general pushing back of chairs as Lord Farrington came over and clapped Aris on the back. 'Right, you're up next after the toasting. Just give them a mo afterwards to quaff more champagne and brandy. That'll get them soused enough to be more generous when it comes to putting their hands in their pockets and getting their supporters to do the same.'

Aris nodded. 'No problem.'

Lord Farrington leaned in, the smoke from his cigar curling up Aris' nose. 'And keep it short, Arnold, there's a good chap.'

Lord Farrington returned to his place and tapped a wine glass with his dessertspoon. 'Ladies and gentlemen, as you know we are here to start the season with our annual fundraiser for…' He looked down at the table. Since that blasted Lord Shaftesbury had made fundraising fashionable you had to be seen to be supporting some cause or other. He had let Aris choose this year's charity, but couldn't remember now what the darned thing was called. He surreptitiously glanced at the card by his plate. 'For the Anchorage Mission of Hope and Help which,' he gave up pretending and read from the card, 'receives and assists penitent young women who have gone astray, but are otherwise of good character,' he frowned at the last part, 'whether pregnant or not.' He shook his head. *Whatever next!* 'So, dig deep and remember all that I've done for you over the years.' This received the requisite polite titter of amusement around the room. 'Before we start in on the speeches, raise your glasses, please.'

The assembled company did as they were bid and then followed the toast with the bite-sized square of chocolate fudge placed next to each plate by the footman. Lord Farrington set his glass down and a waiter immediately refilled it. 'Now, to kick off, I give you Arnold Aris, Independent Member of Parliament for Chipstone and District.' As he spoke there was a commotion at the end of the table. He turned to find the said Member of Parliament collapsed over the table.

In the ensuing shocked silence, the butler discreetly checked Aris' slumped form and then slid back round to Lord Farrington. 'Mr Aris is dead, my lord.'

'Oh, for goodness' sake!' Lady Farrington muttered to her husband. 'You do pick them, don't you!'

CHAPTER 1

'Botheration!' Lady Eleanor Swift just had time to think that this was likely to hurt, before she flew over the handlebars and landed awkwardly in a thicket of hawthorn. 'Ow!'

Whizzing down the hairpin bends at full tilt to the village of Little Buckford had seemed like a good idea when she'd mounted her bike at Henley Hall. But how was she to know that her wretched bootlace planned to spite her? And by deliberately coming undone and getting itself wrapped around the chain on the sharpest, steepest corner in the whole of the Chilterns and Cotswolds?

Eleanor cursed loudly to the hedge sparrows and blackbirds peering down at her suspiciously as she crawled out of the hawthorn. She wrenched her tangled red curls from the bushes' spiky clutches so that she could pull down her skirt that had somehow got caught over her saddle. Oh, double botheration! Inelegance personified. *You're supposed to be a lady, Ellie!*

She righted her bicycle and shook her head at the front basket twisted into the wheel. At least her dog trailer was intact, save for a slight scraping down the left side. Luckily Gladstone, her recently inherited bulldog, had chosen to forgo the wind tickling his jowls this morning and continue snoring in his comfy bed by the warm kitchen range instead. No doubt, also artfully biding his time to steal a sausage when the staff were otherwise distracted.

No stranger to misadventure, and never one to turn back, Eleanor soon had everything fixed to her satisfaction. Giving it a quick once-over, she continued with her ride down into the valley, her scraped arm haphazardly bandaged with her emerald scarf.

The good people of Little Buckford held quite a different view of her handiwork. Respectful tutting and concerned clucking followed her into every shop and offers of ointments, repairs and lifts back to Henley Hall followed her out.

'So thoughtful of you. But any damage to my bicycle, or myself, is much less serious than it looks,' she insisted at each offer. She couldn't help but marvel for the hundredth time at how these kind-hearted country folk had accepted her into their close-knit community after her recent inheritance of Henley Hall from her uncle. Even the flint walls of Little Buckford's shops and cottages felt homely to her, which she found odd. She had only visited three or four times as a child and only moved to the Hall six months ago.

Perhaps it was simply the kindness of the villagers, or maybe it was the contrast of being in one place after travelling for years? In truth, it was most likely that the gaping hole she had carried in her heart throughout her adolescence and adult life was finally beginning to heal. She had started to know what it felt like to belong.

Tuning back in to the circle of attentive faces, she pointed to the next shop front along the picturesque flint and black-beamed high street. The swinging sign above the door promised 'Penry's Butchery, the finest cuts'. 'I have only Mr Penry's fine establishment to visit and I shall be home in the shake of a lamb's tail.'

Used to her rather unorthodox behaviour, the farmers' wives merely exchanged glances and bade her farewell. She waved back, leaned her bicycle along the inside of the stonework porch of the butcher's shop and walked in, the shop's bell dinging musically.

Inside, the hum of gossip wafted over to greet her.

'I took my Johnny last week, he's been that bad, but once I'd paid me seven shillings to see the doctor, I could only afford a week's worth of medicine what he prescribed for him. Johnny's supposed to take it for at least a month, the doctor said, but where am I going to get the money for it, I asked him?'

This brought a round of indignant support. 'You should see your MP. Get him to do something.'

The lady who Eleanor assumed was Johnny's mother shook her head. 'Can't, can I? Not till they replace him.'

'Face down in his fancy pudding, I heard,' a stout middle-aged woman said, shaking her head.

The other three, who could all have been sisters, took a collective sharp breath.

'A terrible business.'

'Death so often is, dear.'

Eleanor mentally clapped her hands over her ears. She'd had enough of being caught up in deaths in the short space of time since moving to the Hall. Her wonderful staff would no doubt inform her of who had passed away and the appropriate condolences for a lady in her position would be sent in due course. It obviously wasn't anyone she knew, or Clifford, her butler, would have informed her at breakfast. Still, she thought sadly, someone will be in mourning.

'Mr Penry, good morning to you,' she called as she perused the three glass-fronted cabinets of precisely sliced meat cuts separated by thin lines of fresh green herbs.

Behind the counter, a large, ruddy man in a pristine blue and white striped apron turned and beamed a genuine welcome. The lilt of his voice was unmistakably from the other side of the Welsh border.

'Lady Swift, what a pleasure, or should I say, Lady Van Gorder?'

The whole shop laughed at his reference to the character she had played opposite him in the annual amateur dramatics performance not long back. This had been her first concerted effort to be a part of the village life and it had gone better than she had hoped.

She smiled and struck a dramatic pose, careful not to knock the neat stack of carefully-sized wrapping papers on the counter.

Penry wiped his hands on his apron. 'Now then, firstly my apologies that you've got to trouble yourself to come here for your order, although,' he scratched his head, 'a lady doing her own errands I'll never get used to, if you don't mind my remarking, m'lady. As I explained to your excellent cook, Mrs Trotman, though, my poor wife is still too laid up to make her usual deliveries and I can't leave the shop unattended.'

Eleanor frowned with concern. 'I hope she feels better soon. And really, it's never a problem to pop down—' She glanced round, her frown deepening. 'Oh gracious, I seem to have jumped the queue!' She turned to the nearest woman: 'Please do continue.'

This brought on exuberant head shaking.

'Not at all.'

'Father Time's not due at my door at all today, m'lady, there's no rush.'

Penry spread his sausage-like fingers on the counter. 'In that case, how can I be of service this delightful autumn morn? Mind, there's more than a drop of rain hanging over us, waiting to please the ducks on the village pond.'

Eleanor smiled at the image. 'Well, fortunately for our feathered friends, I don't have duck on my list today. I do, however, have many other things which the combined skill of your good self and Cook will be transformed into dishes too delicious to sample just a little of, I fear.'

'Too kind of you, m'lady, however any credit is due to Mrs Trotman working her magic in your kitchen.'

Whilst he was talking, Eleanor patted her pockets for the list entrusted to her by her housekeeper. 'In that case, might I trouble you for these, ah... I appear to have dropped the, er, list through the tiny hole in my skirt pocket.'

Penry chuckled. 'Oh dear, oh dear, but never mind. What say between us we conjure up something of a menu that won't cause too much consternation and difficulty in the kitchen?'

Eleanor nodded with relief.

Penry counted out on his fingers. 'Now then, it is Monday, and a full roast on Sunday… and probably game pie on Saturday, am I right?'

Eleanor's face creased in confusion. 'Frighteningly so. How on earth do you…?'

'Ah, it is a professional tradesman's business to know pertinent facts about his customers, m'lady.'

Still baffled, Eleanor listened to him rattle off a series of suggestions for the remainder of the week. She nodded dumbly as he concluded with something about a special pork loin to go with the forthcoming apple sauce.

'Delightful, I'm sure. Thank you, Mr Penry. I didn't realise you were branching out into homemade sauces.'

He leaned forward slightly. 'We do forget sometimes that you're new to the village, m'lady The sauce will be from the apple harvest, as is tradition.'

'Oh yes, yes, of course, silly me!' More baffled than ever, she did her best to wait patiently as the butcher created a mountain of beautifully wrapped parcels, each labelled with a day of the week.

'So kind, but might I trouble you for one more thing?'

The twittering further along the counter, which had turned back to the original gossiping, halted instantly as ears wagged once again.

'Anything at all.' Penry threw his arms wide. 'Name your poison.'

'Actually, I'd like to buy a jolly long length of your parcel string, please. But not a word to Mr Clifford.'

Penry laughed hard enough for his sturdy shoulders to shake. 'Celtic honour, m'lady, your secret will be safe with me.' He slid his eyes towards the women and gave them a subtle shrug. Then he tilted his head slightly at Eleanor. 'But my curiosity might eat me up and as you can see, I can barely afford to lose a pound.'

She laughed. 'Let's just call it an unladylike spot of bicycle bother.'

'Ah, say no more, my lady. Understood. Take the rest of the roll, I have more.'

'Gracious, thank you, but mightn't you run out?'

To Eleanor's ears, Penry's lilt seemed to thicken as he dismissed her concern with a wave of his hand and a broad smile. 'As we say in the valleys, everything you have in this world is just borrowed for a short time.'

His parting words were flowing lightly round Eleanor's mind as she emerged from the shop only to find the promised rain had arrived. Taking advantage of the shop's porch, she balanced the bags Penry had packed for her along the bicycle's frame whilst she made room in her trailer. Through the half-open door, the gossip resumed.

'Not a day over forty, I'd say he was.'

Eleanor shivered and mentally counted her blessings.

'They've dismissed her, you know.'

'I heard the police questioned her for an hour!'

'But even if they don't press charges, where'll she ever find another position with that hanging over her?'

'It must have been an accident. Who'd want Mr Aris dead?'

Eleanor had heard enough, but suddenly she froze. *Had she misheard that name?*

Johnny's mother spoke again. 'Mr Aris did a lot for our area, no question. His wife must be distraught.'

The voices moved away, leaving Eleanor shaking her head. She hadn't known Aris well, but she'd been at a dinner party with him and his wife only a few days before hosted by her friends, Lord and Lady Fenwick-Langham. He'd seemed an odd mixture of bull-headed politician and sympathetic women's rights supporter.

His wife hadn't said much. Eleanor had the impression that she was only there to support her husband. She sighed. *Poor woman!* Condolences needed to be at the very top of her list, just as soon as she had beaten the darkening clouds back to Henley Hall.

CHAPTER 2

On the pavement, Eleanor set to work weaving a 'that'll-do' patch to her basket and lashing it more securely to her handlebars with the string Mr Penry had given her.

With everything as shipshape as it was likely to get, she gave a mighty heave and backed her bike onto the cobbled street.

From behind, she heard the unmistakable rattle of milk bottles bouncing in their wooden crates. She straightened up and turned to see twinkling hazel eyes under a mop of red-brown curls.

'Good morning, Lady Swift. What a fine day we've not been promised.'

Eleanor smiled. 'Good morning. Mr Stanley, isn't it?'

'Close enough, Stanley Wilkes, m'lady, at your service.'

'Forgive me, I've only met you once at the back door of Henley Hall and I have a terrible memory for names.'

'No matter there. Most folks call me Milky.' He grinned and thumbed the collar of his blue and white overcoat as he leaned in to whisper, 'Not very imaginative, but 'tis a tiny village.'

She whispered back, 'You're not a Buckford man then?'

'Me? I'm not even a Buckinghamshire man!'

She gave a mock intake of breath. 'Don't you fear being burned at the stake one dark Lammas Eve by an angry rabble waving pitchforks?'

Stanley guffawed. ''Tis a worry every August first, but I've made it through another year unscathed as the offcomer from afar. Mind, there's always Bonfire Night to watch out for. I'll be sure to lock my doors come dusk on November fifth.'

Eleanor smiled at his effortless charm. 'What nonsense! I'm a total interloper and yet we've both been taken in wonderfully by the Little Buckfordites, haven't we?'

'That we have, m'lady.'

Two ladies passed them, their heads bent together conspiratorially. Eleanor just caught their words.

'Reckon they'll have another election soon now poor old Aris is gone. How are we going to vote?'

'What do you mean? You know as well as I do, if you bother to vote, you'll vote the same way as your husband, and so will I. Anyway, that's not what I meant. I heard Aris' death might not have been entirely natural, if you get my drift…'

They faded out of hearing. Ellie shook her head. *Gossip!* Although she was partial to it, she was trying to stay away from anything that might get her mixed up with any more murder cases. She held her hand out and watched a few fat drops of rain fall into it.

'I imagine the weather is better for you, Mr Wilkes, now that we're out of that scorching summer? For your milk deliveries, I mean.'

He nodded. 'There's less worry of it curdling, for sure. Less trouble for my customers with the birds too, of course.'

She had grown up in the wilder, woolier parts of the world, with most of nature trying to eat her, so this sounded rather quaint. 'The birds?'

Stanley's eyes twinkled. 'Can't blame the kids, really. Those cardboard tops on the milk, "pogs" they call them, keep the birds off, but the kids creep up and take the cardboard tops for their collection, see. That's when the birds have a field day. Blue tits, they're the main culprits, just mad for the cream they are.'

'I had no idea of the peculiarities of nature you have to contend with, Mr Wilkes.'

'Makes for interest, as they say, m'lady.' He nodded at her trailer. 'Now, at the risk of speaking out of turn, that's a fair bit of weight there you'll be needing to haul up the hill. Can I play the role of gentleman and take it for you?'

'Gracious, that is kind, but I'm quite self-sufficient, really.'

'So I've heard, m'lady.'

His comment surprised her, but his smile was genuine as it reached up to his twinkling eyes. He lowered his voice. 'If you can keep a secret, I have a date with your wonderful Mrs Butters on the back step of Henley Hall in about forty minutes. Can you believe your own housekeeper left me a billet-doux in a milk bottle?'

Eleanor's curiosity got the better of her. 'Gracious, really! Whatever did it say?'

Stanley leaned in. 'Six pints and a large pot of cream.'

Eleanor laughed. 'Outrageous! I shall have words with Mrs Butters. And as to your kind offer, do you know I would be most grateful. I have purchased rather a lot and been given more and… well, the details don't matter.'

'Fair play to you. I can put your trailer over there by shifting the empty crates and I'll deposit it all safe and shipshape with the notorious Mrs Butters, how's that sound? There's room for yourself and the bicycle too, if you wish.'

'Just the trailer would be perfect, thank you. I definitely need some fresh air to blow away the cobwebs.'

Eleanor waved as she rode off, unencumbered, determined to get to the Hall ahead of him and leave a gift with her housekeeper to give him for his kind gesture.

She wondered if she ought to have given some sort of hand signal as she'd pulled away. The government had just made hand signals compulsory for all drivers and she figured it wouldn't be long until they introduced them for cyclists. *Honestly, Ellie, once those politicians start legislating, they don't know where to stop!*

Setting a steady pace, she soon rounded the end of the high street and took the right fork that ran alongside the village common. Lines of beech, the county's favourite tree, added swathes of autumnal yellow, gold and bronze to the otherwise green vista. A single quack from the pond made her look over. She noted the wilting bulrushes that had stood so proudly throughout the hot months, their velveteen ends looking so soft and inviting. Now the clumps had a forlorn and bedraggled air. The season had definitely turned. Summer was through for another year.

The overheard conversation in the shop came back to her: 'Not a day over forty, I'd say he was.' The shiver that ran down her spine made her handlebars wobble. Today of all days, she had been determined not to think about death, or the passing of time. For today was the 18 October 1920, the twentieth anniversary of her parents' disappearance. The grief had finally eased as she reached her twenties. The regret of not knowing what had happened, however, stayed with her, even though she was now twenty-nine.

Come on, Ellie. You've dealt with this before! Giving her legs an extra turn of speed, she began the long, tortuous three-mile climb up to Henley Hall. Here, she knew one of the staff would make a greatly exaggerated display of his disapproval at her state and the others would fuss over her scratched arm and mend her torn clothes as much as her mother used to.

Eleanor shook her head to dislodge more unwanted thoughts. Her mother's nightly words leaped into her mind: 'Don't forget to count all your silver linings as you fall asleep, darling.' The memory brought a smile to Eleanor's face and banished the icy chill creeping in with the rain. She set to cycling up the steep hill with renewed energy as she resolved to do just that.

But where to start? Compared to only last year, life was looking so much better. She nodded and mentally ticked off the lengthy list of blessings as she crawled past the hedgerows. Her staff were loyal and caring. Henley Hall was a beautiful, if enormous, home. Clifford, the butler she had also inherited, kept everything running in impeccable order, which she was grateful for. And then there was that restless feeling that had driven her to distraction, the one that had told her for years that putting down roots would only lead to heartache. That had diminished, and she had managed tentative steps at building relationships.

Ah, that thought conjured up an image of another silver lining, a certain dashing gentleman. Despite breathing hard over the steepness of the rise, she felt her face split into a wide grin. Lancelot, or 'young Lord Fenwick-Langham' as Clifford referred to him, had caught her eye and awoken a longing. One she had buried ever since her ex-husband had turned out to be as trustworthy as a jackal. She was even on first-name terms with Lord and Lady Langham, Lancelot's parents.

She stood up out of the saddle, pushing hard on the pedals to conquer the bend where she had fallen off on her way to the village. Despite the steep incline, without her trailer and shopping she felt like she was flying up the hill. *Oh, don't forget Gladstone in your list of blessings, Ellie!* She now shared her wonderful new home with the silliest, soppiest bulldog that had ever been born. Ball-mad, sausage-obsessed, 'Master Gladstone' was loved by all the staff and already devoted to her. Whoever said diamonds were a girl's best friend clearly hadn't received happy bulldog kisses in bucketloads. She pictured him lying on his back on his quilted bed next to the kitchen range, the ladies working round him, his contented snores filling the room.

The image of the driven young woman who had travelled solo across some of the harshest terrain imaginable popped into her head. Was that really 'Old Ellie' as she now thought of herself back then? 'Back then' being only a matter of ten months.

She laughed. One thing remained the same: she was still no good at doing nothing. She loved her new life, but since inheriting her uncle's estate, she really had no need to do anything except play at being Lady of the Manor. That ignited something that had lain dormant for years, the excitement she had shared with her parents over their projects to support struggling communities around the world. Their work had taken them to dangerous places, yet young as she was when it all stopped so abruptly, she'd recognised even then how it had fulfilled them.

She nodded to herself. *That's what's missing, Ellie. You need to do something that matters, like my mother and father did. Something that changes things for others.*

'Yes!' she wheezed aloud, grinding up the last cruel rise of the hill. What a wonderful epiphany to reach on the anniversary of her parents' disappearance and one that dissolved her wistfulness for what might have been, had they still been around. She blew a kiss heavenwards.

CHAPTER 3

The wind seemed to be at Eleanor's back as she flew under the arch of Henley Hall's imperious gates. She sped on down the half-mile driveway, delighting in the lines of rustling London Planes, their now-russet leaves no longer reminding her of the end of summer. It was a new season, a new beginning. New Ellie was ready to burst forth! Thus it was that she arrived at the entrance to Henley Hall in great, if rain-soaked, spirits, her cheeks flushed with more than just exertion.

As if by an unseen force, the front door opened as she whizzed across the semi-circular drive with its central fountain.

'Ah, Clifford, good timing.' She braked hard, sending a small shower of gravel over his impossibly shiny shoes as he closed the gap to her front wheel.

'My lady.' Eleanor's butler gave his customary half-bow and took the handlebars of her bicycle as she dismounted. 'Forgive my observation, but perhaps you have returned with less than you set out with this morning. Was your shopping trip entirely unsuccessful?'

'Not a bit, actually. Aside that is from returning minus a patch of skin on my arm, a trifling section of my skirt and some unnecessary attachments for my bicycle basket.'

Clifford's gaze went from the bicycle to her dishevelled appearance. 'My error, my lady, I erroneously thought you had also left with some decorum this morning.' He winked.

Eleanor tried to hide a smile. The only thing more unorthodox than her at Henley Hall was her late uncle's butler. As much at home handling an armed assassin as uncorking a vintage bottle of the rarest Romanée-Conti, he'd been her uncle's batman, servant and friend for over thirty years. Tasked by her uncle on his deathbed with looking after his beloved niece's happiness and safety, he fulfilled his duty with a mixture of impeccable butlering, dry wit and steel resolve.

She pulled a face. 'Very droll! I may have had a slight altercation with a hawthorn hedge, that's all. And it came off worse, I assure you. Now, let's get out of this rain. I'm already soaked, but there's no point in you being the same.' He half-bowed and wheeled her bicycle towards the garages. 'Sorry about the shoes,' she mumbled.

Inside, Mrs Butters, her housekeeper, bustled down the hallway to meet her. With her diminutive frame and homely figure, topped off by plenty of smile lines and a motherly air, Eleanor invariably wanted to hug her on sight. She refrained, however, as she had already crossed the line between the lady of the house and the servants on numerous occasions.

'My lady, I hope your ride was enjoyable? Oh, but you're soaked. And you've been fighting with the spikiest of hedgerows again, it seems. And perhaps His Majesty's jury might be out on who won this time?'

Eleanor chuckled. 'Well, looking on the bright side, I shan't need to apologise for causing you more work as I've done on occasion.' She gestured at the long tear in her skirt. 'My favourite member of my wardrobe is no more. Silly of me to wear it on my bicycle.'

'Oh, I don't think we will send out the funeral cards for it quite so soon, my lady. Shall we get you dried off and your arm fixed up and then I'll see what we can do with your poor skirt? By tomorrow, no one will know you and the hedge ever came to blows.'

'Except every member of the village who has just trailed me in and out of the shops, offering sympathy and safety pins.'

Her housekeeper chuckled and took Eleanor's hat and coat.

'Oh gracious, Mrs Butters, I almost forgot two very important things! A small task for you, if I might ask, and one for Clifford.'

'Anything at all, my lady, what is it I can do for you?'

'A half bottle of brandy, please, to be given to the milkman.' She watched her housekeeper's eyebrows rise to her hairline.

'Milky Wilkes?'

'That's him.'

'Very good.' She turned to go, but paused. 'Forgive me, but I think tongues might begin to wag.'

Eleanor winked at her. 'I do believe, Mrs Butters, that they already have.'

Fifteen minutes later, Eleanor had changed into comfortable trousers and a matching cosy, sage cardigan with three-quarter-length sleeves over a cream silk blouse. There was a clatter of a tray being set down outside the morning room door and the sound of muttering. Ah, that would be her maid bringing the tea. Eleanor smiled. She appreciated her staff enormously and constantly marvelled at how so few kept the Hall running to such a high standard.

'Come in, Polly,' she called.

The door swung open, banging against the wall and bouncing back onto Polly's head as she bent to retrieve the tray from the floor.

'Morning again, your ladyship.' The young girl gave an awkward curtsey on her gangly fifteen-year-old legs. 'I was going to knock, honestly.'

'Thank you, Polly. Gosh, those pastries look delightful!' Eleanor clapped her hands. 'I'm quite famished after my bicycle ride.'

'Mrs Trotman said as to tell you,' the maid stared at the ceiling for a moment, 'that the twists are pear and walnut with sultanas and the turnovers are brandied apple and elderfl— No, elderberry.'

Eleanor gestured to the coffee table between the two cream damask sofas, adroitly moving the framed photograph of her late uncle with his beloved bulldog from harm. 'There, a little more room. How's that?'

'Just wonderful, thank you.' Polly set the tray down and then stared in dismay at the splash of spilt tea on the tray. Her chin fell to her chest, her voice a tiny whisper. 'I am trying really hard, your ladyship, really, really hard.'

Fearing tears, Eleanor patted the girl's shoulder. 'I know you are, Polly. That is why I asked that you be charged with the very tricky task of bringing my tea. I think you've done a wonderful job.'

Polly peeped up, looking somewhat unconvinced. Eleanor noticed her eyes settle on the bandage poking from her sweater sleeve. 'You'll never guess what happened this morning, Polly? My shoelace betrayed me and caused me to fall off my bicycle into a hawthorn hedge with...' she leaned in '...my skirt up over the saddle of my bicycle!'

The maid's hands flew to her mouth. 'Your ladyship, you must have been all of a show, with everything out for all the world to see!'

Eleanor nodded. 'It was very unladylike, Polly. I was hanging over my bicycle with my behind stuck out like an archer's target.'

The young girl's horror switched to hysteria as she giggled behind her hands. 'So sorry, your ladyship, but that is a funny picture, isn't it?' She tailed off, eyes wide with fear she'd overstepped the line, again.

'No, Polly, it wasn't funny, it was hilarious. Thankfully, there was no one to see, just the hedgerow birds.'

'Poweee! You were born lucky this morning, your ladyship.'

Eleanor smiled as the young girl left, appreciating her delightful innocence and genuine wish to do her best.

*

In the morning room, Eleanor caught up with Mrs Butters.

'Ah good, so Mr Wilkes made it up with all my shopping then. Was the brandy well received?'

She stopped, surprised by the bright flush to her housekeeper's cheeks. Perhaps Stanley Wilkes hadn't been far off with his description of the doorstep milk order being a billet-doux?

She fell into a daydream about a certain young gentleman writing her billets-doux. Since her parents' disappearance, withdrawing into her own world had become her way of coping. The staff had got used to it and waited patiently for her to emerge again. After a moment or two, she realised Mrs Butters was looking at her quizzically.

Eleanor shook her head. 'Speaking of sausages,' – which no one had been – 'where is our oh-so lazy bulldog? He greeted me when I came in, but now he's abandoned me!'

Mrs Butters shook her head. 'He's trotting round the orchard, helping Joseph collect the apples.'

'Oops, no apple jam this year then!'

'Don't worry, my lady, there'll be plenty spare and, of course, we'll have to purchase some from the village.'

Eleanor was confused. 'Will we? But why? We've a whole heap of our own apple trees.'

''Tis the way, my lady.'

'Ah, yes, naturally.' Eleanor shook her head. 'I'm trying really hard to get the hang of how things are done here, but sometimes…' She held her hands up.

Mrs Butters gave her a reassuring smile. 'And doing a wonderful job, seeing as you was brought up abroad, my lady. Country ways can be mighty confusing for folk who aren't from round these parts. Although,' she added hastily, 'the few times they let you out of that boarding school, you spent the summer here at the Hall, so I think that makes you an honorary local lass.' She turned to leave and stopped. 'Oh, by the by, Mr Clifford mentioned that he has some papers for you, my lady, something that needs your attention.'

'Sounds frightfully dull, but please do send him along when ready.'

Eleanor jumped as a quiet cough came from the doorway.

'Mrs Butters, please add one essential item to my next shopping list,' she said good-humouredly.

'Of course, my lady, what will it be?'

'A large cowbell for Mr Clifford.'

After a quick curtsey, Mrs Butters ducked out of the room, avoiding her gaze, her chuckle echoing down the hall.

Eleanor turned to him.

'I see you come prepared with a raft of letters and the household accounts, Clifford. How large is the heap of ugly tripe I must wade through this morning? Maybe I should have worn my wellington boots?'

He gave her that look she had yet to fathom, the one that made her doubt if he did have a sense of humour. She suddenly remembered the overheard gossip from the shop.

'Before we start, I heard something distressing in the village this morning.'

'Yes, my lady?'

'It—'

The chime of the doorbell interrupted her.

CHAPTER 4

The drawing room's gilded mantelpiece clock struck the quarter hour as Eleanor entered. Her visitor, sitting stiffly in a high-waisted blue wool suit, jumped like a scalded kitten. In her late thirties, she patted her mouse-brown hair, tucking a stray strand back into the tight chignon at her neck.

'I am sorry to call unannounced, Lady Swift.'

'No trouble,' Eleanor said. 'Ah, here is the tea. Please do pour, Clifford.'

Whilst Clifford engaged her visitor in deciding on milk and sugar, Eleanor stole another glance at the woman's calling card: 'Miss Dorothy Mann, Women's League' was handwritten in neat but spiky strokes.

With the ceremony of tea serving done, Clifford melted into the rear of the room, correctly interpreting Eleanor's nod as 'stay here, I may need rescuing!'

Eleanor wiggled backwards into the deep seat of the button-backed cream and silver striped settee, balancing her cup. 'So, Miss Mann, to what do I owe the pleasure?'

'No, the pleasure is mine, Lady Swift. You see, I am here officially, as it were, as a, er... representative of the Chipstone area Women's League. I've been sent along with a... a proposition.'

A proposition? Eleanor blinked. 'I'm confused, but intrigued. Please do continue.'

Miss Mann took a deep breath.

'As I'm sure you know, your local Member of Parliament was Mr Aris.'

'Indeed. I met him and his wife recently at a dinner and was saddened to hear this morning of his passing.'

Miss Mann took a sip of her tea. 'Well, since Mr Aris' recent, and—'

'Oh gracious, are you alright?'

Clifford stepped forward with a glass of water to ease the woman's sudden and violent spluttering as Eleanor slapped her back.

Red-eyed and flame-cheeked, the woman gulped air as if she'd been locked in a box for a month. 'Oh dear, how unladylike! I do apologise, Lady Swift. I fear my tea went down the wrong way.' She sat up straight, coughed and swallowed hard. 'I'm fine now, thank you. Er, where was I?'

Eleanor handed the water back to Clifford. 'Mr Aris' recent demise?'

'Oh, yes. Due to Mr Aris' recent, and unexpected, demise, there will be a by-election shortly. Mr Aris was an independent MP, and quite sympathetic to our cause. We now have the opportunity to put forward an independent candidate ourselves.'

Eleanor nodded. 'I see.' She recalled the snippets of conversation she'd heard in the village.

'Lady Swift, times are changing. Only this month the first women were admitted to study for full degrees in the hallowed halls of the University of Oxford, no less.'

Eleanor nodded. 'I know, I read that the ladies who studied previously but weren't permitted to receive degrees have recently been allowed to do so retrospectively.'

Miss Mann nodded back. 'Exactly, but change is slow and unequal. The Representation of the People Act two years ago may have given some women the right to vote, but the true legacy is a greater divide between men and women.' Her pale cheeks flushed.

'How can it be correct that women need to be of thirty years of age, yet men over twenty-one are eligible? It is disgraceful!'

'Naturally, I agree. Despite inheriting Henley Hall, I myself do not have the vote for that very reason, but change takes time,' Eleanor said. 'And with ladies like yourself dedicating yourselves to the cause...'

Her visitor put her cup down. 'Oh dear, my apologies, but unless our candidate is successful, there will be no one who will champion women's issues in the area.'

'Absolutely! And you could count on my vote, only as I said, I'm not allowed to vote. Rather ironic. Who, by the way, is your candidate?'

Miss Mann leaned forward eagerly.

'That's just it, Lady Swift, we know we have found the perfect person. We are all very excited about it. It will be a landmark event.' She cleared her throat. 'What do you think?'

'Well, I wish you every success. What name shall I look out for in the canvassing literature I am sure will soon flood in?'

'Lady Swift.'

'Yes?'

'No, I mean, Lady Swift. Or gracious, perhaps you prefer to be addressed differently?'

Eleanor scratched her head. 'Miss Mann, forgive me but we may have our wires crossed?'

Behind her, Clifford gave the softest of coughs. Eleanor stared at him and then back at her visitor perched on the edge of her seat, expectation consuming her face. The penny dropped.

'Me! You want me to stand?' Eleanor sat back in her chair, feeling winded.

Miss Mann nodded vigorously. 'Why, yes! Forgive the direct-ness of my observation, but you are considered to be a progressive woman. Just imagine what that would do for the local population and women's rights. The first female MP in the Chilterns and Cotswolds. Indeed, the first British-born woman MP!'

Eleanor's mind jumped to the euphoria she had felt at the end of her ride. Hadn't she only recently decided that on the anniversary of her parents' disappearance she needed to follow in their footsteps? *But politics!* Eleanor shuddered. It would be like putting a chicken in a fox pen, if there was such a thing.

Miss Mann was right, she was a progressive woman for 1920. She had cycled around the world (although she wasn't the first), and earned her living working in South Africa as a trailblazer for Thomas Walker, the foremost travel company of the day. She prided herself on being fearless in the face of wild animals, belligerent officials and treacherous terrain because she was in her element.

Since returning to England and polite society, however, she'd found herself completely out of her depth. Entering politics with its backstabbing, double standards and archaic traditions would undoubtedly see her sink without a trace. She needed help, and fast. She stared at Clifford, but he pretended to be busy examining his cuffs.

Her words tumbled out. 'But I can't be an MP, I'm titled. Surely that precludes such things? Clifford, you're a walking encyclopaedia, please back me up.'

He stepped forward again. 'Apologies, my lady, but you may stand despite your title. Nobility of the Irish Peerage have always been able to sit in the House of Commons. The 1801 Act of Union creating the United Kingdom did not give them the right to sit in the House of Lords, but did not exclude them from sitting in the Lower House. The well-known prime minister from the 1800s, Lord Palmerston, was such a titled Irish lord who sat in the House of Commons.'

Eleanor stared at her butler. *Had he lost his senses?* 'That's all very splendid, Clifford, but I don't happen to be Irish nobility.' She smiled apologetically at her visitor, who seemed suspiciously unmoved by the information.

Clifford coughed gently. 'Actually, my lady, your late uncle, Lord Henley, held a second title, which has also passed to you. That of a small baronetcy in West Ireland which would permit you to enter Parliament, although you may have to renounce your English title.'

'Right, I see…' She wasn't that surprised. Since coming to Henley Hall, Clifford regularly informed her of some strange legacy of her late uncle that he hadn't seen fit to make her aware of before. Her brow furrowed. Clifford was a veritable library on legs, but even for him that reply had suggested a degree of research before the fact. And to give up her title? It wasn't that she cared much for titles, but carrying the family name of Swift gave her a connection to her parents she didn't want to lose.

She looked back at Miss Mann. 'Well, that, er… obstacle seems to be surmountable.' She took a deep breath. 'However, I'm really sorry, but I am not in any way sure I am the woman for the job. I am not designed to be a political animal. I truly fear that I would do you, and your cause, a disservice if I said yes.'

Her visitor's face fell. 'But, Lady Swift, we are counting on you.'

'And so you may for anything I can do to help. Except actually stand as a candidate in this by-election.'

She rose.

Miss Mann rose too. 'Please reconsider. The future of woman-kind in this area is in your hands. We have until tomorrow afternoon to register a candidate. Please, at least consider it until then?'

At the back of Eleanor's mind a small voice was telling her she was about to break her recent promise to herself. She sighed. 'Alright, I'll consider your offer and give you my answer tomorrow.'

By the time Clifford returned from showing Miss Mann out, Eleanor had worn a clear path in the deep-pile patterned rug.

'How curious!'

'Curious, my lady?'

'No, you're right.' She nodded thoughtfully. 'That was dashed peculiar.'

He looked blank.

'Oh, come on! Surely you didn't wake this morning imagining I wonder if her ladyship will choose to stand for Parliament today?'

'Not on first arising, my lady.'

She scanned his face, but infuriatingly, his expression gave nothing away.

'However, you seem to have spent the morning reading up on obscure laws to facilitate just such an eventuality!'

Clifford coughed. 'Actually, my lady, you are correct.'

She spun round. 'Clifford! Don't expect me to believe that you anticipated Miss Mann's visit?'

'Naturally not. I rang her and suggested it after you left to run your errands.'

She collapsed back onto the sofa and fixed him with a questioning stare.

Clifford ran his finger along his starched white collar. 'This morning, I learned of Mr Aris' demise. Too late, unfortunately, to pass on the news.' *That explained it*, thought Eleanor. Clifford continued: 'I knew that a by-election would be called and that Mr Aris was the only man of any standing in the area who was sympathetic to the issue of women's rights. Therefore, I deduced that the Women's League would have to look to a woman as a candidate. If you'll excuse my presumption, my lady, you were the obvious choice.'

Eleanor threw her hands up. 'Clifford, I know we've only known each other for a little under a year, but I thought you understood me fairly well. How can you suggest that I am "the obvious choice"?'

Clifford coughed gently. 'Perhaps you are right. The young lady who first arrived at the Hall would certainly not have been an obvious choice, but…' He cleared his throat. 'When you returned from your ride to the village earlier, your usual enthusiasm was infused with such animation, I concluded that you had, perhaps, been considering a… change?'

'Clifford… I…' She blushed. 'I didn't realise you could see the inner workings of my mind as clearly as you understand the mechanics of the Rolls.'

An awkward silence hung in the air. Clifford adjusted his cuff-links. Eleanor straightened the buttons on her cardigan to line up with each other. 'Oh, dash it!' she burst out. 'Yes, you're right.'

He nodded. 'I was hopeful. Given the date, of course.'

A lump jumped into Eleanor's throat. Her words came out close to a whisper. 'You mean… you realised that today is the twentieth anniversary of my parents' disappearance?'

He nodded. 'It has been on my mind for a great many weeks, my lady.'

Lost for words, tears prickled behind her eyelids. 'That means a great deal,' she managed. 'And perhaps, Clifford, perhaps one day you might tell me more about my uncle. I've always had such a jumble of thoughts, but so few memories of him to make any sense of things.'

'With pleasure, my lady.' He tidied the tea tray. More, she thought, for something to occupy his hands than to ensure the milk jug lined up with the teapot and the sugar bowl. 'However,' he continued, 'a rather timely, if assisted, visit from Miss Mann, one might conclude? Perhaps, your ladyship, you might reconsider her proposal?'

She shook her head. 'Oh, Clifford, I'd love to, but have you seen a fish hooked out of water and hurled three miles inland? Because that would be me trying to make it in the murky world of politics. Bad smell and all. You probably haven't noticed, but I'm not brilliant at saying and doing the right thing.'

She glanced at him.

'No, don't, that was a rhetorical question. I suspect, if I did say yes to the Women's League, it would quickly end in an unladylike row. They would certainly end up disowning me, which would hardly further the cause of women in any form of a positive light. And, as I keep being reminded by all the faux pas I make, I'm still very much the new girl in town with little grip on how things work here. The few summers I spent here as a child don't qualify me as being "local". I have absolutely no clue what the good ladies of the area really want, or need. All in all, I'm convinced it would be a truly terrible idea to accept this proposition.'

Clifford bowed his head. 'Artfully won, my lady, if I may say so.'

She frowned. 'Won, Clifford?'

'The argument with yourself. It is not often easy to find so many reasons against oneself.'

Eleanor felt a flush of heat rush up her neck. *Is that the real reason, Ellie? Are you just trying to wriggle out of being the one to step up?*

She stood up. 'I'll sleep on it. It's the best I can do. I would never forgive myself if I rushed into this and ended up making things worse for everyone.'

'Indeed, my lady.' Clifford picked up the tea tray and then turned back to her. 'But there is a further complication whether you decide to accept Miss Mann's offer or otherwise that I have not yet had time to inform you of.'

CHAPTER 5

Eleanor followed Clifford into the kitchen, where she was surprised to see a woman she judged to be in her mid-fifties, in a woollen shawl, sitting at one of the high-backed chairs. Salt and pepper hair that had slid out of the bun on top of her head framed her pale and puffy face like a broad-brimmed hat.

'Ladies.' Clifford nodded to Mrs Trotman, Mrs Butters and the mystery visitor, who had all jumped up as Eleanor entered the room. Polly let the saucepan she was scrubbing slide into the water and hastily dried her hands on her apron.

Eleanor smiled round the kitchen. 'Good afternoon, everyone.' At the sound of her voice, Gladstone opened his eyes and lolloped out of his cosy bed and leaned against her legs so she could ruffle his ears. 'Hello, my friend. Had a pleasant lie-in after helping Joseph collect all those apples?' she whispered.

'My lady.' Clifford stepped forward and gestured to the stranger amongst the group. 'This is Mrs Martha Pitkin.'

'Delighted.' Eleanor smiled cordially, noticing the red rims of the woman's watery blue eyes.

'Your ladyship.' Mrs Pitkin gave a stiff-legged curtsey. 'So sorry to disturb you.' With a stifled sob, she pulled a handkerchief from the sleeve of her cotton blouse.

Eleanor was at a loss and stared at Clifford, who gestured discreetly to the three staff that they should leave the room.

Mrs Butters ushered Polly over towards the back door. 'Fresh pot of tea and shortbread's finished cooling, already on the table, Mr Clifford.'

Mrs Trotman hung her apron on the hook by the range and gave Mrs Pitkin's arm a squeeze on the way out to join the others. The door closed quietly behind her.

Unsure of the correct protocol, Eleanor gestured to the chair Mrs Pitkin had risen from. 'Please do take a seat. How about a cup of tea?'

'Goodness, sitting in front of a mistress of the house is bad enough but drinking tea with your ladyship, I couldn't!'

'Well, I'm absolutely parched,' Eleanor lied, trying to put the obviously flustered woman at her ease. 'Besides, the walls of this kitchen might have seen me sharing tea with the ladies on more than one occasion but no one has found out yet, so we should be fine.'

'Very kind, m'lady, but I do beg your pardon for even being here without your permission and all, it ain't right.'

'Really, don't worry about it.' Eleanor nodded to Clifford to pour them all tea. 'Mrs Pitkin, am I right in thinking that you are a friend of Mrs Trotman's?'

'Oh yes, m'lady, she's been a ducky to me since forever. She was very good to me years back, you see, when my mother got taken into the mental asylum, God bless her, and we've been friends ever since.' She wiped her eyes with her handkerchief. 'That's why I came here…' Her head fell to her chest with a sob. Gladstone gave a soft whine and padded round to her side. He laid his head in her lap. She ran her hand down his back, a tear plopping onto his nose.

Eleanor pushed a cup of tea closer to Martha. 'Now, now, take a sip and have a bite of shortbread, I insist.'

Mrs Pitkin accepted her tea with a trembling hand and gave a wan smile. 'Bit more together now, m'lady, so sorry.'

'Good, but there's no need to apologise. Firstly, any friend of Mrs Trotman's is welcome at Henley Hall, it is home to all of us, after all.'

'Mrs Trotman has said many times as how kind-hearted you are.'

'Thank you, and I have to say the same about Mrs Trotman and all the ladies. Secondly, though, you seem to be struggling with something. Did you come to ask for my help?'

'Oh no! Goodness me, that would be a fine thing. A ragged old cook approaching a lady of the house like yourself for help, especially a domestic who's gotten herself into such trouble. Oh, lummy!' This brought on more tears and sniffling in the handkerchief. 'I came because I didn't know where to go and Mrs Trotman—'

Clifford gave a quiet cough. 'Perhaps I might assist, Mrs Pitkin?' She nodded gratefully and took a gulp of her tea.

'Very good.' Clifford turned to Eleanor. 'Mrs Pitkin has been the cook at Farrington Manor for a number of years.'

The woman stifled a sob. 'They had to let me go, Mr Clifford. I understand. 'Tis no blame on the lord and ladyship, though I didn't do anything wrong, I swear I didn't.'

'Farrington?' Eleanor said. 'What a coincidence! I shall see Lord and Lady Farrington tomorrow at a luncheon.'

Clifford nodded. 'Indeed, my lady. Perhaps I should explain that Mrs Pitkin has been "released" from their service following the demise of Mr Aris.'

A quiet groan came from Mrs Pitkin. She put her hands on the table and peered dolefully up at Eleanor. 'M'lady, I swear on my mother's grave I didn't do it.'

Eleanor tried to choose her words carefully. 'Didn't do what?'

'Kill him!' Her shoulders began to shake.

Eleanor looked helplessly at Clifford and mouthed, 'Kill?'

He nodded. 'Mr Aris was deemed to have died after ingesting peanuts, my lady.'

'And that was a known allergen for him?' she asked, quite sure she'd already guessed the answer.

Mrs Pitkin jerked upright, making Gladstone shuffle back round to lie at Eleanor's feet. 'But that's just it, m'lady. I'm always careful and I know the Manor's kitchen inside and out. I couldn't have done it wrong. I can make chocolate and peanut butter fudge, with or without peanuts, blindfolded. The recipe's my own. And I took out all of the peanuts from the larder myself and asked Mr Clements to lock them in the butler's pantry so as to be sure of no accidents happening. And I made doubly sure all surfaces and hands were scrubbed. It's such a hassle when that Mr Aris comes to eat, I don't understand why their lord and ladyship invite him, I'm sure I don't.'

'Quite.' She remembered the conversation she'd overheard in the village. 'And yet Mr Aris' pudding was found to have peanuts in it?'

'His fudge, m'lady. The police said so. The poor gentleman passed away, with his face down in his dessert bowl. Oh, what a way to go and in front of all the other fine ladies and gentlemen! God rest his soul.'

Reflecting that this was turning out to be a most extraordinary day, Eleanor looked across at Martha, who was stirring her tea once again, repeatedly sniffing and wiping her eyes.

Helping people doesn't have to mean getting embroiled in another potential murder case, Ellie. You can leave this to the police. But Martha's next words threw that thought to the floor.

'Mr Aris had been to Farrington several times afore. Why would Lady Farrington think that I would cook dishes for him so carefully all those occasions, but this last time go and finish him off with an apprentice's error? Because he made a comment afore about what I'd served? If I'd taken umbrage every time critical words had come back from the table, I'd have an entire dinner table's worth of murder to my name.' She shook her head. 'I've worked as a cook all my life, m'lady. Anyone could stick a blindfold on me and a peg on my nose and make me taste just a morsel of anything. I'd tell them exactly what was in it, how fresh it be and likely even if it came from the estate or outside of it. I know my business inside and out. I've licked a thousand spoons in my time and there weren't no peanuts in that fudge.'

Eleanor frowned. 'Mrs Pitkin, have there been any other incidents of perhaps a mix-up of ingredients before?'

The cook straightened. 'Never, m'lady. Ask Trotters, oh beg pardon, Mrs Trotman, she knows how I work. Had the pleasure of sharing a kitchen with her once years back when I was at Wendlebury Estate and the only daughter, Lady Margery, was having her coming-out ball. Mrs Trotman got called in temporarily like, on account of the number of guests. Never seen the like afore nor since, mind. But that was in 1906 when food was easier to get, of course.'

'Of course,' Eleanor agreed, trying to marshal her thoughts. 'At the risk of asking an indelicate question, what will you do now, Mrs Pitkin?'

'I don't rightly know, m'lady. A cook what's been dismissed on account of having killed a gentleman... why, even if the police don't charge me with Mr Aris' death, I'll never work again. I've no wish to live out my days in the workhouse, if they'd even take me, m'lady. Or huddled under a bridge, scouring the rubbish for a mouthful if they won't.'

Eleanor leaned forward and put a hand on the woman's arm. 'Good Lord! There's no need to think like that! Have you no family who can help?'

Mrs Pitkin pulled her shawl closer round her neck. 'None. That's why I came to see Mrs Trotman, she's the nearest to family I've got.'

Eleanor had heard enough. 'Mrs Pitkin, despite being a lady, the staff here at Henley Hall, including Mrs Trotman, are the nearest thing to family I also have. I would never forgive myself if you were punished for something you never did.'

Unexpectedly, Mrs Pitkin rose and snatched up the felt hat from the chair beside her. 'Thank you for your time, m'lady, I do appreciate it, but the likes of me is going to get punished whichever way and no matter what the truth is. I got dismissed, which I understand they had to do to save themselves from the scandal. That's the way of a life in service. But a woman on her own, at my age, from the lowest classes with no family to take her in?' She gave a thin smile. 'She's better off dead and no mistake.'

Eleanor rose and held her hand up. 'Mrs Pitkin, wait! I'm sure we can find employment for you here. If not, I know—'

'So kind, but I won't take up any more of your time, only to thank you for listening and for your hospitality. It's heartening to see Mrs Trotman working in such a splendid home as this. Good day, m'lady.' She bobbed another stiff curtsey and hurried out of the back door before Eleanor or Clifford could stop her.

Eleanor turned to Clifford. 'We should go after her. Suppo—'

'Mrs Pitkin will be fine, my lady. Mrs Trotman has just emerged from the kitchen garden, where I suggested she wait in case of such an eventuality.'

Gladstone pottered back to the table, having followed after Mrs Pitkin, his stumpy tail as downcast as Eleanor's mood.

She sat down heavily. 'Oh, Clifford, what a terrible state of affairs! The poor woman appears to be genuinely distraught but, without wishing to be uncharitable, part of me is wondering if it might have been purely over her situation. And that would be with excellent reason, Clifford, she's destitute.' She glanced up at him sharply. 'Do you think she's…?'

'Telling the truth? Like you, my lady, I find my own judgement to be vacillating. I am, however, reminded of the words of Voltaire, if I may paraphrase: "It is better to risk saving a guilty cook than to condemn an innocent one."'

Another groan escaped Eleanor's lips. 'Why do the wisest of words have to surface just when I had promised myself I was done with mysteries and murders?'

'It is always possible to ignore wise words, my lady.'

'Not,' she stood up again, 'if you have a conscience.'

'Such a burden for the bearer, but a blessing for everyone else.'

'Thank you, but I shan't sleep tonight for worrying about what Mrs Pitkin is going to do if she isn't cleared of responsibility for this tragedy.' She closed her eyes but saw only an image of the distraught woman standing on the edge of Chipstone Bridge. She sighed. 'Of course, you said Mrs Trotman is with her. I'm sure she'll look after her. Tell Mrs Trotman, she's welcome to let Mrs Pitkin stay in the spare room in the staff quarters and to repeat my offer of employment.'

He nodded.

'It seems, Clifford, that I, actually *we*, are once again caught up in investigating a potential murder. For that must be the first thing for us to ascertain. If it was murder or misadventure.'

Clifford adjusted the perfectly aligned seams of his white gloves. 'Indeed, it might be advisable before employing Mrs Pitkin?'

Eleanor gasped. 'I hadn't thought of that!' She shrugged. 'But it seems she won't take up my offer. The important thing is, either Mrs Pitkin made a mistake, or someone deliberately set out to kill Mr Aris. If Mrs Pitkin *is* to be believed, it seems that the only possible conclusion is one of murder.'

Clifford pursed his lips. 'Perhaps I should speak to Abigail and ask her to keep her ears open for any information that comes her way?'

'Excellent idea, Clifford.' Abigail was the niece of Sandford, the Fenwick-Langhams' butler. She worked as a typist at Chipstone Police Station, the nearest town, and had helped Eleanor and Clifford solve a murder at Langham Manor earlier that year. 'And I'll see what I can learn from Chief Inspector Seldon. As the Farringtons are very influential, I assume the main investigation is being carried out from Oxford.'

DCI Seldon's office was in the town's main police station. He'd been in charge of the investigation into the murder at Langham Manor. He also had a soft spot for Eleanor. As he'd arrested Lancelot Fenwick-Langham, Eleanor's on-off beau for the murder, their relationship was rather cool at present, but Eleanor knew she'd need all the help they could muster to prove Mrs Pitkin's innocence. She shook her head. 'There is a raft of questions that need answers, however, before we can draw a conclusion.'

'Indeed, my lady. We need to ascertain exactly when that fudge was made that led to Mr Aris' unfortunate demise.'

'And not only when it was made, Clifford, but also who, apart from Mrs Pitkin, would have had the opportunity to meddle with it. Although it could have been substituted for one with peanuts at the table itself.'

'Assuming, of course, that the dessert item was responsible.'

'What do you mean, Clifford?'

'I wonder if the police are assuming that the peanuts in the dessert were the cause of Mr Aris' death. Suppose, however, that Mr Aris was actually poisoned?'

'And the fudge used to cover it up?' She frowned. 'That seems a tad unlikely, if you think about it. I mean, why go to all the trouble to put peanuts in Aris' fudge and then poison him? Given his violent reaction to a mere suggestion of peanuts, it seems fairly certain that he would die anyway?'

Clifford nodded slowly. 'That is an excellent point, my lady.'

Eleanor hesitated. 'Do you think... you know, that Mrs Pitkin herself might have done it... deliberately?'

'Indeed, my lady. And came here merely to ensure she acted the part of the desperate innocent. Her seemingly distraught state of mind may be nothing short of an act.'

'Well, I hope for Mrs Trotman's sake at least that I can find out something tomorrow.' She groaned. 'Lady Langham will be horrified if I turn her meet-the-Farringtons-for-luncheon into a full-blown murder investigation at the table. That can't be the done thing at all!'

Clifford cleared his throat. 'I am sure, my lady, you will manage to do it discreetly.'

CHAPTER 6

The following morning, Clifford eased the Rolls along Langham Manor's two-mile drive. Lined with aged maple trees, resplendent in their autumnal red, pink and burnt orange foliage, it led to the grand horseshoe entrance.

Once there, Clifford pulled up at the base of the sweeping stone staircase and turned to Eleanor: 'Happy investigating, my lady.'

Keenly aware of her hostess' firm views on punctuality, Eleanor was pleased to see she was the first to arrive. Sandford, their long-time butler, led her into the blue drawing room to await her hostess. Exquisite, powder-blue tapestry chairs were set against the backdrop of the finest embossed wallpaper in duck-egg and silver. Choice porcelain pieces dotted the walnut tables and a line of silver-framed photographs sat in a perfect circle on the grand piano. Her emerald silk dress with matching sheer sleeves seemed oddly loud in this tranquil space.

'Her ladyship will be with you presently, my lady.' Sandford picked up a silver tray and offered her a crystal flute glass. 'Perhaps you might wish to partake of a soupçon of champagne whilst waiting?'

'For fortification purposes only, thank you. You know me well, Sandford. I just hope I'm not in my cups before the fish course.'

Sandford and Clifford had been firm friends for years and Sandford had always accepted Eleanor's frequent etiquette faux pas with a twinkle of his hazel eyes. He gave a half-bow Clifford would be proud of and retreated backwards, closing the double oak-panelled doors in front of him.

Eleanor felt a pang of guilt at deceiving her hostess over her real reason for being there. Although, she consoled herself, she always loved seeing Lancelot's parents. And their French cook was a master of his craft!

Whilst waiting, she thought back to the information they had been able to find out so far. Abigail had confirmed that the investigation into Aris' death was being handled by Oxford Police, which they'd already guessed. With that settled, she'd rung the station and asked for DCI Seldon. She had his direct number, but was strangely unwilling to use it. At first, he'd been reticent about Aris' death, especially as she refused to disclose why she was interested. She didn't feel she could tell the police that she was trying to prove their main suspect innocent. Grudgingly, he'd finally admitted that he was leading the investigation. He assured her that, at the moment, the police were treating the case as death by misadventure. Whether the cook would be charged or not, hadn't been decided. And that was all he'd been willing to say. After a couple of awkward pleasantries, he'd ended the call. A small part of her wondered what life would have been like if she and the inspector hadn't found themselves on opposite sides of a murder investigation that involved Lancelot, her wayward beau?

She sighed and forced herself back to the matter in hand: how to execute a murder investigation over luncheon without being thrown out on her ear. She sipped at her champagne, which gave her instant tummy gurgles.

Oh, dash it, Ellie, you're supposed to be a lady at a society luncheon!

She jumped as the doors opened.

'My dear, dear Eleanor, how are you?' Lady Langham rustled into the room, arms outstretched, her lavender taffeta-silk skirt and matching jacket setting off her tight, greying curls and cornflower blue eyes.

Eleanor had become firm friends with the Langhams even before becoming their darling, having helped clear their only surviving son, Lancelot, of a murder charge just three months before.

'Augusta, what a treat to see you! I have to say you look positively radiant. Thank you so much for your kind invitation to luncheon.' She wondered how she would bring up Mr Aris' death. And which course would be most fitting to discuss murder? 'Who will I have the pleasure of dining with this afternoon?'

Her hostess took her arm. 'To be brutally honest with you, my dear, I've asked you here partly for support.'

Eleanor looked at her in surprise. It wasn't often the formidable lady needed support. 'But why?'

Lady Langham grimaced. 'The thing is, we are quite the small party today, which is why luncheon is in the second dining room.'

'How wonderful, then we shall have the best view of your beautiful rose garden.'

Roses were Lady Langham's passion. 'Absolutely! Now, two of our guests are a most delightful couple, I can't wait for you to meet them. We've known Baron Ashley and his family for years. And he has a wonderful new wife, Baroness, Lady Wilhelmina.'

Eleanor waited, knowing there must be more.

Lady Langham spread her hands. 'Well, Baron Ashley has married for love and not duty, which Harold and I totally agree with. However, our other guests, Lord and Lady Farrington, feel the Baron has married beneath his station and somewhat beneath his age! We had to invite them because Harold and I had to cancel dinner at Farrington Manor on Saturday night on account of Harold having an attack of gout.'

'I'm so sorry to hear that,' Eleanor said. Then she caught on. *That was the dinner where Aris died, Ellie.*

Lady Langham waved her hand. 'Oh, he's fine now, it's Manet, that French chef of ours. He insists on cooking that rich, continental food. That's fine for dinner, but for luncheon! I've told him he can prepare simpler food during the day, but he just sniffs and tells me that's not what he studied for ten years for.'

Eleanor laughed. 'Why don't you just get a cook who will prepare what you, and Harold's gout, wants?'

Lady Langham put her hand on Eleanor's. 'I keep forgetting you were brought up abroad and have only been in this country a short time. You simply have to have a French chef these days. And the sniffier, the better. We couldn't possibly get rid of him. What would we do when we entertain?' She shook her head. 'Anyway, it was rather a good thing we cancelled. By the sound of things, we got off lightly.' She looked thoughtful for a moment. 'Where was I? Oh, yes, Baron Ashley and his new wife. Harold and I believe Lady Wilhelmina is a delightful young woman. Her father is, well, I forget what her father does, something manual, I think. Or he runs a company or two, where they do manual things. Anyway, I shall be most grateful for your support at luncheon as I know you take the modern view on all things and approve of marrying for love, above all.'

Eleanor thought back to her own brief, disastrous marriage six years previously. She had indeed married for love after falling for a dashing officer in South Africa. Only it turned out he wasn't dashing, or an officer. Everyone believed he had been killed in the war, which was true. It was naturally assumed, however, that he died at the hands of the enemy, whereas he'd been shot by his own side for selling arms *to* the enemy. She shook the memory out of her head. 'Of course you have my support, although I may not be the best example for them!'

Lady Augusta laughed. 'Nonsense! We'll also have Harold's support. If he can tear himself away from the shoot, that is. I've sent Parsons out to snare him and drag him back.'

Harold, better known as Lord Langham, was devoted to three things: his wife, his son, and his hunting, not necessarily in that order. Eleanor found his unpretentious company most congenial.

'Has the shooting season started again then?'

'Pheasant season opened just days ago, my dear, but oh, bother of bothers, partridge season started on the first of September. We are simply drowning in the wretched things! I took the liberty of asking Cook to wrap several braces for Clifford to take back to Henley Hall. I do hope you don't mind?'

'Of course not, what a kind thought, it will be an absolute treat! I haven't had partridge for ages. Lancelot isn't joining us then?' She tried to sound casual.

'Oh, don't, he's such a terror! He said something about needing to work on his plane.'

Eleanor laughed to cover up her disappointment at the news. Then again, he would only have made her inquiries into Aris' death so much harder with his constant jokes and ribbing.

Lady Langham clapped her hands. 'Come, my dear, we'll meet the four of them on the terrace.'

Outside, the lightest of breezes brushed Eleanor's face with a warmth rarely experienced on such an autumnal day. By the time they arrived at the sweeping, balustraded terrace the first couple had finished the tour of Lady Langham's prize rose garden and reached the top of the stone steps. Lady Langham threw on her impeccable-hostess smile.

'Lord and Lady Farrington, do meet Lady Swift! Eleanor has become quite the family friend, just like her dear, sadly departed uncle.'

'Good afternoon.' Eleanor smiled at the two of them, pretending not to notice Lady Farrington's intense scrutiny of her outfit. Every inch the aristocrat, Lady Farrington's ash-blonde hair, set in tight finger waves, nudged her alabaster complexion. Her long angular frame gave her the appearance of the most elegant of ghosts.

In contrast, Lord Farrington had the ruddy complexion and robust physique of a man who had excelled at sport in his younger days. His indifferent expression soured his otherwise classically handsome features.

The Ashleys hurried up the last of the steps and unhooked arms as they each held out their hands to Eleanor. Standing beside her husband, Lady Wilhelmina's dainty frame exaggerated his tall and slender build as he towered a full head and shoulders above her.

'Lady Swift.' Baron Ashley looked to be in his early forties and thus close to eighteen or so years older than his wife. He gave her a warm smile that brightened his already personable demeanour. 'Absolutely delighted to meet you! We've heard so much about your exciting adventures.'

Eleanor laughed. 'All brushed with a little fictitious glamour, I hope.'

Lady Farrington tilted her chin up and peered down her long nose.

Baron Ashley gestured to his wife, his face alight with pride. 'May I present Lady Wilhelmina.' As she nodded in greeting, Wilhelmina's natural honey-blonde curls, pinned loosely with a flower hair clip, bobbed against her flawless rosy cheeks, shining as brightly as her deep blue eyes. The epitome of an English rose, she seemed totally unaware of how radiant she was.

Eleanor recognised the young woman's uncertainty over the correct protocol and stepped forward to scoop both of her hands into her own. 'Lady Wilhelmina, my congratulations on your recent nuptials! Did you have the most wonderful day?'

Like her demeanour, her voice was gentle: 'Lady Swift, it is so lovely to meet you and yes, thank you, we had the most beautiful and special day. It was like a fairy tale wrapped in a dream.'

'So delightful!' Lady Langham said with a contented sigh. 'A day to remember throughout all your many, many auspicious years to come. Now, shall we retire to the dining room and await Harold's arrival? I do apologise, he must have become engaged in a fearful tussle with a brace of winged beasts.' With a strained tinkling laugh, she turned and led the way.

*

To Eleanor's eyes, the second dining room was no less opulent than the main one she'd dined in previously. The chinois theme covered the walls with exquisite silk wallpaper designs of oriental flowering trees, brightly painted birds and insects amongst the branches. Lacquered side tables topped with highly detailed china vases punctuated the marble columns that rose up to meet the intricately plastered ceiling, from the centre of which hung three glittering chandeliers, throwing intricate patterns along the length of the long dining table, dressed in the finest starched linen.

Lady Langham nodded to Sandford to sound the gong. She gestured to the table.

'Shall we?'

As they took their places, Parsons, the tall first footman, filled the doorway and nodded to Sandford.

The butler announced, 'His lordship is arriving, my lady.'

His announcement was unnecessary as the booming voice could already be heard.

'Luncheon, how spiffing! Simply famished. Trying to outwit wily pheasants will do that to a chap.' Lord Langham paused, halfway into the room. He smoothed his impressive moustache. 'How goes everyone's morning?'

'It is well into the afternoon now, Harold dear.' His wife sniffed from the head of the table.

Lord Langham bent and gave her an affectionate peck on the cheek. He looked round at the guests. 'Bit short on numbers, aren't we? Some of them scarpered already?'

'Harold, please be seated! Sandford, his lordship will take a fruit juice.'

Lord Fenwick-Langham gave a mock pout and then winked at Eleanor. He took his place at the opposite end of the table.

Baron Ashley cleared his throat. 'Harold, how was this morning's shoot?'

'Top hole, thank you, Clarence, old man. Not really a shooting man yourself, I seem to recall?'

'Never quite felt the urge, actually,' Baron Ashley said, returning his wife's smile.

Lady Langham clapped her hands. 'How delightful! We are all together, finally. Let us begin.' Her words were the signal for the staff to present the first course. A morning-suited figure appeared behind each chair with a silver salver, covered in an ornate matching dome. These were then placed in front of each guest.

To her horror, Eleanor noticed in her reflection, she had a smudge on her nose. *Where on earth did that come from, Ellie?* Rubbing discreetly with her napkin, she thought she had got away with it until Lord Langham gave her a big thumbs up.

With a nod from Sandford, the silver domes were removed in perfect unison to reveal confit leg dressed with celeriac. The clink of cutlery rang round the table. Eleanor noticed Lady Wilhelmina hesitate over the long line of forks before peering at the one her husband held up discreetly for her to see.

She took a delicate mouthful and then busied herself with her napkin. 'Simply delicious, Lady Langham! What a delightful treat to be here for luncheon.'

Their hostess beamed. 'Dear Wilhelmina, the pleasure is all ours. And do call me Augusta.'

Lady Farrington threw a thin smile to the young woman. 'Being new to society, perhaps you haven't had the chance to attend many functions yet?'

'No, not really,' Lady Wilhelmina said, her cheeks scarlet.

'No time,' Baron Ashley rushed to her rescue. 'We've been rather caught up settling in at home together. So much to do after the wedding, you know.'

Lady Langham nodded. 'Absolutely! How is married life at Castle Ranburgh treating you, Clarence?'

'Absolutely wonderfully,' Baron Ashley replied. 'Wilhelmina has had some exciting ideas for decorating, which is long overdue. The place does have something of a forlorn bachelor air, after all.'

Lady Langham smiled at the young woman. 'Do tell us some of your ideas?'

'Oh, gracious. I… well…'

Her husband came to her rescue. 'Wilhelmina would never admit it, but she is the most incredible artist. I shall insist that she fills the castle with her own works.'

Lady Wilhelmina blushed again but gave him a loving look.

Eleanor remembered Lady Langham's plea for support. She turned to Lady Wilhelmina. 'I've never really tried the arts, but I don't think I would master any of them terribly well. Patience isn't my forte.'

'Regular dynamo, this one. Always on the go,' Harold said proudly to the rest of the table.

Lord Farrington fixed Eleanor with a slightly derisive look. 'I've heard you are quite the modern lady?'

'I really couldn't say,' she replied blandly.

His wife was still staring at her. 'Lady Swift, do tell. What does a "modern woman" occupy herself with these days?'

Okay, Ellie, this is your chance. 'Well, the Women's League have asked me to stand as an independent candidate as poor Mr Aris' successor.'

Lord Langham harrumphed from the depths of his brandy glass. 'Well, if you get elected, see if you can't do something about those blasted death duties, won't you?'

She laughed. 'I'll try, but I haven't actually agreed to stand yet.'

Lord Farrington shook his head. 'Governing this country should be left to those with the natural aptitude to do so, which isn't women!'

Harold rose and tottered over to the drinks table. 'My dear Eleanor, I think you did the right thing in saying no.'

The Farringtons and Lady Langham nodded in agreement.

Eleanor felt her face flushing. 'I haven't actually said I won't stand either... yet.'

Lady Farrington nodded frostily. 'As that wretched American, Lady Astor, has clearly shown, Alexander is right. Parliament is no place for a lady.' She smiled thinly at Eleanor. 'Although, if you were elected, you could keep each other company.'

'I'm sure we'd get along wonderfully,' Eleanor replied sweetly.

Lord Farrington snorted loudly. 'And would you get along with that criminal disgrace, Pankhurst? I heard she's now been charged with sedition after calling on workers to loot the London Docks! How is that furthering your so-called women's rights?'

Before she could reply, Lady Langham interrupted. 'I think that's enough talk of politics at the table, please, Alexander!'

Lord Farrington rolled his eyes, but said nothing. Eleanor also held her tongue.

'Quite right, Augusta old girl, let's change the subject.' Harold turned to Lord Farrington. 'How's the hurly-burly of property treating you, old chap?'

Lord Farrington pursed his lips. 'Portfolio's strong enough but suffered a wretched setback on a recent venture. Terrible timing!'

His wife shot him a look and addressed no one in particular. 'Investment opportunities are so varied these days, don't you find? I've even heard of quality people actually considering the entertainment industry a respectable option. Can you imagine?'

Harold chortled. 'Modern times have arrived, you know. We're going to have to lift up the portcullis and let the rest of the world in at some point.'

Lady Wilhelmina's eyes widened. She opened her mouth but seemed to think better of it and took a sip from her glass instead.

Lady Farrington was staring at Eleanor. 'Perhaps Lady Swift can give us the modern woman's view again? Especially one so travelled?'

There was something about her tone that rubbed Eleanor up the wrong way. She kept her voice level. 'Oh, I doubt it. I've become quite the contented country girl, you know.' *How to turn the conversation back to Aris' death without making it too obvious, Ellie?* She was saved the trouble by Lord Farrington unintentionally coming to her aid.

'I can imagine you had to eat all manner of unmentionable things on your adventures across the world?'

Eleanor grasped the opportunity. 'Beyond unmentionable, actually. Unrecognisable as even meat or vegetable all too often, but I was always grateful for the hospitality of people everywhere. Only trouble was, of course,' she mentally apologised to her hostess again, 'one never knew if one was going to have an adverse reaction to a food, and out in the wilder spots that was a concern.'

'Gracious, you mean like that chap Aris?' Harold said. His wife shook her head. Eleanor gave him a silent cheer.

Oblivious to his wife's horror, Harold rolled on: 'Wasn't even out of the Home Counties, never mind the woolly wilds of the world, but that didn't help him. Went blue around the lips and snuffed it in a heartbeat. In his main course, isn't that so, Alexander?'

Eleanor felt for her hostess but couldn't let the conversation drop. But she didn't have time to throw out a line as Lord Farrington did it for her.

'I'd say they were purple, actually, Harold. And it was dessert. The fudge, the police chap said.' He ran his hand through his hair. 'Not the finest hour on the estate, but there you are. These things, as you say, do happen.'

From the corner of her eye, Eleanor saw Baron Ashley squeeze his wife's hand.

Harold harrumphed. 'Of course, we missed it all because of my damned gout. Apologies again, old man, for letting you down.'

Eleanor jumped in. 'Gracious, my heartfelt sympathies! For the gentleman and his family, but for yourselves equally, Lord and Lady

Farrington. That must have been a terrible thing to go through. However did your other guests react?'

'Lots of fainting from the ladies, naturally,' Lord Farrington replied haughtily.

Charming! Eleanor tried to keep the frown from her face.

Harold drummed his fingers on the table. 'That the reason for your property investment hiccup, Alexander?'

Lord Farrington nodded. 'Aris was a good man to know, if you know what I mean.'

Eleanor saw her chance. 'I only met poor Mr Aris once, at a luncheon here, actually. Was he a popular man in the area?'

Lord Farrington eyed her oddly. 'This would have been his third successful election, don't you know?'

Harold was nodding along with this. 'Course. Tedious what, now you'll have to hold another swanky dinner to drum up support again to push the bally housing scheme through or it'll never happen.' His chuckle died as he caught his wife's glare.

Lady Farrington set her glass down with a little too much force. 'Actually, Harold, it was a charity dinner. We were fundraising for the Anchorage Mission of Hope and Help.'

Eleanor grabbed the opportunity. 'I do hope the tragedy didn't affect your guests' generosity?'

Lord Farrington guffawed. 'I didn't allow anyone to use the incident as an excuse not to put their hand in their pocket, if that's what you mean.'

Eleanor tried again. 'It was such an unfortunate mix-up. It was an allergic reaction to peanuts, wasn't it?'

Lady Farrington nodded. 'The cook knew of Mr Aris' extreme allergy to peanuts and yet she still served them. She's been dismissed, of course, pending the police's decision whether to press charges.'

Eleanor shuddered. She tried to gather her thoughts. 'I guess then the by-election will be fiercely fought, as the candidates must each feel more hope of being successful now that poor Mr Aris has passed?'

'Carlton for one,' Lord Farrington said. 'I swear he looked like the cat who got the cream when Aris was pulled up out of his dessert.'

Interesting, Ellie! Remember that name.

'Alexander!' Lady Farrington's voice cut into her thoughts like a scythe.

'What?' her husband snapped back. 'You spent the entire following day telling me just how vociferously he'd rowed with Aris throughout the evening.'

'That is enough!' said Lady Farrington. 'Mr Aris' unfortunate death has occupied too much of Lady Langham's luncheon. I'm sure no one has any interest in discussing such an indelicate subject. Please move on.'

Their hostess nodded gratefully.

Eleanor had the good grace to blush and avoided her hostess' eye.

CHAPTER 7

The Langham Manor lunch was still sitting like a heavy brick in Eleanor's stomach as Clifford manoeuvred the Rolls through the southern outskirts of Chipstone on the return drive home.

'Well, Clifford, I made a slight impression on the questions we raised this morning.'

He leaned across and held out her notebook and pen. After their discussion that morning, she had written everything down.

Flipping to the right page, she cast her eye down her list and tutted. 'Actually, I haven't made a dent in them at all. I've simply a few more to add.' She brightened. 'Still, we have our first suspect.'

Clifford raised an eyebrow. 'I would imagine, my lady, that anyone who was present the night of Mr Aris' demise and had access to Mr Aris' dessert would be a suspect at the moment?'

'Of course, Clifford, that goes without saying. We need a list of those above, and below, stairs who could have interfered with Aris' dessert. Until then, I've found out that Aris had a series of verbal spats with a Mr Carlton, so we can put him down as our first suspect. And, yes, he was at the dinner that night.'

She wrote 'Suspects' on a fresh page and the name 'Carlton' underneath. It had become her habit in murder investigations to draw a doodle of each suspect to aid memory. As she hadn't yet set eyes on this Carlton fellow, however, she put nothing.

Underneath his name she wrote Lord and Lady Farrington, each with a turned-up nose next to it.

She glanced up and caught Clifford's raised eyebrow. 'I also found out Lord Farrington had some business connection with Aris. And not necessarily the kind you openly acknowledge, so him and his frosty wife are definitely under suspicion as well as Carlton.'

'Agreed, my lady. That would explain why they were so quick to blame the cook.'

'Exactly! But hang on, you must have come across this character, Carlton? You know everyone around these parts.'

'I'm acquainted with Mr Carlton, certainly. He has been the Labour Party's candidate for Chipstone and District for some years. I have, however, only exchanged pleasantries on meeting him in the street, nothing more.' He gave her an enquiring look. 'And despite raising the indelicate subject of Mr Aris' demise at the luncheon table, you are still persona grata at Langham Manor?'

'Absolutely! Lady Langham gave me a parting hug that quite squashed the lobster rissoles into the veal Toulouse.' She rubbed her middle. 'I'm still so full I'm fighting the need to collapse onto a chaise longue.' She yawned so hard her jaw creaked. 'I think I need a walk.'

'If it would suit, I have several errands requiring the facilities of Chipstone that could be brought forward to today?'

'Perfect. Splendid show, Clifford! Let's stop here at the top of the high street and meet up in, say, an hour?'

The town's midweek bustle failed to filter into Eleanor's chattering thoughts as she ran over and over the discussion at lunch.

If Aris' allergy was widely known, anyone at the table might have slipped him a fudge square with peanuts concealed inside. But then again, only if they'd prepared one in advance? But what were Aris and Carlton arguing about? Who else had a grudge against Aris? And why was Lady Farrington staring at her so intensely throughout lunch?

She sighed. What on earth did she need to do to live the quiet life she had envisaged on moving into Henley Hall? This was the sleepy Chilterns after all!

She remembered Lady Wilhelmina's passion for painting. *Who knows, dabbling with a brush and a palette of gorgeous colours might calm your brain when it starts climbing the walls, Ellie?*

With added purpose now in her walk, she tightened the belt on her long wool jacket and picked up to a good pace. She scanned either side of the street for the first art materials supplier suitable for a novice with little patience. But further on, she stopped short at the sight of a new shop. *Yes, that was right, Mrs Butters had been excited about its opening.* Eleanor stepped back and looked up at the sign: 'Mrs Luscombe's Linens and Haberdashery'.

An emerald-and-olive patterned scarf in georgette fabric drew Eleanor's eye. She pressed the skirt of her dress against the glass. *Ooh, a perfect match!* Now *that* she had to have! Hurrying inside, she offered a cheery, 'Good morning.'

From behind a Chinese screen, a voice called back, 'One moment, please.' A minute later, an elderly woman appeared, dressed in a sensible navy cotton long-sleeved dress and owl-like spectacles. Her thick white hair was pinned into a meticulous bun.

'Can I help you, Lady Swift?' the woman replied coolly, eyeing Eleanor's outfit as if she thought it rather ostentatious for a shopping trip round Chipstone.

Eleanor started, then mentally shrugged. Since so many people she'd never met knew who she was it had ceased to bother her, although she still found it surprising. Feeling no compulsion to explain she had come from a formal luncheon and, as the woman seemed disinclined to chat, Eleanor simply pointed to the scarf in the window.

'I should like to buy the emerald one, please. I can't resist the colours! Did you make it yourself?'

The woman nodded. 'I did.'

'Then you must be Mrs Luscombe.' She held out her hand, which was received like limp lettuce. Eleanor continued on, giving her best smile. 'Your shop is new, I believe. Have you recently moved here?'

The woman tapped the cloth tape measure hanging round her neck. 'I was born and raised in Little Buckford, but retired to Chipstone. Now, I provide the ladies of the area with well-priced and sturdy linens and sewing items. I also offer a repair and tailoring service.'

'How very adept of you!' Eleanor's thoughts flew to her wardrobe. 'That is actually splendid news. Might I commission you therefore to make me a matching shawl for evening wear?'

'To what would you like it to match?'

Eleanor gestured to the window. 'Why the scarf, of course.'

The woman drew a sharp breath. 'Regrettably, that is not possible.'

'Why ever not?'

'Because the scarf is fabricated from georgette and is thus too sheer for a decent shawl.'

'Too sheer to last you mean, as in not durable enough?'

'No, Lady Swift, as in not modest enough. Now, would you still like to purchase the scarf?'

Eleanor nodded. *This is 1920, not 1820. Honestly! Are all Chipstone women this traditional?*

She watched Mrs Luscombe retrieve the scarf from the window, which apparently necessitated adjusting the entire display. This fussing and fiddling did however also reveal an election poster Eleanor hadn't noticed from the outside.

Making another brave stab at conversation, she said, 'I understand this election might be more of an event than in previous years, Mrs Luscombe?'

The woman finished putting her shopfront back in order and turned to Eleanor: 'And why would that be?'

'Well, with poor Mr Aris' demise, the other candidates must feel they have a greater opportunity to succeed. Mr Carlton, for example? He's stood several times, I'm told. Perhaps he will pick up where Mr Aris had to leave off in supporting some of Mr Aris' work on women's rights?'

This brought a sharp scoff. 'Ernest Carlton is the least likely man on earth to think of supporting anyone other than his own interests! I would prepare for resounding disappointment if you are hoping he will champion that cause.'

'It sounds as though you know him well?' Eleanor said nonchalantly.

'I was his teacher through the latter part of his school years. Unlike his classmate, Arnold Aris, Ernest Carlton was a demanding and calculating pupil who grew into a demanding and calculating man. He is a predatory tiger hiding behind a pussy cat's smile. Too many women have fallen for it.' She held up the paper-wrapped parcel. 'Good day, Lady Swift.'

The contempt in the woman's voice blew any further questions from Eleanor's mind. Mumbling a goodbye, she stepped from the shop but lurched backwards with the force of a heavyset man barging into her.

'Watch where you're going, can't you!' The man's nostrils flared like an angry bull, his small dark eyes lost to flaccid jowls and thick eyebrows.

'I beg your pardon but actually you bumped into me,' Eleanor said.

'Nonsense!' he scoffed. Undoing the bottom two buttons of his brown suit waistcoat, he bent with a grunt to retrieve his trilby from the pavement, ignoring her paper-wrapped parcel which lay next to it. 'I was walking along this thoroughfare, you were emerging into the pedestrian traffic. Thank goodness women can't drive cars!'

'We can, actually, and jolly competent we are too!'

'More nonsense! Stick to shopping. In fact, stay inside altogether, you'll be less of a menace.'

'Do you know you might just be the rudest man I've ever met.'

He shrugged. 'I didn't come out to make new friends, I am on important business.'

Eleanor gestured up and down both sides of Chipstone High Street. 'Everyone you can see is on business important to them.'

This made him snort. 'They are merely wasting time. I, on the other hand, am attempting to pull society back from the brink of insanity.'

For a brief second, Eleanor wondered if this man's apparent belligerence was in fact a side effect of having lost his mental faculties.

'Well, I suspect that whatever it is I am keeping you from is frightfully important so I will bid you good luck and good day and continue about my business.'

'I sincerely doubt that! Meddlesome women like you can't keep from poking their noses in where they have absolutely no place being, Lady Swift.'

Eleanor sighed. Another complete stranger who knew who she was. She took a deep breath. 'Thank you for your uninvited character assessment but I am not, in fact, meddlesome. However, you are entitled to your opinion, baseless as it is.'

'Baseless, eh?' He gestured up and down the street. 'A man can't even walk down the pavement without becoming entangled in your web of interference. Emancipation? Ha! Nothing more than an attempt at seeking an easy life, being treated like overindulged children.'

Ah, so that's his beef, Ellie.

'I'm sorry, Mr... but your name really isn't necessary. Women do not have "webs", they aren't spiders.' She leaned forward and whispered, 'They have a great many less legs for one thing.' She bent to retrieve her parcel but on straightening up, found the man had had the effrontery to block her path.

'Now,' she pointed past his shoulder, 'you see how complicated this navigation of the pavements can be. We are both facing in the opposite direction to that which we wish to go. I shall repeat my earlier and cordial salutation and wish you every success in your endeavours whilst I continue about my own.'

'But your "endeavours" are precisely the issue. I recommend you stop, Lady Swift, before you regret it!'

Eleanor froze. *Who was this man?* And how had he learned of Miss Mann and the Women's League's suggestion she stood as their candidate? Assuming that was what this was all about?

It seemed he couldn't leave without trying to further intimidate her, however. 'A word of gentlemanly advice: stop asking questions about Mr Aris. It is none of your concern and could be bad for your health!'

He spun on his heels and marched off.

She hurried back along the high street to find Clifford standing by the bonnet of the Rolls, pocket watch in hand.

He gave his customary half-bow and opened the passenger door. 'Your walk was successful, my lady?'

'No, not at all.'

She turned to him as he slid into the driver's seat.

'My stomach is no better and my thoughts are now burning like acid. Clifford, what would you call indigestion of the mind?'

'Cerebral dyspepsia, my lady?'

'Well, I hope you have one of your foul concoctions for that.'

He patted his pockets. 'Regrettably, not about my person. Shall we?'

CHAPTER 8

Even Gladstone's exuberant welcome that pushed her backwards onto the hallway settle didn't soothe Eleanor's thoughts. With his short, stocky front legs on the green silk of her lap, he bashed her nose with the battered leather slipper he'd brought as a homecoming gift.

'Oh, Gladstone, I'm so sorry, boy. I've been completely caught up with everything.' She buried her face in the soft wrinkles of his forehead and closed her eyes. They sighed together. 'Life has got complicated again. But,' she lifted one of his stiff little ears and whispered, 'how about this afternoon, you and I go play ball?' She pulled away and smiled at the sight of his stumpy tail shimmying with excitement.

'It's a deal.' She yanked her shoes off with a grunt. 'But first, I had better change out of this fancy frock and have some tea to refresh my thoughts. Doggy biscuits in the morning room in ten minutes?'

At the 'b' word, Gladstone let out a husky 'woof' and spun in a wobbly circle.

'I'll take that as a yes then.'

She was halfway up the grand staircase when Clifford appeared from the kitchen end of the house.

She called down to him. 'I'm afraid my walk didn't really give me any new insights into Aris' death, Clifford. However, I discovered that Carlton has a reputation as something of a ladies' man.'

Standing at the bottom step, he called up to her. 'Interesting, my lady. Forgive me for changing the subject, but I thought you might like to be forewarned.'

She stared down at him. Gladstone leaned sideways into her leg. 'Clifford, not more unwelcome news? Please say it isn't.'

'That might depend on the nature of the visitor's visit, as it were. I saw someone approaching the end of the drive as I parked the Rolls in the garage.'

'Visitor? Now? It's all getting rather hectic with all these unannounced callers. Besides, Gladstone and I have just made a date for tea and biscuits.'

'Perhaps you would care for your visitor to join you both there, my lady?'

'Really, I am too full, too tired and too frazzled by my own thoughts for visitors. Do you know, I met the rudest man in the world and he had the audacity to say that women want to be treated like overindulged children. Ugh!' She flopped theatrically onto the stairs. This made her stockinged feet slip out from under her and she slid smartly down the bottom half of the staircase, landing at Clifford's feet.

He looked at her impassively. 'I can't imagine how the gentleman might have come to that conclusion.'

'Very droll, but I haven't told you the most interesting part: the man threatened me if I didn't stop asking questions about Aris' death.'

Clifford raised both eyebrows, a rare occurrence. 'It seems, my lady, that you are already making waves.'

'It would seem so, which suggests we should make some bigger ones. Alright,' she picked herself up and adjusted her skirt, 'I shall change into more suitable, and less slippery, attire and receive the visitor in five minutes. Who is it, by the way?'

'Miss Mann, I believe, my lady.'

'Gracious, Clifford! What answer am I going to give her?'

*

Her visitor was standing with her back to the door over by the French windows that overlooked the rear lawns. Now changed into simple, wide-legged linen trousers and a matching grass-green cardigan that fitted her as perfectly as it had her mother, Eleanor hovered in the doorway. As Miss Mann bent to smell the vase of white viburnum and strawberry-and-cream asters, Eleanor noticed that the woman's figure was far more feminine than her shin-length navy wool suit credited.

Eleanor stepped forward. 'Good afternoon.'

The woman let out a squeal and spun round. 'Oh, forgive me, I was in quite a daze.' She smiled nervously. 'Good afternoon, Lady Swift. I do hope you were expecting me?'

'Of course,' Eleanor fibbed. 'Please, do take a seat.'

'Your gardens are truly splendid. Such a calming view.'

'Thank you. I'm afraid I can't claim any credit. It is all due to my late uncle's wonderful gardener, Joseph. It is his passion.'

'But doesn't your uncle's passing make him *your* gardener now?'

Eleanor nodded slowly. 'I still feel like the new girl at Henley Hall. I sometimes forget that I am the lady of the house.'

Miss Mann ran her hand over the knee of her skirt. 'Such an unassuming attitude, Lady Swift! You must see that is exactly why you were the Women's League's immediate choice to represent women countywide?'

This pulled Eleanor up short. At their last meeting, she hadn't imagined asking why the League had picked her. Fortunately, Clifford arrived at that moment with a surprisingly laden tea tray and a very excited bulldog, which he held back with one leg stretched across the threshold.

'Forgive me, my lady, did you wish to keep your promise to Master Gladstone?'

'Absolutely!' Eleanor replied, clapping her hands to call him over as Clifford released him. 'Gladstone, old friend, we have company.'

At this, the dog turned on his stiff legs and seemed to spot Miss Mann for the first time. With extra gusto he charged over and threw the top half of his body into her lap, giving her hand a welcoming lick.

'Oh dear!' she managed in a strangled voice.

Eleanor made a face at Clifford. 'Miss Mann, I do apologise. He is rather enthusiastic at times and, I fear, a little too long in the tooth to be taught too many new tricks, or indeed, better manners.'

Her visitor was pinned in the cream and silver striped chair, hands up as if being held at gunpoint. 'Perhaps he might like to sit elsewhere?' she stammered.

Clifford took control. 'Master Gladstone, stand down.'

The bulldog sat, his back legs sticking out sideways.

Clifford placed the tea tray on the table and picked up a white china bowl with a gold rim and draped a towel over his forearm. At Eleanor's questioning eyebrow, he gave a discreet cough. 'I took the liberty, my lady, of anticipating Master Gladstone's enthusiasm for the "LT",' he said with a conspiratorial nod, 'and brought Miss Mann a finger bowl.'

'Oh, gracious, I didn't realise Mrs Trotman had made him his favourite liver treats! Ah, that explains his extra bounce.'

Ears pricked, the dog scrambled over and sat at Eleanor's feet. She scooped up a jar from the tray and set out a line of hard-baked grey mini biscuits on the rug. 'Good boy! You dig in.' She turned back to her visitor, who had finished drying her hands and swapped the towel for a cup of tea.

Eleanor smiled. 'Pantomime over. Now, where were we?'

Miss Mann quickly finished her biscuit and put down her tea. 'I'm sorry, I couldn't resist. I so love baking myself, but I suppose your cook made these?'

Eleanor nodded. 'Mrs Trotman is a wonder in the kitchen. I can't cook for toffee! Although Mrs Trotman does sometimes let me help her in the kitchen, I fear she's just being polite and I'm really rather under her feet.'

Miss Mann shook her head. 'That is exactly what I am talking about, Lady Swift. I had just mentioned that we of the Women's League have noted you carry your title with extreme modesty. We feel that will greatly appeal to the ladies of the lower classes, which are precisely those we are trying to reach.'

'Then why not choose a lady from that sphere? Surely, they would hold greater appeal to their peers?'

Miss Mann's cheeks flushed. 'Yes. Regrettably, however, none of them have either the education nor standing in the community.'

'Ah, I see.' Eleanor marshalled her thoughts. 'However, what I said to you before stands. I do not consider myself to be the best person to lead the charge at the front as it were.'

'But you have inspired the ladies of the Women's League so much. Your reputation for adventure and your independent attitude has not gone unnoticed. Surely you must agree that it is unfair that even though it was the women who kept Britain working during the war whilst the menfolk were away, now, after only two years, they are considered nothing more than menial labourers? Equal work deserves equal pay and equal respect.'

Eleanor took a long breath. 'Miss Mann, I cannot shake the disquieting feeling that I am not the woman the Women's League imagines me to be.'

Miss Mann stood up. 'Lady Swift, I have no desire to persuade or cajole you. I therefore respectfully accept your decision.'

Eleanor shook her head. 'I don't see how.' She ran her hand down the sleeve of her cardigan. 'You have not heard my decision.'

Miss Mann dropped back into her seat. 'But you said…'

'What I said was the truth. It is important you know that I had already made my decision before I entered the room. And I do not bow to pressure, however emotively or eloquently it is presented.'

Miss Mann's eyes widened. 'Are you saying you... you intend to stand?'

'Miss Mann, I intended to all along.' In truth, she had decided to stand immediately after her meeting with that objectionable man outside Mrs Luscombe's shop.

Her visitor gasped. 'Thank you, Lady Swift! That is wonderful news, I can't wait to tell my fellow members.' She stood again. 'I won't take up any more of your time for the moment. I'll be in touch tomorrow.'

At the front door, she paused. 'I'm sorry, but I feel there is something I should pass on.' She bit her lip. 'Perhaps I should have mentioned it before.'

Eleanor ignored Clifford's discreet cough. 'There's a thing,' she muttered. 'And what is that, Miss Mann?'

'There is a powerful group in the area – councillors and men of influence – who have formed a cabal to fight what they see as the threat of the Women's League. They are trying to put up their own independent candidate, who is as anti-women's rights as they are. Between them, they can exert a great deal of influence. And trouble. They are led by a Mr Blewitt, a councillor, local business owner and a most obnoxious man.'

'I see. Don't worry, Miss Mann, I believe I may have met that very gentleman today.' She described the man who had been so rude to her earlier. Miss Mann confirmed that it was indeed Mr Blewitt.

Eleanor nodded slowly. *At least you know what, and who, you're up against, Ellie.* 'Now, before you leave, I've a question.'

'Of course.'

'I believe you were at the dinner the night Mr Aris had his unfortunate accident?'

The blood drained out of Miss Mann's face. Eleanor groaned inwardly. She could have been subtler. It must have been quite a trauma for the woman. She obviously knew Aris to some extent, through her work with the Women's League, of which Aris was a supporter.

'I'm so sorry, Miss Mann, I really shouldn't ha—'

'That's fine, Lady Swift.' Some of the colour had returned to her cheeks. 'It was just such a… a… shock. One minute, Lord Farrington was proposing a toast, and then Mr Aris just collapsed.' She rummaged in her handbag and pulled out a handkerchief, dabbing at her eyes with it.

Oh, Ellie!

She instinctively put her arm around the other woman. 'I really am sorry, I should have thought.'

Miss Mann smiled weakly. 'It's really not a problem. Mr Aris was a good man. We'll all miss him at the Women's League.'

Much as she wanted to, Eleanor couldn't abandon her intention of quizzing her guest in detail over the night Aris died entirely. After all, Mrs Pitkin's future was at stake. Instead, she drew up a heavily censored version. 'Absolutely! Although, perhaps not everyone will miss him as much as the Women's League.'

Miss Mann looked up sharply. 'What do you mean?'

'Oh, I heard that at the dinner, one of the other guests seemed to be in disagreement with Mr Aris ov—'

'Mr Carlton.' Miss Mann nodded, her eyes flashing. 'That man appreciates no one. We at the Women's League have nothing to do with him. Neither did Mr Aris.'

'Really? Apart from your work with the Women's League, is he someone of your acquaintance?'

Eleanor's visitor flushed. 'I think you will find, Lady Swift, that every right-thinking woman would do their level best to avoid becoming acquainted with a man of his reputation. Politically, he is not overtly against women's rights simply because he does not realise women exist, aside from indulging his personal proclivities.' She patted her chignon. 'If you will forgive my indelicate observation.'

Eleanor shrugged. 'He doesn't seem to be wholly beloved by the few people I've mentioned his name to.'

'As I have been rather harshly reminded myself, one has to be loveable to be loved, I have always heard.' She gave a wan smile and held out her hand. 'I doubt Mr Carlton will be a significant threat to your success, Lady Swift, but he will doubtless make a nuisance of himself on the way, I am sure of that.'

With Miss Mann gone, the tea replaced with something stronger, and Gladstone sprawled along his back on the chaise longue by the fire in the drawing room, Eleanor sighed. It had been an eventful afternoon.

'Here we are again.'

'Might I enquire as to precisely where you consider that "we are", my lady?'

'On a mission, Clifford. Actually, two missions now, I suppose.'

'My congratulations on your decision, my lady. I assume that is the first mission. And the second?'

'Thank you, Clifford, but as you had a hand in setting me up, I expect your assistance in seeing it to a successful conclusion.'

Clifford bowed. 'With pleasure, my lady.'

She smiled; she'd anticipated nothing else. 'The second is doing all we can to help poor Mrs Pitkin, assuming she didn't deliberately kill Mr Aris, of course.'

'Of course.'

'How is she bearing up? I wish she had agreed to stay here, although I understand her thinking she was already putting us to enough trouble.'

'I would not fret, too much, my lady. After she refused to stay here, Mrs Trotman insisted she stay with her sister in Chipstone, who promised to keep an eye on her. It cannot be denied, however, that the quicker her innocence is proved, the less danger there is of her doing anything foolish.'

'And Mrs Trotman conveyed my offer of employment, again?'

'Yes, my lady, but Mrs Pitkin refused.' He coughed. 'I understand her position. She has worked as a kitchen maid, and then a cook, her whole life. Even though she is friends with Mrs Trotman, it is difficult to see how it would work out.'

'A case of too many cooks?'

'Exactly, my lady. I also believe Mrs Pitkin is very distressed and not thinking, or acting, rationally.'

She nodded. 'So, we'd better make some progress on our second mission, and fast.'

Something in his usually impenetrable expression pulled her up short. 'What is it, Clifford?'

He cleared his throat gently. 'I merely wondered, my lady, if in fact they are two separate missions?'

She frowned. 'I don't follow you?'

'If we are to clear Mrs Pitkin's name, we will have to assume, until events prove otherwise, that Mrs Pitkin is telling the truth. Therefore, it seems someone maliciously fed Mr Aris peanuts with intent to kill. We do not yet know the motive. However, the majority of people, and thus suspects, who were at the table that night, are also now your political rivals. If the motive for Mr Aris' murder was politically motivated...'

Eleanor grimaced. 'Oh bother! I hadn't looked at it like that. If this anti-women's rights cabal is half as bad as Miss Mann is making out, I suppose it's perfectly feasible they did away with Aris as he supported the Women's League.'

Clifford cleared his throat. 'Then how much more unfavourably are they likely to look on you, my lady, now you are standing in Mr Aris' place, possibly denying their candidate success?'

Eleanor snorted. 'I can't believe anyone would credit me with much chance of success, Clifford. Only one woman has made it into Parliament so far. And no disrespect to her, but Mrs Astor was elected by her husband's supporters when he was forced into the House of Lords. She stood on the understanding that she would carry on her husband's policies and remain only until her husband could sit in the House of Commons again.'

'True, my lady, and I was only conjecturing.'

She nodded. 'At the moment we have no evidence at all that Mr Aris was nobbled for a political motive. In fact, we don't know much at all.' She brightened. 'But think about it. By standing, I'll have access to the very people who knew Aris best. I think I'll start with Carlton. Even the polite and mild-mannered Miss Mann seemed to think he is a bounder.'

'Might I suggest that there is another association you might wish to further as well?'

'With whom?'

'Lady Farrington.'

'Must I? She doesn't like me at all and was rude enough to show it.'

'Regrettable, my lady. However, she happens to live at the scene of the crime, and you mentioned her husband had some undisclosed dealings with Mr Aris?'

'Okay, Clifford. I'll get myself invited to Farrington Manor and you think up a ruse to go mingle with the staff.'

He gave his customary half-bow. 'Both are already in fact accomplished, my lady.'

'What? How?'

'Lady Farrington telephoned whilst you were engaged with Miss Mann. I accepted on your behalf. Tea at Farrington Estate is arranged for three o'clock tomorrow. And I have a hunch that the Rolls will suffer a most inconvenient breakdown on the premises.'

'One you can fix in a jiffy when we've the information we need?'

He nodded. 'And we can then assess, back here, exactly where we are in the investigation.'

'Agreed. And, as a bonus, if I survive Lady Farrington's venomous tongue, the world of politics should be a doddle.'

'I shall be sure to pack the Rolls' glovebox with a half-bottle of the finest distilled French brandy and a suitable crystal-cut glass.'

'Perfect! And I shall rant all the way home about how awful and sniffy she was.'

'Very good, my lady. I look forward to it most heartily.'

'Fibber!'

CHAPTER 9

The next afternoon found Eleanor at Farrington Manor. As instructed by Clements, the butler, Eleanor sat on a red velvet chaise that Henry VIII likely ordered several of his wives' executions from. The yellow ochre walls stretching three tall floors up to the elaborate glass-domed ceiling brought little cheer to the overall atmosphere of a medieval castle's armoury. Meticulously arranged fan-shaped displays of swords, battle shields, pikes and muskets rose up to the galleried second floor. Here, a regiment of suits of armour on silver horses stared defensively over the marble balustrade that ran the full perimeter of the hall. In the very centre of the room two white marble statues of horseback knights embroiled in a joust stood on plinths, the steeds rearing up for added drama.

The click of heels on the white marble floor echoed round the immense hall, making it hard to know which of the many passageways the noise came from. Eleanor hoped this would be a short meeting.

'Lady Swift, so good of you to call.' The crisp voice made her look up with her best guest smile ready.

'Ah, Lady Farrington. So kind of you to invite me.' Even with her longer-than-average legs, Eleanor had to shuffle forward in the velvet seat for her feet to reach the floor before she could stand and greet her hostess. 'Such a remarkable hall, I've been quite caught up in imagining all kinds of stories that might have played out in here.'

Lady Farrington's ash-blonde finger waves did not flinch as she swept a cursory glance around the enormous room. 'Alexander likes it. Very masculine, of course. It appeals to the warrior he still believes is surging through his genes somewhere.'

Eleanor feigned polite interest. 'It's quite fascinating.'

'No, Lady Swift, it's like living in a blasted museum! Do follow me.'

Feeling like the less-than-welcome cousin from the country, Eleanor adjusted the collar of her serge georgette tea-dress and trailed after Lady Farrington's ivory silk form.

Every inch the graceful lady of the house, her hostess led her through several miles of corridors. At regular intervals, staircases swept upwards and elaborate recesses were decorated with antique tapestries and gold-framed oil portraits.

Eleanor had formed a vague plan of action on the drive to the Farrington Estate, but something about Lady Farrington's cold manner made her doubt this would wash for a moment.

Eventually, Lady Farrington stopped at a bank of six oak doors which concertinaed back against the inside wall of the most exquisite sitting room Eleanor had ever seen.

'Wow!' she muttered, staring round her, the enchanting ambience leaving her feeling she had tiptoed inside the exotic tent of a princess.

'It appeals to my inner heroine in distress,' Lady Farrington said with surprising honesty, folding her long frame into a claw-footed wingback chair, upholstered in the exact shade of her dress. 'There is a touch of the hopeless romantic in all of us, after all.'

'Samarkand silks,' Eleanor said with genuine appreciation as she gazed round at the delicately patterned drapes, cushions and chair coverings. Each one was an artful variation of the ivory, jade and gold theme that threaded the room into an embroidered scene of cool opulence.

'You surprise, and please me, Lady Swift.' Her hostess tilted her head to one side. 'I wasn't sure you were quite the woman your reputation professes. I concede that I was wrong.'

Eleanor took the seat opposite Lady Farrington. 'My reputation?'

'No need to be coy. It is not an appealing quality, I find.'

A tray of strong Turkish coffee arrived with gold-rimmed cups and a silver dish of almonds and dates dusted with icing sugar. The maid placed this on the central walnut table between the copy of *Pride and Prejudice* and a silver-framed photograph of the Farringtons on their wedding day.

Eleanor seized the moment to decide how she was going to play this meeting. Lady Farrington was far from the delicate porcelain statue her pale complexion and angular frame belied.

'I've a peculiar sense that you have made enquiries about me?'

Lady Farrington's tone held a hint of something Eleanor couldn't quite place. 'Naturally. Why else do you imagine I invited you here so soon after we were introduced?'

'I admit I was surprised.'

'And relieved,' her hostess replied.

Where on earth is this conversation going, Ellie?

She took a sip of her coffee, enjoying the way it transported her back to her days in vibrant Asia, home of the unexpected. *Mind you, Farrington Manor was proving to house a few surprises.* Lady Farrington seemed to misjudge her silence for a moment and surprisingly gave away her next hand.

'I made enquiries, not about your travelling exploits but about your involvement in solving two recent murder cases.'

Eleanor couldn't resist the obvious parry. 'Naturally,' she said with a smile.

Lady Farrington laughed and seemed to relax a fraction. 'Mr Aris died at our annual fundraising event, Lady Swift. Whilst the modern way might be to shrug off the whispers of scandal, I prefer the approach of meeting it head-on and batting it smartly to the floor. I abhor tattle.'

'It can be so damaging, I've heard,' Eleanor said.

Lady Farrington nodded. 'Especially if one has... business dealings.'

Eleanor recalled Lord Farrington's reference to Aris being a useful man to know. 'Did you suspect foul play on the night Mr Aris died?'

'I did, and I didn't. These things are so tedious.'

Eleanor wasn't sure if the reference was to fundraising events or guests inconveniently dying in front of the assembled company. 'Tedious?' she queried.

'Small gatherings are always the worst, especially when they consist of individuals desirous of being seen in the right place with the right people. And with the requirement to be charming and gracious throughout the evening when one is shuddering over the dinner topics and limited etiquette. I mean, rowing at a function. If it hadn't been for Alexander being so insistent that his latest project depended on Aris' support, I would have had the two of them ejected.'

'Ernest Carlton being the other man in the argument?'

'Something quite odious about him.' Lady Farrington nodded. 'One is used to seeing members of the lower classes scurry up any whiff of a social ladder, however precariously it leans. But Mr Carlton appears to have slid willingly and, in fact, deliberately, down the rungs to inhabit those occupied by the working classes.'

Is that what her husband had hinted at over the Langham lunch when he said Carlton was batting for the wrong side, Ellie?

'Did you happen to overhear what they rowed about?'

'What didn't they row about would be an easier question to answer. I was caught up in trying to keep the rest of the table from focussing on their disagreeable behaviour, so most of it missed my ears. I got the feeling that it was borne of ancient history between them, but I couldn't swear to it.'

Eleanor dragged another part of Lord Farrington's comments back from her memory. She threw a question out as nonchalantly as she could: 'Perhaps Carlton disagreed with the principle of whatever property investment Mr Aris was considering with your husband?'

Lady Farrington shook her head. 'That, of all things, should have been one thing Carlton and Aris wholeheartedly agreed on.' She threw Eleanor a knowing look. 'But there is no need to fish, Lady Swift. I need any hint of scandal over Aris' death squashed. I'm sure the cook was guilty of a criminal oversight, but tongues will wag. It's no use trusting the police. There was a time you could guarantee they'd play ball and the word of a lady over a servant meant something.' For a moment she looked wistful. 'You could rely on authorities to be discreet, but since the war, well…' She waved her hand dismissively. 'You, however, Lady Swift, are of our class and understand these things. Therefore, I will assist you in your investigation by offering any information I can.'

'Thank you. I accept your offer of help in establishing just how Mr Aris died, Lady Farrington. But am I really that transparent?'

'Quite the reverse, actually. I left the Langham lunch questioning my intuition that your empathetic concern over our disastrous dinner held anything behind it. But, as I said, I will not tolerate scandal, hence conducting my own investigation of you. Needless to say, I was pleased by what I heard.'

'From whom, may I ask?'

'You may not,' came the crisp reply. 'Now, you can ask me any questions you need, with the proviso I may not answer them all.'

Eleanor didn't like being dictated to, but Mrs Trotman, and more seriously, her friend Mrs Pitkin, were relying on her and Clifford. She forced a smile and took out her notebook. 'First off, why are you really offering to help?'

Lady Farrington smiled thinly. 'I've already told you, I don't want any scandal and that I may not answer all your questions.'

Eleanor sensed Lady Farrington obviously had another reason but she wasn't going to tell Eleanor what it was, so she changed tack: 'Right, I'll start by asking about the chocolate fudge that Aris ate. Did Mrs… your cook, make it often?'

'Yes, it was a favourite of Alexander's. Only when Cook made it normally, she put peanuts in it.'

'I was told that Mr Aris had eaten here before. Wasn't it an awful—'

'Hassle with his allergy? Absolutely! So why did we put up with it?'

The one thing Eleanor hated more than being dictated to was having her thoughts anticipated. Clifford was a master at it. 'Yes, I was wondering that. And since you've removed the need for pretence, I shall also be direct. Was the reason anything to do with the property investment project Aris and your husband were involved in?'

Lady Farrington smiled drily. 'Touché! As the Member of Parliament for this area, Aris was a useful man for being able to weigh influence locally, and in Whitehall. Rather quaintly, he agreed because he believed in the project from an ethical, as well as monetary, point of view. Alexander, however, is in it for the money alone.'

'Which is why at luncheon the other day, Lord Farrington said Aris was a useful man to know?'

'Quite! You will have heard of the Addison Act of last year, as the newspapers dubbed it?'

'Regrettably last year, I was somewhat indisposed in South Africa.'

'Of course,' Lady Farrington replied without sarcasm. 'The Housing Act was passed to burden local councils with the duty to provide improved housing for the lower classes.'

Eleanor smiled. 'Very commendable.'

Lady Farrington snorted. 'The war may be behind us, Lady Swift, but the majority of men sent to the front at the time bore the reduced health and fitness that results from poor housing. In these uncertain times, the powers that be are acutely aware that this time of peace may not last. Our soldiers need to come from healthier stock in the event of another war, which is why the government is insisting councils clear away slums and build the residents better housing. It isn't out of the goodness of their hearts!'

Eleanor pursed her lips. 'Sounds rather callous on paper.'

'Yes, but the families that are given access to the newly-built council housing will greatly benefit, would you not agree?'

'Well, yes.'

'And Alexander and I, will benefit greatly as the housing will be built on land that we own.'

'Ah! That's cleared up why Aris was—'

'Worth the trouble of making sure there were no traces of peanuts anywhere he went? Yes. Although if you have an allergy so severe you are going to die, it's just a matter of when.'

Eleanor mentally shook her head at Lady Farrington's callousness. 'And Mr Aris' allergy was that severe?'

Lady Farrington finished lighting a cigarette. She offered one to Eleanor, who declined. Her hostess drew on the cigarette and blew out the smoke in a long, thin trail. 'The way the man went on about it when he accepted a dinner invitation, you'd have thought just being in a room with a peanut would have been enough to kill him. Men! They are such children sometimes.'

Eleanor hurried on to her next question: 'Who amongst your guests that night was aware of Mr Aris' allergy?'

Lady Farrington shrugged. 'It was common knowledge.'

Drat, Ellie, that doesn't help. 'Well, who amongst the guests would have known that your cook would prepare,' she looked down at her notebook, 'chocolate and peanut butter fudge?'

She realised she was hungry and reached for an almond and a date.

Lady Farrington looked at Eleanor with a hint of grudging admiration. 'I see you really have done this before.' She thought for a moment, tapping her cigarette over a silver ashtray. 'Most of the guests had been to one or two previous functions, I suppose, but whether Cook prepared fudge, I don't know. Even if she had, it wouldn't mean she was doing so again.'

Eleanor looked down at her questions: so far she'd drawn a blank.

'Do you know any reason someone might want to—'

'Murder Mr Aris?' Lady Farrington laughed shortly. 'I rather imagined that was what you were going to find out? You and that butler of yours. I understand that he has assisted you in previous investigations.'

Eleanor shrugged. 'Fabulously unseemly, isn't it?'

Lady Farrington gestured towards the bell rope. 'I assume you wish to visit the room where Mr Aris died? Do you think your butler will have had time to grill my staff yet?'

'Indeed I do,' Eleanor agreed cheerily. 'But wha—?'

Lady Farrington rose as effortlessly as if she weighed less than paper. 'If, my dear, you are going to have your butler fabricate a story about a car breaking down, better not make it a Rolls.'

Eleanor smiled despite herself.

The Farringtons' butler appeared. Lady Langham instructed him to take Eleanor to Clifford, then turned to her: 'I've some things to attend to, so Clements here will see you out when you're done. I hope you live up to your reputation, Lady Swift.' She half turned away, then turned back: 'And I would ask that you don't mention any of this to my husband. Alexander has enough to worry about at the moment. Just keep it between ourselves.'

Having met up with Clifford and Clements departed, Eleanor whispered, 'This is all very peculiar. Lady Farrington has not only given permission for us to snoop, she has offered to pass on any information she can.'

Clifford lowered his voice as well. 'Indeed, my lady. Mr Clements, the butler, had already drawn up a guest list for the night of Mr Aris' murder, including where everyone was sitting.'

He handed it to Eleanor, who ran her eye down the list.

Lord Farrington
Lady Farrington
Mr Oswald Greaves
Mr Ernest Carlton
Mr Arnold Aris
Miss Mann
Mr Stanley Morris
Mr Duncan Blewitt
Mr Vernon Peel
Lord and Lady Fenwick-Langham (cancelled)

She copied the names carefully into a fresh page of her notebook.

Clifford waited until she had finished and added, 'He also informed me that Lady Farrington had instructed the staff to provide us with any information we might require.'

'Odder and odder! Still, might as well take advantage of it.' She stared intently at the names on her list and then at the table. 'I say, Clifford, if we are to believe Mrs Pitkin, then the fudge containing the peanuts must have been introduced up here, at the table, not in the kitchen. Which means those sitting either side of Mr Aris would have had the best opportunity!'

Clifford nodded. 'That is a sound theory, my lady. Unfortunately, it is immaterial as I was informed that before the toasts, the assembled company left the table to mingle and so forth.'

'Blast!' Eleanor looked back at her list. 'Well, I asked Lady Farrington who would know the cook was making that particular fudge beforehand, and she reckoned no one did. But if no one knew, then—'

'No one could have made a peanut-laced substitute. Unless, rather than switch the peanut-less piece for one with peanuts, they somehow added peanuts to the original peanut-less piece on Mr Aris' plate.'

They both considered this option for a moment, before both shaking their heads in unison.

'Too risky and complicated,' Eleanor said. 'I think we have to assume that someone must have prepared a "special" piece of fudge laced with peanuts beforehand.'

Clifford nodded. 'Indeed. Which means that someone at the table must have known Mrs Pitkin would make fudge. And yet, it seems, no one could have.'

Eleanor nodded, and turned around. 'Where does that lead?' she asked, looking at a nearby door.

'Those at the table would have seen their meals arrive through that door. It leads directly to the second butler's pantry, I believe.'

Eleanor made a face. 'Second pantry! Henley Hall is quite large enough for me. Here, I'd feel like a pea left in a canning factory that has closed down.'

'Henley Hall is much more manageable, my lady.'

'It's much more than that, Clifford. It's like a home. Lady Farrington herself said living here felt like living in a museum. It doesn't feel at all homely.'

Clifford nodded. 'I believe that is due to the strained relations above, and below, stairs. At Henley Hall, you have admirably continued the tradition set by your uncle of maintaining harmony amongst the staff.'

'Thank you, Clifford. Although I think I only achieved that after I stopped accusing you of trying to murder me when I first arrived.'

'True, my lady. The point is the relationship between Lady Farrington and the staff is acrimonious at best. She has been through three cooks in three years and as many footmen, maids and gardeners.'

Eleanor sighed. 'Why do some people have to be so difficult? Now, what can you add that you found out downstairs?'

'Apart from obtaining the guest list, and the names of servants that evening, I found out a certain matter that may, or may not, have a bearing on the case in hand.'

Eleanor's eyes were wide. 'Go on?'

He gave a discreet cough. 'At the risk of giving the impression the staff were indiscreet, my lady, there is talk. Talk of there being a substantial rift between his lord and ladyship, which has become something of a chasm since Mr Aris' demise.'

Eleanor let out a long, low whistle. 'She wasn't terribly complimentary about her husband, I have to say. So why...' Eleanor scratched her nose, deep in thought. 'Ah! With Aris dead, they've lost the powerful supporter they needed to make sure this housing plan went ahead on their land. Maybe it's more serious than she made it out to be. Perhaps they are in debt and need the money from the sale of the land to stave off bankruptcy? I can see that would put a tremendous strain on an already difficult relationship.'

'That is how I have surmised the situation to be, my lady.'

Eleanor shook her head. 'Which still doesn't explain why she wants us to find out who killed Aris when she's already laid the blame squarely at the cook's door. And why she wants to keep the fact that she is helping us a secret from her husband.' She looked around the room in despair. 'We're getting nowhere. With the second pantry door being over there and the number of servants coming and going that night, we can't even say if the murderer was one of the guests, or the servants.'

'Actually, my lady, fortune has favoured us, and Mrs Pitkin, there.'

Eleanor stopped examining the table and spun round. 'Well, we could certainly do with some. What have you learned?'

'If you recall, Mrs Pitkin insisted that she had locked all peanuts away?'

'Yes, she said she'd asked your Mr Clements to lock them in the butler's pantry.'

'Exactly, my lady, and Mr Clements corroborated this. And that Mrs Pitkin also insisted all staff scrub surfaces and their hands.'

'She could have been covering herself, Clifford. You know, if she was the one who...'

'Possibly, my lady, but one of the kitchen maids also confirmed that she helped Mrs Pitkin make the fudge. And then Mrs Pitkin left her to finish the decorations on top – the Farrington coat of arms in red icing, I believe. The point is the maid insists she was with Mrs Pitkin the whole time the fudge was being made. And then Mrs Pitkin was engaged in other duties and never returned to the table whilst the maid was decorating the fudge.'

Eleanor frowned. 'But surely the maid told the police all this?'

Clifford nodded. 'As I said, my lady, about the strained relations above and below stairs?' He lowered his voice. 'I cannot imagine that Lady Farrington wanted this information to come out, but Mrs Pitkin has more support amongst the servants here than I think Lady Farrington imagines. After being taken to the depths of the wine cellar, I was told, in strict secrecy, that the kitchen maid was told to tell the police that Mrs Pitkin finished the fudge. And told that she couldn't confirm Mrs Pitkin's innocence one way or the other.'

Eleanor gasped. 'Who told her to say that?' But she already knew.

'Lady Farrington, on pain of instant dismissal with no references. I believe several other staff received similar warnings. As you know, my lady, like Mrs Pitkin, to be dismissed without references is tantamount to a ticket—'

'Straight to the workhouse!' Eleanor shuddered. 'What happened to the fudge after the kitchen maid finished decorating it, though?'

'She gave it to the footman, who was waiting. Apparently, it was already late in the making and was taken directly to the table, where it was put on display, then cut into bite-sized pieces and placed on each guest's side plate. It seems it is a tradition that, as the chocolate fudge has the family crest on, it is eaten as a kind of toast after dessert. Each piece is but a mouthful.'

'And was the toast taken immediately?'

'I had the same thought, my lady. No, the fudge was placed on each guest's plate with the dessert.'

'Was there any left over?'

'A few pieces – they were placed on the larger of the serving tables.'

'I see.' Eleanor tapped her front teeth, deep in thought. 'Then Mrs Pitkin can't be guilty, I feel. Not only because her story is corroborated by the rest of the staff, but also because... unless... But wait...' She frowned. 'Did the police test the remaining pieces of fudge?'

Clifford shook his head. 'I have no idea, my lady. I do see, however, where your mind is going. If there were no traces of peanuts in the remaining pieces of fudge, then again, Mrs Pitkin is innocent.'

Eleanor nodded. 'Yes, because the peanuts must have been introduced after the fudge was cut – and Mrs Pitkin couldn't possibly have done that.' She frowned again. 'But DCI Seldon is in charge of the case. He knows what he's doing.'

Clifford nodded. 'The Chief Inspector is indeed a fine policeman, my lady, but he can only have tested what is there.'

Eleanor gasped. 'You mean...'

Clifford nodded again. 'After Mr Aris' death, the staff were told to wait in the kitchen until the police arrived. All the guests had eaten their fudge, as I said, it was a mere mouthful, but when the footman looked to retrieve the remaining fudge from the sideboard, it had—'

'Vanished!'

CHAPTER 10

Eleanor set off purposefully to the morning room for a hearty breakfast. Campaigning would take concentration and energy and other stuff she imagined was essential but had no idea about.

Whilst campaigning, however, she was determined to continue her investigation on behalf of Mrs Pitkin, especially having established her innocence to her and Clifford's satisfaction. Eleanor had been keen on contacting DCI Seldon and telling him what they had found out. Clifford, however, had sounded a note of caution, pointing out that it would still be the servants' word against that of Lady Farrington. And her husband was an earl and sat in the House of Lords. Even if DCI Seldon believed them, what could he do? His hands would be tied. The only solution was to find Aris' murderer themselves and present it as a fait accompli.

So far, she had Carlton pegged as a suspect and the odious Mr Blewitt after Miss Mann's revelation. She also had the Farringtons listed, but it was hard to reconcile them as suspects as it seemed they needed Aris very much alive for the business deal. Thus, she decided she needed proper fortification this morning if she was going to make any headway in campaigning or investigating.

In the breakfast room, she lifted each of the three silver-topped salvers on the sideboard: sausages, eggs, scalloped potatoes and toast. Just what was needed to get the brain going to separate genuine clues from ill-founded gossip and hearsay.

A hesitant tap sounded at the door.

'Come in, Polly.'

The maid shouldered the door open and wobbled in, red-faced and breathless, bearing a tray with another salver and two round silver pots. The spoons that had left the kitchen smartly set in the pots now seesawed on the rims, threatening to flick a mess of sauce everywhere.

Eleanor blanched. 'Good gracious, Polly! Did you trip on the way here?'

'No, your ladyship, I'm as right as sunshine, thank you.'

'Rain, Polly.'

'Oh, your ladyship, that will be a shame. Rain today, is it? Mind, Mr Wendon will be chuffed, he said the flowers is crying out for a drink.'

'No, Polly, the expression you were looking for is… anyway, it doesn't matter. What have you got there?'

The young girl slid the tray awkwardly onto the sideboard.

Eleanor raised an eyebrow. 'More sausages! Is Gladstone planning on joining me for breakfast?'

Polly looked confused. 'Beg pardon, your ladyship, but Mrs Butters said most definitely he was to stay in his basket. He's snoring by the range, burning his nose again, I shouldn't wonder. He doesn't like it when we ties a cold compress on, but he won't learn.'

Suddenly the young girl clammed up, her hand over her mouth. Between her fingers, she whispered, 'I got it wrong again, didn't I? Why do I always forget?' Banging her forehead with each word, she finished with, 'Not. Allowed. To. Chat. To. Her. Ladyship!'

Eleanor jumped up from the table and put her arm around the young girl. 'Of course you're allowed to talk to me, Polly. After all, I asked you a question, didn't I?'

Polly looked up, relieved, but she still gave a long, loud sniff. ''Tis confusing, your ladyship. I'm trying to follow the upstairs–downstairs rules, honest.' She bobbed a curtsey and scuttled from the room.

'So am I, Polly,' Eleanor said softly after her.

*

Having decided to cycle, the buffeting wind made hard work of the few miles into the village, despite it being downhill almost all the way. It did, however, burn up a fair proportion of the enormous breakfast Eleanor had eaten and the views of the valley, in its full autumnal glory, made it worthwhile.

As she entered the tiny high street, she let out a groan. How had she ended up trying to further women's rights and at the same time trying to solve a murder? The only bright spot was that after the revelations about Lady Farrington forcing the servants to lie and the disappearance of the leftover fudge, she and Clifford were both convinced of Mrs Pitkin's innocence. And, conversely, sure of the guilt of one of the guests around that table. *Guests and hosts*, Eleanor reminded herself.

Despite it being Thursday, Clifford's day off, he'd offered to help her campaign in Little Buckford. Much as she appreciated his offer and his unwavering loyalty and support, she didn't relish the idea of anyone peering over her shoulder as she attempted her first campaign.

She resolved to sound out a few villagers' political allegiances before weaving in some artful questions about Aris' death. And Carlton's possible motive for killing him. Even though she still needed to go through the rest of the guest list with Clifford, the two men rowing in public was at the forefront of her mind.

She paused by the village green, clutching at her lucky emerald scarf as it threatened to blow off across the county.

Not that she thought she needed luck. Everyone knew her in Little Buckford, so were bound to support her stand. At least, that was the reason she'd given Clifford when she'd told him to meet her in two hours and they'd go together to tackle Chipstone. A town like Chipstone was likely to be a very different proposition to Little Buckford.

She glanced at the pamphlet in her, now properly repaired, basket. Miss Mann had given her some literature to ensure she was prepared, but Eleanor's eyes had glazed over on reading. She wasn't convinced she could use any of it and sound, well, natural, or genuine. *Or yourself, Ellie.*

She tutted aloud and shook her head. No matter, she was resourceful and determined. And she was genuine. Women deserved help and here she was, charging to the front to champion their cause. Miss Mann had arranged for her to attend the next meeting of the Women's League, where they would discuss her standing. But as it wasn't for a few days, Eleanor had foolishly, she now thought, insisted she'd be fine starting the campaign ball rolling on her own. *Oh, Ellie, you and your big mouth!*

Pulling out her uncle's fob watch, she calculated that the good village folk would shortly stop gossiping on their doorsteps and come into town to gossip on someone else's. That would give her a captive audience. Small village life had taught her one thing: local news was spread by the village drums and gossip fuelled those drums like lit paraffin.

She would simply inform the villagers she was standing as an independent candidate with the backing of the Women's League. Then they would spread the word of her noble stand for women's equality and those other bits in the literature she'd hopefully remember to tell them.

Before she could decide whether to start at the nearest or furthest end of the high street, a waving hand distracted her.

Eleanor waved back and the Reverend Gaskill, vicar of the local St Winifred's Church, joined her.

After exchanging some general chit-chat, Eleanor felt confident enough to broach the subject of her campaigning.

'Reverend, I have something terribly exciting to share with you.'

She announced her news with a flourish. Strangely, Reverend Gaskill seemed oddly underwhelmed.

'Oh dear, dear, that is rather surprising.' His tone suggested to her he really meant 'disappointing'. He stared at the ground, shuffling his feet. 'The thing is, Lady Swift, I am not convinced that forming divisions under political parties, or gender, will ever result in a great many good deeds being done.'

Eleanor was taken aback. 'But that's exactly the opposite of what the Women's League is trying to achieve. We want to unite, not divide. I rather thought I might count on your vote?'

Reverend Gaskill gently shook his head. 'Gracious, no! I am a vicar, dear lady. Surely you remember Romans 13, verses 1–7? "For there is no authority except from God, and those that exist have been instituted by God". Dear, dear! I shan't be voting, merely praying that the best man, or woman, wins because he has an honest heart.'

'Let's hope that is the case, Reverend. Poor Mr Aris certainly seemed to have won the local people's support.'

'God rest his soul.' Reverend Gaskell shook his head. 'A fine example of compassion and generosity he was and, now, a great loss to us all.'

'Did you know him well?'

'Yes, he was one of the St Swithun's flock. He was always willing to help those less fortunate than himself when the opportunity arose. I was delighted that he chose to celebrate something of a recent prosperity that came his way with our orphans' fund. So kind! Good day, Lady Swift.'

Determined not to be deflated by this early setback, Eleanor walked her bicycle to the first shop in the high street. As she walked, she wondered if Aris' recent prosperity had played any part in his murder. Was it a payment from Lord Farrington for Aris pushing for this housing development to be built on his land?

Through the open door of Brenchley's Stores she could see a positive hubbub of people: the perfect audience.

Walking towards the counter, she offered a cheery wave. 'Mr Brenchley, an extra-fine good morning to you.'

'Lady Swift, you seem in particularly fine spirits. How can I help?'

'Actually, Mr Brenchley,' she let her voice carry further round the shop, 'I come with a request that you might further your already superb services to our wonderful community by displaying this poster.'

Brenchley smiled. 'I'm sure that can be arranged. What event is it you're holding?'

From behind the shelves off to the right, Eleanor heard twittering voices and just caught a whispered, 'Ooh, a garden party up at the Hall!'

Wrong... but not a bad idea if, no, when, she'd won. She made a mental note to file that away for later.

'Actually, Mr Brenchley, I am standing in the election as an independent. I hope to further the excellent work started by poor Mr Aris.' She faltered for a second, then gathered her courage again. Facing deadly predators in the bush was a lot less nerve-racking than this! 'So... so, yes, I would be most grateful if you could display this poster alerting people to the, er... exciting news.'

Brenchley appeared flummoxed. So flummoxed, in fact, that he failed to move his arm sufficiently to take the poster.

'Gracious, I...' He rubbed his forehead. 'Lady Swift...' He tailed off again. Beside him, his son John had appeared, unnoticed, and stood staring at the floor.

A shadow crossed her brow. 'Is something wrong?'

He shot a look at his son and then shoved his hands into the deep pockets of his shopkeeper's overcoat. 'With apologies, my lady, I always remain neutral during the election season. It pays to stay out of such matters in my business. I am sorry.'

'But if you were to display the campaign materials from any party who asked, that would be fair, wouldn't it?'

He sighed. 'My sincere apologies again, it is not a battle I wish to saddle my horse for.'

Eleanor was stunned, but quickly accepted this was just another hurdle to triumph over. She smiled warmly. 'No matter, I understand your position. Shame, though, as I wanted to let all the ladies of our community, such as your dear wife, know they can rely on me in their fight for equality.'

This drew a collective sharp intake of breath.

A voice called from the door. 'Lady Swift? Forgive my intruding on your audience, but I like to be abreast of political matters.'

Eleanor stared at the woman, struggling to place her, although there was something familiar about her. Was this another case of everyone knowing who Eleanor was and yet she knew very few of her fellow villagers? *Dash it, still the new girl in town!* Aha! That thought sparked her memory. She took in the woman's sensible navy cotton long-sleeved dress, thick white hair in a neat bun and round spectacles.

'Mrs Linscombe!' she said cheerily. 'How are you?'

'Luscombe. And sufficiently well, thank you, although I am potentially perturbed by someone waging a war on my behalf, without my knowledge or agreement.' Her last words blew a chill through the shop.

Eleanor kept smiling. 'No one mentioned war, Mrs Luscombe. Let me explain… The Women's League have asked me to stand, and should I be successful, I shall also take the opportunity to further the rights of women, not just locally, but nationally.'

Mrs Luscombe's lips set in a firm line. 'Really? And have you asked the ladies of our happy community if they are seeking "equality"? Because I think you'll find that we are very content with things the way they are.' A tight-lipped smile flashed across Mrs Luscombe's face. 'Lady Swift, I'm sure Mr Brenchley won't mind if the ladies let you hear their views right now?'

Eleanor fought the urge to turn and run. She repeated the mantra her father used to say to her whenever she was faced with an unfamiliar creature in whatever exotic country or island on which they were currently stationed: 'Come on, Ellie, it's more afraid of you than you are of it.'

Eleanor glanced at Brenchley, who had the look of a terrified rabbit outnumbered by a pride of hungry lions. That had been the problem with her father's advice once she'd arrived in South Africa. Most of the creatures inhabiting that country were definitely NOT more afraid of her than she was of them. Brenchley returned her gaze with a sympathetic shrug of his eyebrows, then turned to Mrs Luscombe and held up his hands: 'Go ahead, ladies.'

Mrs Luscombe pointed to two of the other ladies in the shop. 'Mrs Jenkins, Mrs Browne, would you like the opportunity to go to work from seven in the morning until eight at night, as your husbands do? And perhaps have them stay at home and raise the children and keep the house?'

'Mercy, no!' they choroused. The plumper of the two blushed as she nudged her friend in the ribs. 'Can you imagine the mess, Ida? The chaos?' A collective shudder ran through the assembled throng.

Eleanor tried to steer the conversation back to safer ground. 'Well, that is just one example. Let's start with you all having the right to vote at twenty-one like men. Why should you wait until you're thirty to have your say?'

From behind her, Eleanor heard a throat being cleared. 'No disrespect, Lady Swift, I might have the vote now, but I've no time for wading through the newspaper when I've a home and family to see to. And most young 'uns trying to bring up a family don't either.' This brought a round of vociferous nodding. 'I rely on my Tom to tell me what I need to know. If I vote, he'll let me know who to vote for.'

General hubbub of agreement and disbelieving cries broke out at the thought of any married woman voting differently from her husband. The consensus was summed up by a middle-aged woman with rosy cheeks and soft brown curls under her grey felt hat. 'First nugget of peaceful times and we're looking to start a war between us and our menfolk!'

Eleanor had heard enough. That was the second mention of war. Even she recognised when it was time to retreat. 'Thank you, ladies! And you, Mr Brenchley, for the kind usage of your marvellous shop for our enlightening discussion, I really am most grateful. If anyone has any questions or would like to discuss any, er, issues, you all know where to find me.'

Pausing only long enough to nod to Mrs Luscombe, Eleanor escaped out into the fresh air, ignoring the riotous clamouring that broke out behind her.

Well, she conceded to herself, *the villagers were a little more traditional in their opinions than she'd assumed.* This afternoon, with Clifford, she would likely fare better in the bustling metropolis of Chipstone, surely more radical territory?

That Chipstone was a small market town, inhabited by folk with much the same mentality as Little Buckford, Eleanor chose to ignore. After all, her only other option was quitting, and she had no intention of letting herself, or the Women's League, down.

Or Mother and Father, Ellie.

CHAPTER 11

It felt good to have someone with her this time, Eleanor admitted to herself. Nothing wrong with fancying a bit of sympathetic company when campaigning and solving a murder. She peered sideways at Clifford at the wheel, his impeccably brushed bowler hat almost touching the headlining of the Rolls.

He broke into her thoughts: 'Where shall we start, do you propose, my lady?'

Cheered by the 'we' in his question, she opened her mouth and then stared out of the window with the realisation that she had set off without a plan, *again*. She had only visited Chipstone in the past to get items she couldn't buy in Little Buckford. Oh, and to visit the fabulous Winsomes Tea Rooms with its award-winning fruitcake. Making a mental note to reward her and Clifford with several slices once they'd won the town over, she weighed up her options.

She knew no one except the local police, who she'd recently accused (rightly) of corruption, and a gang of urchins not old enough to vote, neither an excellent starting point. So, stop people in the street? Clifford knew almost everybody, but she couldn't fall back on him too much. After all, she was the candidate. She needed to present herself front and centre. *So, Ellie, approach those with a prominent window to display a poster? Or ease in and drop a few leaflets through letterboxes?*

'How about we start at the far end, Clifford? I'll take the left side of the street and you take the right?'

'Very good, my lady.'

Once parked, with a respectful lift of his bowler hat, Clifford crossed the road with a neat sheaf of leaflets in his leather-gloved hand.

Right, who will be your first target, Ellie?

To her left, a puff of pipe smoke billowed out from a moustached, elderly gentleman in a heavily-decorated military uniform. He was leaning on a walking stick and given his advanced years, she concluded he was unlikely to be sympathetic to her cause. In any case, she'd have to bellow into the ear trumpet hanging from a leather strap on his shoulder. Not the best way to ease in.

Looking at the first row of shops, Eleanor decided that the watch mender, the cobbler and the china emporium were as good a set of places to start as anywhere. But then a sign down a side alley caught her eye: Reading Room. All Welcome.

Of course, that's where the enlightened types will hang out, Ellie.

A few minutes later, as she moved on to the next shop, she saw the woman ripping the leaflets up and dropping them into the wastepaper basket by her desk.

Needing a fresh approach, Eleanor paused by the watchmakers. Perhaps she'd do better if she played down her involvement? Now that was a plan! Distribute the campaigning literature without highlighting the fact that the Women's League had clearly lost their minds in proposing her as a candidate. She looked across at Clifford as he doffed his hat to a group of ladies on the opposite pavement. Perhaps she ought to send him back to the Rolls?

You're not quite feeling that brave yet, Ellie!

Instead, she stepped into the watchmakers and beamed a hearty 'Good morning!'

'Supposed to cloud over presently and rain soon enough, though,' came the reply. 'With you in a moment.' White hair and wrinkles topped off the extraordinarily large spectacles on the near-fossilised face that appeared. As he parted the curtain partitioning the front of the shop from the rear, it revealed a poster for the Labour Party filling the entire wall behind him. 'Yes, miss?'

She stared at the badge he sported on his apron: 'Vote Labour'.

'Would you look at my late uncle's fob watch? I believe it's running rather slow?'

Abashed at how quickly she'd bailed out of another campaigning opportunity, she tried to redeem herself by jumping into investigation mode. This man might know something about Carlton, seeing as he was the Labour candidate.

As the watchmaker rummaged in a drawer, she coughed. 'Have you high hopes for Mr Carlton being the man to win the election?'

The watchmaker turned around and shrugged: ''Tis not a case of Carlton being the man, 'tis a case of he's all we've got!' He looked up at her, his eyes boring into hers. 'I distrust Mr Carlton, even though he's a Labour man like myself. He'd do well to remember that us old folk have a long memory.' He held out her pocket watch. 'Three shillings, please.'

It seemed that Mr Carlton was not highly regarded, but that didn't make him a murderer.

At the window of the cobblers, she jumped as a fierce-looking giant in a leather apron moved out of the shadow of the boot rack against the wall. He glared at her, hammer in hand. Behind him, two others appeared to be having something of a disagreement, one waving scissors as large as sheep shears. Perhaps not there, she decided, hurrying into the china emporium next door, where she was rewarded by the welcome sight of ladies browsing and gossiping.

Perfect!

Amongst the artfully displayed but modest-priced tableware lined up on Welsh dressers and gingham covered tables, her ears pricked up as the name Aris was mentioned.

'Course I've not been round to offer condolences, that Mrs Aris wouldn't take kindly to finding me standing on her doorstep. Even though my John's doing well, it's not well enough for the likes of her.'

'Must be hard on her though. I know it's always been said that… well, you know, but still…'

Eleanor nonchalantly stepped to the dresser next to the two women. She judged them to be in their early thirties, both wearing an improbable amount of black kohl around their eyes and distracting lipstick.

The taller of the two leaned towards her friend. 'John said there was talk at the Lamb and Wagon alehouse last night. Folks were saying they reckon those Farringtons probably did it.'

Another woman with a toddler on her hip sidled up to join them. 'Morning! Talking about what I think you are?'

'Whole town's talking about it, what did you expect?'

The newest member of the huddle gave a knowing look. ''Twasn't no frame job. That cook, she's been in trouble afore.'

'How do you know that?'

'Mary at the Post Office. She hears everything. Toffs send telegrams all the time. Not her fault if she happens to remember what the messages say, is it?'

'You mean this isn't the first one she's done in! I've read about her kind. Becomes a habit.'

The quietest of the women tuned in to Eleanor standing close to them. 'Morning?' she said, her tone questioning.

'Morning, ladies, my apologies for overhearing you talk of the big news. Shocking, isn't it?'

The women looked at each other and then back at her.

The tallest spoke first. 'Shocking? Maybe. Mr Aris might have had a big reputation but if you court trouble, it always finds you, that's what my mother used to say.'

Eleanor leaned forward. 'Gracious, you expect potential Members of Parliament to behave better, don't you? Still, power goes to people's heads, I suppose.'

'Wasn't power that made him start a showdown at a public meeting. There's ways of doing things and that's not one of them in my book. My John saw it all, a few weeks back. Said the other fellow was laughing smug like, but Aris went at him like a ferret.'

Eleanor threw on her winning smile. 'That, ladies, is why I believe we need a female to champion our needs. We simply want the job done, don't we? No interest in fighting. That is why I have agreed to stand.'

The women gasped in unison.

'You mean you're...' The shorter of them giggled.

Eleanor hastily placed a leaflet in each of the women's hands. Tucking another in the sticky fingers of the toddler, she nodded a genial farewell. 'Lovely to have met you all. Do call if you have any questions.' She turned to go. 'Oh, who was it I should watch out for with a rash of ferret bites about his person?'

The group's appointed spokeswoman looked up from the pamphlet: 'Oswald Greaves.'

'Marvellous!' She filed the name away and fled.

With one side of the high street covered with little success on any count, and Clifford nowhere in sight, Eleanor wasn't keen to continue on to the end. The most she had achieved was a couple of leaflets begrudgingly taken and a lecture on why Parliament is, and should remain, the province of men.

Few people seemed to have anything positive to say about Carlton. But, annoyingly, very little useful information either. Eleanor was learning that mostly people were indifferent or openly hostile to candidates of any political persuasion.

'So kind,' she called over her shoulder to the greengrocer who had followed her outside to expound on maintaining family values. Apparently, there was no point in giving women the vote as they had neither the need, nor understanding, for it.

She waved cheerily to him as she set off for one couple she had more hope for.

She'd visited their shop once before, looking for help in tracking down a dashedly devious murderer. *Now, which was it?* She held her hand over her eyes and peered along the street. Ah! Pigs' trotters hanging in rows along the front, that would be their grocery-cum-all-sorts store.

The rough brickwork of the shopfront was hidden by a bewildering array of items, including the ubiquitous pigs' trotters she'd noticed earlier. It seemed all of Chipstone must dine on them regularly. She wriggled past the sacks of potatoes and large drums of paraffin.

'Good morning, Mr Wright.'

'Morning, miss. Oh… beg pardon, m'lady. Maud!' The square chap behind the counter called behind him. 'Wife is just coming.' He hummed awkwardly, looking anywhere except at Eleanor until a petite woman appeared at his side.

'You lummock!' she whispered to him. 'Good morning, m'lady. How are you?' Maud Wright snatched at the wilder strands of her grey hair, willing them into submission with a bent hair grip.

'I'm in great form, as I hope you both are too?'

'We're all good here, thank you kindly. Is it Alfie you're looking for again? He told us all about the excitement you gave him and his merry soldiers a few months back.'

Eleanor smiled. 'It's not every day I need to enlist the help of such a fine band of boys in capturing a murderer.'

'Bad business,' Frank muttered and went back to staring at the counter.

Eleanor felt at ease with this couple, yet she barely knew them. She pondered on their age. It could be anywhere from late forties to early sixties.

'Forgive my asking, Mrs Wright, but are your family all grown up?'

She instantly regretted her question as Maud blushed. 'Frank and me, well, we're just Frank and me, aren't we, luv?'

He reached over and squeezed her hand.

'Gracious, I'm so sorry! I didn't mean to pry. Just chatting, oh dear!'

'It's no matter, m'lady. No need to apologise. Life works a certain way for certain folk, which it seems is us in that regard, but we've a great many other blessings.' Maud smiled at Eleanor. 'Now, what is it we can help you with today, m'lady?'

Out in the street, Eleanor concluded it would be a dejected drive back to Little Buckford unless Clifford had miraculously solved the murder and found all the women's rights sympathisers. Even the Wrights had only reluctantly taken a poster from her. Maud had suggested that their affiliations lay with a party more sympathetic to the needs of working-class tradespeople, but there was more hidden beneath.

As Eleanor thanked them for listening to her political endeavours, Frank had hinted the true base of their worries lay in uncertainties of what was happening in Parliament.

'Fingers crossed that we stay in peaceful times… for all the lads that will be old enough to be conscripted afore this government's second term.'

'Amen!' Maud added, patting his hand.

Eleanor, finding no suitable reply, had beaten a retreat.

But that minor act of affection reminded her of her upcoming appointment with the one person who could always cheer her up. Scowling up at the start of the promised rain, she became aware of Clifford at her elbow.

'Don't ask, please,' she said glumly.

'Perhaps a snippet to support the investigation will brighten the morning. I have learned that Messrs Aris and Carlton were once the firmest of schoolboy comrades.'

Eleanor frowned. 'Children are supposed to be the ones who squabble, not grown men who've known each other forever. I wonder what soured their relationship so badly that they would fight so doggedly, and in public?'

'From the pursed lips, raised eyebrows and more descriptive comments, I was led to surmise that years later, there had been a lady at the centre of their falling out.'

'Clifford, you have been gossiping like a fishwife! Outrageous, but well done. I also have some news. Apparently, Aris had a public row with Oswald Greaves. I've heard the name…'

'I believe Mr Greaves is the Communist Party of Great Britain candidate, my lady.'

'Ah!' She peeped sideways, imagining her inscrutable butler in his smart black overcoat, tie and bowler hat surrounded by twittering women. But even that and the jumble of information she had gleaned about the investigation didn't lift her mood. She felt quite dispirited. 'Well, we'll have to have a talk with Greaves, but not today.'

With one look at the still numerous leaflets in his gloved hand, she slapped hers dejectedly into his other. 'Thank you, Clifford, especially for all your support. It appears you are my only ally at present. Please enjoy the rest of your day off in peace. I shall make my own way back to the Hall later.'

He took the umbrella hanging from his wrist and held it out.

'Suitable refreshments will be ready, my lady.'

CHAPTER 12

Surely Joe's yard had never been this neglected? Thick nettles grew through the stacks of old tyres and around the ripped back seat of a car propped against the stone wall. Bits of mechanical gubbins lay rusting in piles dotted about the unpaved area. Even the outbuildings looked to be on borrowed time.

'I say, hello?' Eleanor called out across the yard. *Silence.* Then she thought she heard… yes, the clink of tools.

'Joe? Lancelot? Yoo hoo, anyone home?'

She headed for the huge wooden barn Lancelot hired when his plane, Florence, needed repair. The right-hand side door was ajar. Stepping in, the smell of a hundred years of dust and mould struck her. And was that a waft of long-left chickens or pigs? *Yuck!* She groaned. Having a potential beau with a title and his own wings should be more glamorous than this.

She called into the gloom: 'Lancelot? You here?' But only the blinking of a barn owl in the rafters answered her.

'Dash it!' She cocked her head and stared at Lancelot's plane, looking surprisingly petite in this enormous barn. The shadows failed to do justice to the dragonfly-blue paint or the intricate carving of the wooden propeller. She patted the nose, running her finger along the side. 'Hi, Florence. We've never really been introduced.' Saying the name made her smile. What a soppy ape Lancelot was, naming his plane. 'Good job I'm not the jealous type, I'd think he loved you more than me.'

She craned her neck into the cockpit, but the tops of a row of dials was all she could see. A short set of steps lay against the nearest wall. She dragged them over. Climbing up, she stepped into the single front seat and caught her breath. A picnic basket sat in the rear passenger seat.

Oh, Ellie! Has he taken another girl on a flight? She scowled at Florence. 'Be honest, girl to girl.' But the plane gave nothing away.

'Captain Sherlock, permission to come aboard?'

She jumped at Lancelot's grinning face.

'What, oh yes!'

He ran his hand through his damp ruffled blond hair and chortled as he swung one leg over the side. 'You're like the fox after the chicken, always stealing after me and I have to say, popping up in the most surprising of places. And grilling poor old Florence into spilling the beans on her master's secret liaisons. Bit below the belt! Florence is the most loyal girlfriend I've ever had.'

Eleanor wanted to laugh at his silly joke, but her mouth was too dry and that crease in her brow wouldn't shift. 'You're a terrible rogue, Lord Fenwick-Langham, playing with a lady's delicate sensibilities.'

'Delicate! You! My dear girl, you're about as fragile as a rhino.'

'Is that a compliment?'

'Only for a girl with sensibilities as tough as clog iron.'

She wrinkled her nose as though considering how to take his response. In truth, she was secretly delighted.

'Lancelot?'

'Yes, darling fruit.'

'Can you be sensible for a moment?'

'Not a hope! Sorry to disappoint, I just don't seem to have been born with the earnest gene. Mater's got enough of those for the entire family.'

'Maybe that's because life is very different for women.'

He rubbed one eye. 'Maybe.'

She folded her arms. 'Lancelot, what do you think about equality for women, really?'

'Really?'

'Yes, really, really.'

'Honestly, Sherlock, I can't say I've thought much about it.' At her exaggerated eye roll, he brushed his thumb across her cheek. 'But I do care about how you fillies are treated, scout's honour.'

She shook her head. 'Fillies? Lancelot, you can't go around comparing women to racehorses.'

'Better fillies than frillies, wouldn't you say? Anyhow, you're the one who should understand them, surely? I am a man, a dashingly handsome one admittedly.' He turned his best side to her as if posing for a photograph and offered a cheesy grin.

She pushed his face backwards. 'Hmm, the jury's out on that one!'

'Honestly, you're painting a chap in a horribly bleak light, so unfair! All I said was you're better placed, being female-ish.'

'Ish!' This came out as a much higher-pitched squeal than she had intended. 'Lord Fenwick-Langham, are you insinuating that I am, in fact, mannish?'

'Oh, no.' He leaned in and brushed her lips with his, making her squirm in her seat. 'No, quite the opposite. You're like an irresistible Amazonian Aphrodite that someone dipped in burning gold.'

'Lancelot, I've decided to stand for Parliament after all.'

He laughed. 'I know, old fruit, the roads of Chipstone are paved with your leaflets. "Lady Swift. Progressive Embodiment of something or other". I rather thought you'd got yourself mixed up in nosing about in that MP's affairs. There's a whiff that his ending up face down in his dessert might not be quite the full heart attack ticket.'

'He had a peanut allergy, actually. And, yes, alright, I might be investigating a teeny bit.'

'And dragging poor Clifford into it as well, no doubt. Tsk, tsk! So, still Sherlock the sleuth by day and Member of Parliament by... when? How are you going to progressively embody anything in the least bit respectable whilst nosing about in a potential murder?'

'I'm good at juggling and being organised. Well, maybe not the organising bit, that's Clifford's job. Anyway, I refuse to descend to squabbling with you, I'm too busy fighting the good fight.'

'Oh, always thought girls were better at squabbling than fighting.'

She punched his arm with more force than intended.

Lancelot rubbed the spot. 'Ow! You, Lady Swift, are all class. *Which* class, I'm not honestly sure.'

She turned away. 'I'll be fearfully tied up, you know, with this election business. First, all the campaigning, then debates and then blazing a trail in the stuffy halls of Parliament.' She looked at him out of the corner of her eye. 'You'll probably forget about me and get distracted by someone else.'

'Most likely.'

She spun to face him.

'Joke,' he murmured as he cupped her chin, rubbing noses with her.

'That's not fair. It makes me go all girlie.'

Lancelot held her gaze. 'Sherlock, I've tried to tell you before, what I find so tantalising about you is that you're not like other girls at all. You're deliciously peculiar.'

'Thanks, I think. But I'm serious about this election. People need help, women especially. Look, this might sound gushy, but honestly, I've never done anything worthwhile in my life, not really. Not like my parents. They dedicated their lives to helping people overseas before they disappeared.'

She thought back to that terrible day. They'd been in Peru for what seemed ages to Eleanor, they normally moved around so much. They'd been helping to restore the country's educational and social system after years of troubles. But not everyone in the country wanted the reforms and the stability they'd bring. One night, she'd been shaken awake by one of the local women. The woman had jabbered and gesticulated at her. As Eleanor had only understood a little of the local dialogue, she'd stumbled next door to her parents' room, only to find the bedcovers thrown back and they were gone. She never saw them again.

She tuned into Lancelot's voice.

'What rot! You've helped loads of people. Me, for one. I'd still be stuck in a jail cell, or worse, if it weren't for you.'

She sighed in exasperation. 'Yes, yes, but here I am, lucky enough to have been able to travel and see extraordinary sights and all the rest of it, but I haven't made a real difference to many people.'

'Tosh, you made a difference to Mr Thomas Walker's bank balance! You made his travel company a roaring success, and you earned your own wage.'

'But it isn't about money.'

'Couldn't agree more, darling fruit. I'd give up inheriting the stately pile in a heartbeat. And the title, all a total pain in the behind. But poor old mater would positively expire on the spot if I ever said so, bless her.' He held her shoulders. 'Look, I've told you I like you until I've nearly run out of air, but you're so impossibly independent and busy and all those other wonderful things that reel me in and frustrate me equally. But...' he tilted his head, 'you've got something important to do. And a murder to solve. I can see that. So, I say, we make the most of the time we have.' He took her hand and tied a gold satin ribbon with a tiny charm at each end around her wrist.

'Goggles! That's so sweet.'

'I pictured you the minute I saw it. Now, Florence has had to sit through enough gushing. Poor girl's probably feeling quite nauseous. What say you we go and have that picnic I planned to take you on?'

'Ooh, are we going by plane?'

'Sorry, not today, Florence is lame in her hind quarters. Like all women, she's high maintenance and susceptible to a fit of the vapours at any moment. Don't want to land you in a hedge on our inaugural date.'

She caught her breath. *A date, Ellie!* 'Oh, hang on though, you're not suggesting we picnic here?'

'Absolutely.' He looked around at the dusty, cobwebbed surroundings. 'It's positively dripping in romance.'

'It's dripping in something! Tell me you're joking?'

'Of course, I'm joking. It's totally rank, but Joe is a top egg for letting me do whatever I please here.'

He jumped deftly down backwards from the plane and held his arms up to take her round the waist.

'So gallant! Thank you, kind sir.'

'My pleasure, madam, only stop wriggling for heaven's sake!'

They landed in a heap, with Eleanor on top: 'See, women can be top dog! Now, where are we going?'

'It's my secret place. Come on, Sherlock.' He winked and grabbed her hand, yanking her to her feet.

They burst out into the sunshine, Eleanor wincing at the brightness of the afternoon. 'Hey, the rain's completely gone.'

'I arranged that.' Lancelot grinned and looped his arm around her shoulder, the picnic basket swinging from his other hand.

She glanced around. 'Where's Joe, by the way? I haven't seen him for ages. Even for a car yard, it's looking a bit rundown, wouldn't you say?'

'Haven't noticed, old girl. But the poor chap is struggling to juggle everything. Mrs Joe has been pretty poorly by all accounts. He's spending more and more time at home looking after her.'

'Gosh, whatever is wrong with her?'

'How on earth would I know? Chaps don't go into details about things like that.'

Eleanor's mind skipped from Mrs Joe to Mrs Aris. She knew she needed to interview her about her husband's death, but was putting it off, not savouring the idea of asking a recent widow about her husband's possible murder. She bit her lip, then realised Lancelot was looking at her quizzically.

'You're not going to go all dull and earnest on me, are you?' he asked with a hint of a whine.

She shook her head. 'I was thinking about poor Mrs Aris and her husband's mu— , death.'

'Dash it, what does a chap have to do to be more interesting than a fellow who's gone toes up?'

'Goggles, that's awful!'

'No, darling fruit, it's just the truth.' He jiggled the charms on the end of the ribbon around her wrist. 'Not good for a chap's ego, you know. Now are we going or have you suddenly done that mysterious girl thing of needing to dash off and do something frightfully important?'

'No. I need to talk to Oswald Greaves but he can wait, especially as he isn't even expecting me.'

'Greaves? As in the chap held up before the beak for having the wrong sort of affiliations?'

'No idea. He's just a name to me at the moment. What do you mean, he was held up before the beak?'

'Pater used to be a JP, a Justice of the Peace. Laughable really, he's such a softie. He was hopeless. But I remember him saying he swung his gavel over a man called Greaves.'

'Gracious, what was Oswald Greaves in court for?'

'That Aris fellow tried to get him imprisoned for being a communist.'

'Then I definitely need to see him.' She held her head high. 'There are some women JPs now, you know. That's some progress for equality.'

'Probably fancy themselves in all the gear.' He dodged her swipe at his head. 'Sherlock, promise me you won't lose your sense of humour if you become an MP?'

She nodded. 'Show me this "special place" and I'll go as far as promising not to be earnest this afternoon.'

'Deal.' He pretended to spit on his palm and shook her hand before kissing it and linking fingers with her.

As they left the yard, she saw a young woman hurrying across the road away from them. She entered the small doctor's surgery on the corner of the road. Eleanor thought back to the conversation in the butcher's shop in Little Buckford and Johnny's mother who couldn't afford the seven-shilling doctor's fee or the medicine for her son. Eleanor wondered if the young woman she'd just seen enter the doctor's surgery could afford to pay for her treatment or prescription.

And what about Mrs Joe? With her ill in bed and her husband neglecting his business to look after her, how would they afford the cost of medicines if Mrs Joe's illness was a long one? She sighed to herself, wondering just how long she could keep her promise to Lancelot not to be earnest.

They strolled down the lane, before turning up a narrow, grassy track. Lancelot pointed to the low forest of orange-brown bracken. 'Watch out for late-hibernating adders. They could be grabbing some last sun before they tuck up for a few months.'

'I had no idea you were such a wildlife expert.'

'Pah! It's called growing up as a boy. Even us rich kids grubbed about in the dirt for a while. How else would I have found this place?'

'Whatever were you doing out here on your own? Langham Manor is miles off.' She turned in a circle, trying to get her bearings.

'Three and a half, actually. I had a governess who secretly fancied herself as a watercolour artist. She used to drag me out here on the ruse to my parents that I was getting geography lessons. She'd paint the day away, and I'd have a ball making dens and scrambling up the rocks. Best time of my life... until today.'

Looking through the gap in the branches, she could see flint hamlets clinging to the rolling Chiltern Hills, framed by the misty blue horizon. Lancelot's 'special place' had turned out to be a treehouse, hidden high up in the crook of an ancient English oak. The tree was in full autumnal glory and Ellie paused as she climbed to marvel at the golden, russet and yellow leaves.

'I bet you never imagined you'd be sitting here with girls when you made this all those years ago.'

'Girls! Yucky!' Lancelot held his nose and grimaced.

'We all thought the same of you boys, then. Horribly icky and sticky!'

'Whereas now, some of us are irresistibly dashing and manly, and give you vertigo just looking into our eyes.'

'Good job I don't get vertigo, you oaf! You didn't check before you dragged me up here.' She turned the gold ribbon he'd tied round her wrist.

'Not sure "dragged" is quite the word.' He pointed to the wicker basket. 'Picnic time. Peel her open, Sherlock.'

Eleanor fought with the buckles. 'I hope there's more than champagne in here, otherwise I seriously doubt either of us will make it back down this tree.'

'Well, we'll have to spend the night staring at the stars and cuddling up for warmth.'

She tingled at the image, but then frowned. 'Yes, and blow me if Clifford wouldn't come blundering up halfway through the evening, having miraculously tracked me down. And all to tell me that it wasn't wise to sleep out without a suitable bedcover and I'd thrown the meal schedule out entirely.'

Lancelot roared with laughter and took the bottle of champagne she held out to him.

'Hauling it up here fizzed it up good and proper.' He uncorked it and held it to her mouth so she could suck up the bubbles, which gave her instant hiccups.

'What was it you were saying, old girl?'

'Well, I was wondering if you've, you know, made up to many girls up here?' she blushed.

Why, oh why, did you ask that, Ellie?

He took her hand and kissed it. 'Darling fruit, how many girls do you imagine I would have managed to entice up here? I haven't found anyone game enough to try until today. Now, pass the fizz and the pâté, and let's celebrate just how deliciously peculiar you are.'

CHAPTER 13

The following morning, the Rolls stopped outside a narrow, wooden-fronted building that had all the hallmarks of an old mill despite being nowhere near a river. Clifford gestured towards the steep stairs up to the windowless door.

On the airless fourth floor, Oswald Greaves sat bent over a long table strewn with papers and bottles of ink.

Eleanor knocked on the open door. 'Afternoon.'

The hunched figure was so rapt in concentration that he continued muttering, fervently scratching his pen across the paper in front of him.

'Mr Greaves?'

He nodded to himself and re-dipped his fountain pen without taking his eyes from his work.

With a shrug to Clifford, Eleanor stepped forward. 'Mr Greaves!'

The man spun in his seat, his hand clasped to his heart. 'What? What a fright... oh, hello! Wasn't expecting students today. What day is it?' His voice was surprisingly rough, given his soft boyish face and bright green eyes.

'It is Friday, but we are not students.'

'Ah! Then apologies, I'm caught up with all this, right now.' He waved at the papers on the table.

Eleanor walked over to his side. 'Mr Greaves, we are colleagues of sorts. Perhaps you have heard of me? I'm standing under the banner of the Women's League.'

He looked up. 'I have a terrible memory for faces. Have we met? I don't...'

She squatted down to his eye level. 'I joined after the Town Hall debate on Monday, so we haven't met. Until now.'

He peered at her and then reached for a pair of wire-rimmed spectacles. 'Monday, Monday… ah yes, the debate.' He cleared his throat. 'It's a terrible habit, but I tune out entirely at those wretched things. But they're usually well-attended events and I always end up with some interested would-be converts afterwards.' He tapped his chin with his fountain pen, oblivious to the splatters that dotted his face and shirt collar. 'Which candidate were you there supporting again?'

Eleanor frowned. *Was he being deliberately obtuse?* 'No one, Mr Greaves. I am standing for election, just as you are.'

'Really? Well, good luck and all that, but I must be cracking on.' He slapped a hand on the papers, wafting a large sheaf to the floor in the process.

'Mr Greaves, I wanted to stop by and make your acquaintance. I imagine we will be seeing rather a lot of each other at the forthcoming debates.'

He turned, now chewing on the end of his pen. 'But does that mean we have to become acquainted? I don't see the need myself. Too busy.'

Eleanor wrinkled her nose. 'Yes, me too. Frightfully caught up in all the stuff. Especially since Mr Aris' passing.'

At the mention of Aris' name, he put down his pen. 'Aris, of course. A shame and all that. Can't say we saw eye to eye on anything, but that doesn't mean the world's better off without him.'

'Really? You surprise me.'

'And why would that be?'

'Oh, only because I had heard that you and Mr Aris had a rather public argument? And that Mr Aris tried to have you arrested and imprisoned?'

Greaves chuckled. 'Yes, the stupid old goat!'

'You seem very calm about his efforts to destroy you and your party, Mr Greaves?'

'You think so? A word of advice, if you fancy it.' He spread his delicate, white hands wide. 'Fear not those who disagree with you, but those who disagree with you and are too cowardly to let you know.'

'Karl Marx?'

'Napoleon, well, the second part, but close.'

'And Mr Aris, I take it, was never too cowardly to let you know he disagreed with you?'

'Exactly.'

Already knowing the answer, she asked airily: 'Perhaps you were at the fundraising dinner where poor Mr Aris died?'

'Hmm... Aris was always sucking up to the rich and titled. Might as well have been one of them, the way he went on. Disgusting display it was.'

'Forgive my confusion, but what display are you talking about?'

'The wealth. The privilege. The status. Disgusting!' He thumped the desk.

Eleanor thought he probably wasn't much fun at parties and wondered why the Farringtons had included him. 'Er, yes, but did you see anything suspicious?'

'What would I possibly have seen! Lord Farrington called him up to speak and Aris nosedived to the table before he could.' He let out something close to a snort. 'I saw Carlton make such a great show of trying to revive him, like the charlatan he is.'

'Whereas you on the other hand seem to bear Mr Aris no malice at all?' Eleanor gave him a cordial smile. 'Well, Mr Greaves, thank you for your time. I'll leave you to work on your, er... cause.'

'It's Oswald. I'm not one for formality of any kind.'

'Neither am I, so please call me Eleanor.'

He sprang up from his chair as Clifford handed him the sheaf of papers collected from the floor. 'Where the devil did he come from?'

Eleanor blinked. 'He's been here the whole time. Surely, you must be the only person alive who doesn't know Clifford, my uncle's, well, my butler?'

Greaves shook his head. 'Butler!' He looked from Eleanor to Clifford and back. 'Who the deuce are you, really?'

She shook her head. 'I'm Eleanor. Eleanor Swift. My name is all over the campaigning material. It's no secret.' She held out the leaflet Clifford passed to her.

Greaves peered at it and then pulled off his spectacles to look again. 'Lady Swift. Lady, as in entitled? Privileged?'

'Mmm, it seems so.'

He handed back the leaflet. 'Then you are the enemy!'

CHAPTER 14

'It's midday. No time like the present, Clifford. What do you say?'

'Let us hope Mr Carlton is ready for us, my lady.' He adjusted the cuffs of his leather driving gloves and eased the Rolls out onto the road towards the farthest end of Chipstone. 'If I might offer my congratulations on your successful questioning of Mr Greaves.'

'Thank you. I've already added him to our suspect list. As we've eliminated Mrs Pitkin, thank the Lord, we've now got three suspects: Lord and Lady Farrington, I'm counting them as one, labour candidate Ernest Carlton, and now Oswald Greaves.' She closed her notebook and sighed. 'Dash it! Somehow Greaves has left me feeling that unless I can become a mind reader, I shall never know if he is telling the truth.'

She stared out of the window at the start of the long rows of basic terraced housing which gave this end of Chipstone a whisper of the forlorn. Clifford braked hard for the scruffy brown dog which limped off the pavement in front of the car. A woman with her hair knotted in a scarf glanced up at them from her apathetic beating of a rug hung on a makeshift washing line. With a huff, she turned her back and continued to beat the rug in a desultory fashion.

Eleanor bit her lip. 'I've got a long way to go to understand these ladies, Clifford.'

'Possibly, my lady, but it is my belief that almost everyone's most heartfelt wish is to be safe and to see justice done. If we solve Aris' murder, you will achieve that for one woman, Mrs Pitkin, at least.'

'To work then! Perhaps Carlton will make it easy and break down and confess?'

'That would certainly be a help, my lady. We might even return to the Hall in time for luncheon.'

'Lady Swift, forgive me, my secretary failed to inform me of your intended visit.'

'Well, don't chide her too much, I failed to call ahead.'

Ernest Carlton offered a smile that didn't quite reach his eyes. She studied his face, pitching a guess he was in his mid-to-late forties. He was also incredibly handsome to some women, she imagined. He gestured to a worn button-backed chair in dark green velvet in the plain white study.

'I see… Well, I imagine perhaps a pot of tea will be required?'

'So kind, if that doesn't constitute fraternising with the enemy?' She remembered Greaves' parting words.

'Not at all.' He called out. 'Mr Jones, visitors! Fifteen minutes!'

Unsure if the fifteen minutes referred to the time she was being granted for an interview or the time before tea arrived, Eleanor decided she'd best jump straight in.

'What a delightful working space.' She waved an arm towards the only window which gave onto the rear wall of the public house next door.

'This is just my operations office. You were lucky to find me in.'

'Yes, lucky me. This is Clifford, my—'

Ernest nodded. 'Mr Clifford.'

Eleanor sighed. 'You've met?' It seemed everyone in the known universe was acquainted with her late uncle's butler.

Carlton looked up at the blue china mantelpiece clock. 'Lady Swift, your late uncle was a prominent resident of the constituency. Condolences on your loss.'

'Thank you. He does appear to have left quite an impression.'

'And a fine legacy. Are you enjoying life at Henley Hall?'

'Absolutely! Now, if you don't mind me asking, what line of business are you in?'

'Property.'

'How splendid! In what capacity, pray?'

He answered with a thin smile. 'The details of one's opponents' business interests are all available to view at the Town Hall upon request throughout the election period.'

'Gracious, I'm not here to snoop, Mr Carlton, I'm just not very good at chitter chatter. Mr Aris, though, was quite the opposite, I've heard. Perhaps having a more succinct counterpart at debates will be refreshing?'

'Tea is refreshing, Lady Swift. On the table there, Mr Jones, thank you.'

Undeterred by her host's reticence, she ploughed on: 'Such a blow, losing Mr Aris like that.'

'Like what?'

'Why, suddenly, and unexpectedly, of course? Most inconvenient fo—'

'I've observed that death is always inconvenient for someone, whenever it occurs, but maybe not for others?' Carlton sat back in his chair and crossed one leg over the other.

Eleanor ploughed on. 'It must have been a great shock. I mean, you were sitting next to Mr Aris, I believe.'

'You've been doing your homework, Lady Swift.'

She nodded. 'I believe being prepared is half the battle, don't you agree?'

A puzzled frown passed over Carlton. 'I don't follow you?'

'I mean, for a man to collapse and die like that. Right next to you. For most people, that would be a great shock. And the manner of his death was very—'

Carlton raised a hand, cutting her off. 'Lady Swift, a question for you.'

'Oh absolutely, shoot!' Eleanor took a sip of the strong, sweet tea. She shuddered slightly.

'Why are you here?'

'I merely called to be cordial. It will inevitably end up as a head-to-head between us in the election, I imagine.'

Carlton slid his eyes towards Clifford and back to her. 'Do you, indeed? That is one way to envisage things.'

'Well, now that poor Mr Aris is gone, your chance of being successful in the upcoming election must have risen considerably, I expect.'

'Rather pointed of you. So much for the delicacy of manners. And the answer is Aris beat me aided by a not insubstantial amount of election rigging, so as that won't happen this time, I suppose my chances have increased.'

She smiled back at him. 'Gosh, you think there was something afoot in the polls? I confess I am greatly troubled by the rumours that Mr Aris' death is suspicious. Will I need to stare over my shoulder at every turn when I'm the new MP for Chipstone?'

'If, Lady Swift, if you are successful. The race has not yet been run.'

'Quite! But you were sitting next to Aris the evening he died, weren't you? Are you sure you saw nothing suspicious?'

'Not from where I was sitting. A perfectly ordinary fundraising event. I've been to so many.' He held her gaze. 'Nothing struck me as odd in the slightest.'

She heard Clifford's cough. She pulled her uncle's fob watch from her pocket. 'Gracious, look at the time! I've detained you too long, my apologies.' She rose and held out her hand. 'It has been a pleasure.'

He rose with her. 'Lady Swift, if you really want to find out who had reason to do the late Mr Aris harm, I suggest you ask his erstwhile business partner, Mr Peel. Good day.'

CHAPTER 15

Outside Carlton's office, Eleanor turned to Clifford: 'Do you believe what he was saying about Aris only winning because he rigged the elections? It sounded like sour grapes to me.'

Clifford nodded. 'I agree, my lady. I am sure there is a fair amount of underhand tactics employed by all parties, and I imagine Mr Aris was simply more adept at it than Mr Carlton.'

'My thoughts exactly. Carlton struck me as a man who believes it's his God-given right to have whatever he wants in life.'

'And one who has been bitten by the disappointment of that not having proved to be the case?'

'Spot on, Clifford.'

A coal merchant's cart rumbled towards them and mounted the pavement to avoid two children playing with a hoop in the road.

Eleanor and Clifford jumped back through a nearby garden gate to avoid getting their feet squashed.

At that moment the front door opened behind them and a rotund rear in flannel trousers shuffled out backwards, navy blue braces forming a lopsided 'Y' over a hand-knitted jumper.

'Morning,' Eleanor said.

A smiling, moon-faced man turned to them. 'Morning.'

The man was hauling hard on the handle of a pram-like contraption that Heath Robinson himself would have been proud to include in his cartoons. He grunted. 'He gets stuck sometimes, so he does.'

Clifford stepped forward. 'Allow me to assist, Chester.' He took hold of one side and on the count of three, the two men gave the handle a hearty yank, which pulled the back wheels over the doorsill. Eleanor peered into the pram.

'Oh, gracious!' She held a hand over her mouth.

Clifford maintained his unflappable air. 'There you are, all free now.'

The moon-faced man beamed. 'Right helpful, thank you, Mr Clifford. If you'll excuse us, we're off for our walk, aren't we, ladies and gentlemen?'

Eleanor and Clifford each took a step backwards to give the man the space to turn the contraption around, allowing them full view of the mountain of motley cats inside. The rotund form bent over the handle and tickled the chin of a ginger tom. 'What do you say, Thomas, is it the park or the fields today?' At the mewled reply, he nodded and plodded on towards the gate. 'Okay, fields it is. Come on, everyone. Esther and Miriam, paws inside, please.'

Eleanor waited for the click of the gate before spinning round to Clifford. 'You know that man?'

Clifford gave a rare smile. 'Everyone knows Mr Cecil Broughton.'

'I thought you called him "Chester"?'

'That is Mr Broughton's local nickname. Everyone calls him Chester.'

'Not Cat Crazy Chester, then?' At his disapproving stare, she threw her arms out. 'What? He must have had over twenty cats in that contraption.'

'Likely well over thirty, my lady. All exceptionally well-cared for and taken in out of compassion.'

'He rescues street cats?'

'Indeed. He has been heard many times proudly declaring that he has never turned away a needy cat nor abandoned one who turned out to be fickle with their affections.'

'But what is he doing with them all in that pram-cum-trolley thing then?'

Clifford stared at her. 'Taking them for a walk.'

'That's perfectly normal, is it? So, he nobly takes in all the urchin cats, but what about the rats then?'

Clifford inclined his head. 'Obviously, with no street cats to keep them in check, they are naturally a total menace in this area. There are great packs of them marauding in the backstreets.' He raised an eyebrow. 'Shall we?'

Suddenly realising how hungry she was, she peered up and down the road. 'Look here, we've been at this investigating lark for hours now!'

'Three to be precise, my lady.'

'Exactly. It must be time for a rewarding pot of tea at Winsomes Tea Rooms, surely?'

'A splendid idea, my lady, but I have an alternative suggestion, if it might suit you?'

She shrugged.

'We are but a street away from the offices of Aris and Peel, Law Firm.'

'You clever bean! Shall we?'

The door of the brick-fronted Georgian office gave the building an extra haughty air in its coat of dark grey paint.

'It would appear that Mr Peel did not feel the need for a period of mourning, my lady,' Clifford said, pointing to the shining new brass plaque on the railings.

The Law Office of Mr V. Peel, Barrister LLD.

The name of Aris was nowhere to be seen.

Eleanor frowned. 'But Aris only died a few days ago?'

Inside, the atmosphere in the sterile waiting room was most unwelcoming. Eleanor looked around at the blank white walls and hard wooden chairs. Leaning across to Clifford, she whispered, 'I thought legal bods liked the high life. This feels like we're the ones on trial.'

The sharp-nosed secretary, who had shown them in, reappeared in the doorway, her demeanour in keeping with the office's austere atmosphere. She pushed her narrow glasses up her nose. 'Mr Peel will see you now. He has another appointment in seven minutes.'

Eleanor beamed. 'Does he? How wonderful to be so busy.'

An unremarkable-looking man in an unremarkable suit rose from behind the desk. Only then did she realise that he was almost the same height standing as sitting, that being a little under five feet. 'Lady Swift, I am Vernon Peel. Called to the bar twenty-one years ago. Please be aware I uphold the law to the letter.'

Fighting the less-than-charitable thought this man was unlikely to be any more fun at parties than Oswald Greaves, Eleanor took the hard-backed chair in front of his desk.

'Mr Peel, I appreciate you are very busy so I will come straight to the point. Are you aware that I am standing as an independent candidate in Mr Aris' sadly, and suddenly, vacated place?'

'I am, but I fail to understand the connection with your visit here. Arnold kept his political matters entirely separate from our legal practice.'

'Of course.' Eleanor was racking her brain for a way in. 'However, you would have known him better than anyone in his professional life, even amongst his political colleagues. I understand you were business partners for some time?'

Peel wrinkled his nose. 'Eight years and seven months.'

'How splendid! Oh, forgive me, my condolences naturally. It must have been very difficult for you being there at the time of his passing, especially in such tragic circumstances.'

At this, Mr Peel sat down and steepled his fingers. 'Thank you. It was a shock, of course. But why are you interested in my former partner, Lady Swift? If you are researching his popularity or otherwise amongst the electorate, the obvious place to make such enquiries would be outside,' he gestured towards the window, 'amongst them.'

'Absolutely!' She leaned forward on the desk, oblivious to his shrinking backwards in his seat. 'But that is why I came to you. I didn't need to see the numerous letters after your name to know that not only are you an exemplary barrister but also a man of intelligence.'

Out of the corner of her eye she saw Clifford discreetly adjust his cufflinks.

A fraction of a frown crossed Mr Peel's brow. 'Go on.'

'You see, Mr Aris was very successful in his political career, having been re-elected several times. Coming from the backward position of being a woman, I wish to emulate as much of his approach and attitude as possible, thus continuing his legacy. I won't pretend, Mr Peel, I seek to be a loud and outstanding voice for the constituents.'

'I see.' He peered at her with obvious mistrust. 'My next appointment will soon be with me, Lady Swift. I am not sure I can help you other than to say Arnold was a sincere, dedicated and knowledgeable man of strong values and even stronger opinions. It would appear you must be early in your research otherwise you would know that latterly he made some unpopular decisions which lost him some vital support, not only in politics.'

Eleanor shook her head and tutted. 'Perhaps it is true then.'

'What is?'

'Oh, forgive me, did I say that aloud? I suddenly recalled hearing the suggestion that poor Mr Aris might not have died of natural causes. But you would be aware of anything suspicious. I took tea with Lady Farrington recently and she made sure I knew that you were at the fundraising event.'

Peel sat up straighter. 'Did she? Well, that's hopeful,' he ended distractedly.

'But you would have noted anything suspicious, of course. Perhaps something has come to your mind after the awful event? Isn't it strange how the brain seems to chew things over and produce an answer at the most unexpected moment?'

'I have a very keen and observant mind, Lady Swift. Nothing has subsequently "come to mind" as you put it because it would have done so at the time. However, as I did not observe anything untoward whilst Arnold was eating the meal, I am not of the opinion that there is anything suspicious about his passing.'

'That is reassuring. Then they are nothing but unfounded rumours. Still, so sad Mr Aris was not able to be revived, even after Mr Carlton rushed round to his aid.'

Peel shook his head. 'It was Lord Farrington who reached Arnold's side. Mr Carlton was nowhere to be seen by then.'

'Mr Carlton had left, you say? I believe Mr Aris and Mr Carlton had some sort of dispute during the meal?'

Peel shrugged. 'Arnold and Mr Carlton always had some ongoing dispute.'

'Such a shame! I was told that at one point they were inseparable?'

'That must have been before my time, Lady Swift. Ah, my secretary…' He nodded at the tap on his door.

Eleanor rose and held out her hand. 'Mr Peel, you have been most helpful. An inspiration, in fact. Thank you for your time.' She paused at the door. 'Oh, one last question, in case I should ever need to call upon your legal services, which areas does your own practice specialise in?'

'Commercial, insurance and criminal law.'

'So, I guess Mr Aris worked in the complimentary spheres of family, wills and trusts and what else is there, insolvency?'

He gestured towards the door dispassionately. 'Personal injury and property. Good day, Lady Swift.'

Outside, Eleanor pulled her jacket collar up against the chill. 'I think, Clifford, we've just been given a display of Mr Peel's expert powers of deflection.'

Clifford nodded. 'Indeed, my lady. If I might suggest we add his name to our list of suspects. And his remark about Mr Carlton disappearing whilst they were trying to revive Mr Aris is interesting, assuming it is true.' He was interrupted by the clang of the bell in the Town Hall's medieval-looking tower.

'Might I suggest we discuss the details after your richly-deserved tea and fruitcake at Winsomes Tea Rooms? Unless you might prefer lunch, given that it is the appropriate time for lunch.'

'Watch and learn, Clifford. The amount of fruitcake I intend to devour will most definitely fit the definition of "lunch". It is quite simply the most divine substance on this earth, after everything Mrs Trotman conjures up, of course.'

'If you feel that will suitably fortify you for your first election rally, which commences in precisely an hour and a half.'

She groaned, but then slapped her wrist. *Hardly the attitude, Ellie.*

'Let's get one of the tables up in the galleried section at Winsomes if we can and then we can discuss all our findings on the case so far. Dash it, though! I wish I had brought my notebook.'

Clifford reached to his inside coat pocket. 'Perhaps this will do, my lady?'

'My notebook! Thank you. After Carlton's name, Vernon Peel's is one I shall be most happy to add. There's definitely something he's hiding.' She waved the notebook at him. 'What a shame the scouting movement started so recently! I rather think if Lord Baden-Powell had thought of it years before, you could have been their star member. You are the epitome of always being prepared.'

'I take the essence of your statement as a compliment, my lady, although I am not sure the uniform would have quite suited me. As Twain paraphrased from Shakespeare, "Clothes make the man."'

Eleanor nodded. 'Yes, but you've missed the second line: "Naked people have little or no influence on society." Insightful fellow… Now, which way is lunch?'

CHAPTER 16

'All quiet!' The rotund, beetroot-faced, civic master-at-arms banged his gavel on the edge of the long candidates' table. Looking around, he addressed both those standing for election and the tightly-packed crowd. 'This will be an orderly debate. Best behaviour and no exceptions, otherwise you'll find yourself out in the alley. Roll call, candidates, please rise as your name is called. For the Communist Party of Great Britain, Mr Oswald Greaves. Thank you, Mr Greaves. For the Labour Party, Mr Ernest Carlton, I thank you. Independent candidate, in place of Mr Aris, Lady Eleanor Swift, er, thank you, madam. Order there! Silence! For the Liberal Party, Mr Stanley Morris. Silence! I insist on…'

Three hours! Three table-thumping, headache-making, argument-filled hours later, all that had happened was the whole debate had descended into a brawl. At that point Eleanor had had enough. No one had heard a word of her speech, of that she was sure.

She left quietly, unnoticed in the melee, and pushed through the jostling crowd, which was still trying to scramble onto the stage. It had all started well enough. Eleanor had attended her first meeting of the Women's League and they had accompanied her to the debate. And then…

She needed air like she needed Clifford to magically appear and take her away from it all. Mostly, she needed to gather her thoughts together.

How on earth did that get so out of hand so quickly, Ellie?

As she strode out of the Town Hall and down the steps, she shook her head at a reporter for the *Chipstone Gazette*. She glanced up and down the road. Where on earth was Clifford? But standing there on the bottom step, she had the distinct impression that she was being watched. Glancing over her shoulder, she caught sight of a familiar, heavy-lined face poking out from a straw hat, held in place by a scarf of purple, white and green, the colours of Mrs Brody's militant women's group.

'Mrs Brody, how are you?' Eleanor tried to pull on her best smile.

'Perfectly fine, thank you.'

'Doesn't it seem an age since we were in Little Buckford's amateur dramatic performance together?'

Mrs Brody sniffed. 'If we'd gone with my choice, we would have done more than entertain. We would have—'

'Yes, thank you for sharing your views. But perhaps old arguments are best buried and forgotten?'

Mrs Brody laughed. 'Well, someone buried an argument with Aris, good and proper too.'

Eleanor started. 'You think his death wasn't an accident?'

Mrs Brody shrugged. 'Rather convenient timing, isn't it? It is ancient news that Aris beat Carlton in the last three elections. What is far from common knowledge, however, is that this is Carlton's last chance. If he loses this election, his party has declared categorically that they will throw him out.'

'Are you accusing Mr Carlton of killing Mr Aris?'

'What I am saying, Lady Swift, is that that man Carlton is capable of anything. He's not just a fraud, he's also a womaniser. I'm surprised Carlton's not the one dead, the way he's been carrying on with Stanley Morris' wife, amongst others. Ask Morris, he's well aware of it, poor soul! Carlton is making a total fool out of him, and her, just as he did with the others before.'

She turned and looked back at the Town Hall, where the police were trying to break up the opposing factions. 'Looks like my ladies have done their work well.' At Eleanor's gasp, she smirked. 'My group didn't start the brawl, we merely fanned the flames. You didn't doubt we would support you, did you? We need a woman in charge and it seems you're the best we've got, heaven help us!'

Before Eleanor could reply, she stalked off, slowing only to turn and glower at a man who doffed his hat to her as she turned onto the main road.

A cough heralded the arrival of Clifford. 'It would seem, my lady, that you have found your first supporter.'

Eleanor grimaced. 'Aren't I the popular one!' She let her chin drop to her chest for a moment and let out a long breath. 'What a day! Three interviews, three conflicting stories, three more motives and now three more suspects on the list. And a disastrous and humiliating first attempt at addressing the electorate at the rally which,' she tapped her ear, 'I believe has permanently damaged my hearing. I think Mrs Brody's radical women's group supporting me might just be the death knell of my campaign!'

As they walked to the Rolls, she turned to Clifford. 'She might be derailing my election campaign, however unintentionally, but she's helping our investigation no end! I think the time has come for me to pay a visit to Mrs Aris to offer my condolences.'

On the way, Eleanor recounted Mrs Brody's contention that Carlton killed Aris as Aris had beaten him three times in previous elections.

'Which, as Mrs Brody rightly said, is old news, Clifford. What isn't is that, according to her, the Liberal Party candidate, Stanley Morris, was one of Carlton's conquests. Or rather Morris' wife. I remember Miss Mann hinted that he was a womaniser as well. And Morris apparently found out about it and scrapped with Carlton.'

Clifford shifted the Rolls into gear as they cleared the high street. 'Interesting, my lady, if Mr Carlton had been murdered instead of Mr Aris?'

Deflated, Eleanor sunk back in her seat. 'True, Clifford…'

CHAPTER 17

Eleanor paused in front of a Queen Anne-style mansion set in manicured gardens. As the gate clicked behind her, a maid in an immaculately starched apron appeared on the front step.

'May I help you?'

'Mrs Aris, please.'

'I will see if Madam is home. Your card?'

Unlike many titled ladies, Eleanor had never bothered to get printed calling cards, finding them pretentious. Rather than trying to explain, she pretended to fumble in her jacket pocket. 'Do you know I've made such a lot of social calls lately, I fear I've run out. I am Lady Swift.' She emphasised the 'Lady'.

The maid bobbed and disappeared. Eleanor wished Clifford could have been with her but with all that was going on, he'd had some errands to run. Sometimes she forgot that he had to keep the Hall running despite murder investigations and elections. The maid quickly returned and led Eleanor along the central hallway. They passed the grand staircase and continued out to a charming sunroom with full-length sash windows throwing long shafts of light across the turquoise wool rugs.

'Lady Swift, delighted to see you!' Mrs Aris stepped forward, tall and elegant in a delicate, cornflower-blue dress and a double string of black pearls.

'Mrs Aris, do forgive me calling unannounced. I simply want to pass on my rather late condolences and offer any assistance.' She held out the potted arum lily she'd spotted in a quirky florist on the way past.

'So kind! What a beautiful bloom, I have the perfect Spode planter to set it off. Clare, tea. Do you take Earl Grey, Lady Swift?'

'Only under extreme duress, I'm afraid.'

Mrs Aris smiled at this. 'Clare, two separate pots. Shall we sit? I've rather holed up in this room since Arnold's passing. It's hard to feel totally gloomy in such a bright space.'

Eleanor eased onto the sofa. She looked at the woman opposite her with genuine sympathy. 'It can't have been easy, not with everything happening so... suddenly.'

Mrs Aris stared at her hands and fingered her wedding ring, turning it against a cut sapphire engagement ring behind it.

Eleanor shifted uncomfortably. How could she have imagined this was a good idea? Trying to pump a grieving widow for information? *Oh dear, Ellie, on reflection perhaps not your finest hour!*

The arrival of the tea ended the awkward silence. As the maid set out the fine bone china cups and saucers on the low table between the sofas, Eleanor was struck by her hostess's obsession with blue. Looking round the room, she couldn't find a shred of any other colour, just every shade from sky through to the deepest ocean.

'Mrs Aris, you've such an eye for blending a single colour. It creates a wonderfully restful atmosphere.'

Her hostess gave a wan smile. 'Arnold always told me I overdid it. He said it was like living underwater. Looking back, I imagine he found it rather claustrophobic.'

'Hindsight is a wonderful thing.'

'My husband was a remarkable man, Lady Swift. Driven, passionate and dedicated. Too late, we recognise the errors we make. "The fool who persists in his folly will become wise", only not so it seems.' She laughed awkwardly. 'Do you enjoy William Blake, Lady Swift?'

'He's a little like Earl Grey for my taste, rather strong and intensely flowery.'

'Fair point, he could do with a hefty squeeze of lemon at times.'

Eleanor toyed with the delicate handle of her cup. *Oh well, in for a penny...*

'Forgive my asking, Mrs Aris, I don't wish to speak insensitively... but... do you suspect something was amiss with your husband's... passing?'

The woman stiffened and took up her tea. 'Why ever would you think that?'

'Gracious, it was your choice of Blake quote! I'm sorry, I misread your thoughts. That's what comes of being a poetry philistine.'

Mrs Aris looked across to her maid, who had finished busying herself rearranging the multitude of blue cushions and had moved on to dusting a row of indigo orchids.

'Clare, that can wait, thank you. That will be all for now.'

The girl collected her caddy of cloths and bobbed a half-curtsey, clearly disappointed at not overhearing the rest of the conversation.

As the door clicked shut behind her, Mrs Aris edged forward on the sofa to face Eleanor across the tea table. 'Lady Swift, I do not wish to alarm you, but politics is a barbarous world. Arnold had a rhinoceros' hide and was so blinded by his determination that he failed to see how dangerous the enemies he was making along the way became.'

'Do you think he may have been threatened at all?'

Mrs Aris' lips twisted into a rueful line. 'A million times, but Arnold was too strong for that. If someone had wanted to get rid of him, they would have needed to use more drastic measures. Arnold wouldn't change his mind for anyone, even for that dreadful man Blewitt, who resorted to all manner of underhand tactics to oust him. All so that Blewitt could halt the work Arnold was doing for women's rights. I think Duncan Blewitt believes we women should all be manacled to the kitchen. And then that Communist, Greaves, turned up on the doorstep one day in a fearful temper, but Arnold sent him away with a flea in his ear.'

Eleanor's ears pricked up. 'Interesting… but the police are satisfied that all is in order and presumably the doctor who attended the, er, scene saw nothing wrong?'

Mrs Aris shook her head. 'No, Arnold had an allergy to peanuts. It was so severe that just a trace was potentially lethal for him.'

'Was your husband's allergy common knowledge?'

'He played it down. He felt it was a weakness. If anyone asked him, he'd make a joke of it.' She smiled at Eleanor and shrugged. 'Men!' She sighed. 'Anyway, those closest to him, such as the Farringtons, knew. When we first married, I worried constantly about it. I hated him eating anywhere except at home, but after nearly sixteen years together, I became less vigilant.' She smoothed the skirt of her dress over her knees. 'And now it's happened, I've resolved to accept what is.'

The widow's sangfroid amazed Eleanor. 'A truly admirable attitude. My apologies again for reopening any wounds.'

'It's quite alright. Time, they say, is the greatest healer.' Again, there was that awkward laugh. 'Besides, what choice do I have? I can't change the past. Not any of it…'

'I so admire your compassion, especially at this difficult time. It would be very easy to blame someone.'

Mrs Aris held her gaze. 'Enough people knew that it would be hard to know exactly who to blame. I believe, however, that it was a simple, if tragic error, made by the Farringtons' cook.' She gave a delicate sniff. 'I imagine she feels terrible.'

Eleanor struggled with her conscience. She was on a mission to find who murdered this poor woman's husband, that was true. On the other hand, she desperately didn't want to make things any more painful for her when it seemed clear she didn't suspect her husband's death was suspicious.

If you're going to solve this murder, Ellie, you'll have to do it without disturbing this woman's grief any more. She swigged the last of her tea. 'Mrs Aris, thank you for your gracious hospitality. I merely wanted to pay my respects and assure you that I intend to carry on your husband's excellent work.'

Her hostess rose and offered her hand. 'Tread carefully, Lady Swift. There is no love or honour in politics. It brings out the most merciless behaviour in people.'

Eleanor nodded. 'Yes, I've experienced some of that already, even amongst those groups I thought would support a woman standing.'

'Mrs Brody?' The words seemed to pop out unintended.

Eleanor started. 'Well, I rather meant the women of Chipstone and Little Buckford in general. But why did you mention Mrs Brody?'

'She is well-known for, well...' She looked away and then back to Eleanor. 'Forgive me, it's just that she was a staunch supporter and volunteer of my husband's for several years.'

'Was?'

'They had a falling-out. I believe she turned up at Farrington Manor to cause mischief, but Arnold spotted her and had her ejected. We have said over tea, one cannot always pin down the vagaries of opinions and perceptions. Thank you so much for your kind call.'

Eleanor frowned as she collected her jacket from the maid. They hadn't once discussed the vagaries of anything...

CHAPTER 18

Eleanor's grey silk house pyjamas swished against the balustrade as she trod softly down the stairs.

'Oh, my stars!' Mrs Butters leaned against the wood panelling of the hallway. 'My bones almost jumped out of my skin.'

Eleanor smiled sheepishly. 'I'm so sorry to startle you. It is earlier than I'm usually up, I suppose.'

The housekeeper peered at the grandfather clock in the alcove. 'It is but five and twenty past six, my lady. Polly hasn't started on the fires yet, the morning room will be colder than the pantry.'

Clifford, already immaculately dressed and groomed, came to Mrs Butters' rescue. 'Would you care to join Master Gladstone in the snug, my lady? Perhaps with the addition of a warming pot of tea and a blanket whilst the breakfast preparations are finished?'

'Wonderful, thank you! Sounds better than hanging out with the hams and cheeses in the pantry. Mr Snoozy in there, is he?' said Eleanor. She peeped round the door and softened at the sight of the sleeping bulldog, full-length on the Chesterfield, his feet and jowls twitching as he chased imaginary rabbits.

Clifford coughed. 'May I enquire, my lady, as to the reason for you being up at this unusually early hour?'

'I simply couldn't sleep. I couldn't get Aris' murder out of my mind. And this wretched election... I can't lie in bed, staring at the ceiling any longer. So, tea and a blanket will be lovely. But then a breakfast tray in here whenever it is ready, to save you the faff of laying out the morning room. That way, you can join me sooner.

I need your insights. We're a team when it comes to investigations and such like, remember?'

'Very good, my lady.'

In the snug, Eleanor had a fruitless stand-off with Gladstone, who was too cosy to be cajoled into sharing any part of the Chesterfield. He dug his sharp knees into the cushions and went too stiff for her to move. Finally, she secured enough of the end cushion to sit cross-legged with one knee stuck up in the air.

Mrs Butters tapped at the door and tutted at her mistress being ousted by a bulldog.

'Here, perhaps you'll be warmer in this long wool cardigan and blanket until the fire catches, my lady.'

'Splendid!'

'And this should do wonders for your tootsies.'

'My what?'

The housekeeper blushed. 'I mean your toes, my lady. "Tootsies", have you never heard them called that before?'

Eleanor shook her head.

'Ah, perhaps your mother played "This Little Piggy Went To Market" with you though?'

That made Eleanor's eyes fill. Her voice was quiet. 'That takes me back. I always favoured the little fellow who ate roast beef.'

'Me too.' Mrs Butters gave her that motherly smile that made everything right in the world.

Eleanor wriggled her toes. 'Gosh, that's toasty! Is it a hot water bottle?'

'No, my lady, your late uncle said he was all for modern advancements but tired of the rubber seams leaking and found a simpler, more effective solution. It's two halves of a flowerpot, heated in the range. They'll stay warm for hours.'

This made Eleanor chuckle. 'Honestly, Mrs Butters, this being the lady of the house isn't at all as I imagined it would be. Here I am at the mercy of a stubborn bulldog, wrapped in a blanket with my feet in flowerpots.'

'Can I let you into a secret, my lady? The older I get, the more I realise that nothing is like I thought it would be. Breakfast will be along as quick as a jackrabbit if you can distract yourself for a bit.'

And what a breakfast it was.

'Wow!' Eleanor clapped her hands in childish delight. 'That's genius!'

She held up the artfully formed open bread boat with its crisp brown-crusted edges. Inside was filled with egg-and-cheese soufflé liberally sprinkled with succulent pieces of bacon, tomato, mushroom and black pudding. Gladstone's nose twitched, and he rolled one eye open, before hauling himself up onto one paw with his most innocent face on.

'None for you, Mr Greedy! This is art, not cooking. What does our wonderful cook call it?'

Mrs Butters sniffed. 'The Trotman Breakfast Tugboat.'

Eleanor started to laugh but then glanced at her housekeeper. 'Oh dear! Has there been another disagreement in the kitchen?'

'A silly tiff, I'm sure, my lady. It's just that, well, it was my idea. Only I didn't come up with the name… and perhaps not the black pudding.' She tailed off, biting her lip.

'Well, I love it. How would it be if we renamed this joint masterpiece the Ladies' Launch? It looks like one of those elegant slipper launches one sees on the river.'

Mrs Butters smiled and nodded. 'Ladies' Launch it is. Thank you, my lady.'

Clifford waited until Eleanor stopped smacking her lips. Gladstone, meanwhile, had slumped back into a sleep, grumpy at not receiving the merest morsel.

'You know, Clifford, you really must put your order in for one of these. That was simply divine!'

'Thank you, my lady, but I favour something substantially lighter in the morning, especially before seven o'clock.'

She stared at him, still ignorant about his personal routine despite her having lived at the Hall now for nearly six months. There had to be a normal man in there somewhere. One who ate hearty food, enjoyed a stiff drink and a belly laugh with good friends?

Like the rest of the household, Clifford was used to his mistress drifting off into her own world. 'I believe, my lady, you were asking me to join you in discussing Mr Aris' demise?'

'Yes, yes! It would really help if you took a seat.'

He drew up a long-backed, wooden chair.

'Now that we're both comfy,' she glanced at him sitting as stiff as a poker on the edge of the seat opposite her and shook her head, 'let's get to the bottom of this wretched murder business.'

'How quickly we seem to have returned to this situation.'

She nodded. 'You know, I've worked out village life is like a millpond. On the surface everything seems calm and normal, but underneath currents of scandal, disgrace and dishonour run deep.'

The corner of Clifford's lips twitched. 'Might it be that some people just live a quiet life in the country, my lady?'

She thought about this. 'At best, a handful. The vast majority consist of three groups: those who have committed unspeakable acts, those who dream of committing them, and those who make up malicious gossip about the first two.'

He bowed. 'My congratulations, you have assassinated the good character of the entire rural population.'

Eleanor shook her head, 'Not at all, Clifford, I wasn't just talking about those who live in the countryside. Now, we've seriously digressed, and I've forgotten what I was going to say. Wait! That's it. Yes…'

She picked up the notebook and pen Clifford had placed beside her plate. She turned to the page where she'd copied down the list of all those who were at the table on the night of Aris' death. She'd originally started a list called 'suspects' on another page with a doodle for each suspect. She briefly thought of redoing the doodles in this new list, but decided for once to do without. There were more important matters to get on with.

'Right, Clifford, let's quickly go through everyone at the table the night of Aris' death, not just our suspects, and then see if we've got the same suspect list at the end as we started with? Agreed?'

'Agreed, my lady.'

'Right, Mr Oswald Greaves.'

'Aris tried to have Mr Greaves imprisoned and his party disbanded.'

'And he lied to us, Clifford. He told us he wasn't angry at Aris, yet Mrs Aris told me he turned up on their doorstep in a fearful temper.'

'Certainly enough to keep him on our suspect list, my lady.'

'Now, Ernest Carlton. The man had come second to Aris forever and was about to be deselected by his party, according to Mrs Brody. That's good enough reason to kill Aris, for me. With Aris out of the way, he had a much better chance of winning. There's no prize for coming second, as they taught me all too brutally at St Mary's School. Honestly, every test, every sports event, was like a caged bout.'

'Little did you realise what good training it would be for your forthcoming political career, my lady.'

'It was hell and I'm not a wallflower when it comes to getting what I want. Carlton also seems to be universally disliked, and a known womaniser, although as you pointed out, neither seem relevant to Aris' murder. Last on our suspect list, Blewitt.'

'Mr Blewitt heads a cabal intent on replacing Mr Aris' liberal women's right's policies with a candidate of a very different persuasion. Cause enough for murder?'

Eleanor nodded. 'I met the man and he threatened my health if I carried on investigating Aris' death. He struck me as the kind of man who'd kill his own grandmother if she boiled his egg too long!' She looked back down at her list. 'That pretty much covers our chief suspects. Everyone else at the table seems to have no motive to want Aris dead.'

Clifford nodded.

'Well, let's cross Lord and Lady Langham off as they didn't even attend.' She did so with a certain satisfaction. *One down, eight to go, Ellie.* She ran down the list. 'Lord and Lady Farrington.'

Clifford cleared his throat. 'Aris was supporting Lord Farrington's bid to get a large housing estate built on land owned by Farrington Manor. Since Aris' death, it now seems this deal might be in jeopardy, and the Farringtons' finances too. Hence, it seems that both Lord and Lady Farrington had no motive to murder Mr Aris, rather a motive to keep him alive, at least until the deal had gone through.'

'The complication?'

'The complication is that Lady Farrington forced the staff to lie to the police, seems to have destroyed evidence, id est the remaining fudge, and has asked you to look into the murder without telling Lord Farrington.'

'Your thoughts?'

'It seems Lady Farrington is either covering her own tracks, or covering the tracks of another, but who, and why, I really have no idea at the moment. There is also the rather curious matter of her ladyship asking you to investigate Mr Aris' death, and yet to keep your involvement a secret from her husband.'

Eleanor sighed. 'Indeed. However, we still can't find a motive for either of them wanting Aris dead, and to kill him at their own table, that just seems too unbelievable. Now, Miss Mann. She is head of the very party, the Women's League, that Aris supported. I can't see what she would gain from having him dead. Next is Stanley

Morris, the Liberal Party candidate. Apparently, his wife had an affair with Carlton, not Aris, so there's no motive there. Vernon Peel… Now, Carlton told us that he had issues with Aris. But one, I don't trust anything Carlton says, and two, he could have been trying to incriminate Peel to hide his own guilt.'

Clifford nodded. 'I agree, my lady. However, when we interviewed Mr Peel, I felt he was definitely holding something back. It certainly isn't enough, yet, to place him on our suspect list.'

'Once again, Clifford, I agree.' She cast her eye down the page:

Lord Farrington – no known motive – needed Aris' support for a housing project on his land – possible bankruptcy if not?
Lady Farrington – same as Lord Farrington, but told servants to lie. Why? Protecting someone? Who? Why?
Oswald Greaves – Communist Party – Aris tried to get him imprisoned and his party banned.
Ernest Carlton – Labour Party – lost to Aris three times. Could be dumped by his party if lost again. Also fell out with Aris over a woman.
Arnold Aris – Independent – Dead (poisoned by peanuts).
Miss Mann – Women's League – no known motive – Aris' main supporter of Women's League and women's rights in area.
Stanley Morris – Liberal Party – no known motive.
Duncan Blewitt – Councillor – head of cabal that wants to put anti-women's rights candidate in seat Aris held. No known motive.
Vernon Peel – Aris' partner in law firm – no known motive but definitely hiding something.
Lord and Lady Fenwick-Langham (cancelled)

'So, we still seem to have the same suspects as before. Greaves, Carlton and Blewitt. And the same puzzle that the murderer needed to know beforehand that Mrs Pitkin would serve that fudge, and yet it seems no one at the table did.'

Clifford raised an eyebrow. 'Except Lady Farrington. Mrs Pitkin would certainly have informed the lady of the house of the menu for the evening.'

Eleanor nodded. 'Good point. So maybe we should look more closely at Lord and Lady Farrington as well as Greaves, Carlton and Blewitt.'

Clifford cleared his throat. Eleanor looked up and caught his eye. 'Yes. yes, I know. I'm putting off interviewing Blewitt like I did Mrs Aris, but for very different reasons. My one meeting with Blewitt made my flesh crawl, and that was out in the open. I have no wish to meet the man again, let alone in some confined space like his office.' She stared at the scribblings in her notebook. 'Why on earth did I think I could solve this?' She wrinkled her nose. 'What are we going to do, Clifford?'

He seemed to consider this for a moment. 'Firstly, I would note that your crime-solving skills are considerably sharper than you are crediting yourself with. You have beaten the police to the punch on several most complex murders.'

'Thank you, but *we* solved them. Without your infuriating methodicalness in analysing and dissecting every clue, the killers would still be running around free.'

'Thank you, my lady. Might I therefore suggest that we adopt the same approach here?'

She laughed. 'Maybe we should go into business?' She swept her hand through the air as if reading a sign. 'Swift and Clifford, Private Investigators.'

Clifford waited, his expression as inscrutable as ever.

A thought struck Eleanor. 'You know, we should be adding Mrs Brody as well. She was vociferously scathing about Aris.'

'But Mrs Brody was not at Farrington Manor that night, my lady.'

'Actually, she was. Briefly, it seems. Mrs Aris told me Mrs Brody turned up at Farrington Manor bent on causing mischief. Lady Farrington had her removed.'

Clifford raised an eyebrow. 'And yet she is not on our list for the evening?'

'No, that list is just the seating plan for the table. As she was never officially invited, she was never on the plan. The only trouble is, as she was never at the table and had left before Aris died, I can't see she had the opportunity, whether she had a motive or not.'

She added the name 'Pearl Brody' to the bottom of the list. 'I think we'll keep an eye on her.' She laid down her pen and sighed. 'I don't know what state of mind poor Mrs Pitkin is in at this precise moment. I do, however, know we need to find Aris' killer and prove her innocence as soon as possible before she decides to do something foolish.'

CHAPTER 19

'Watch out!' a disembodied voice yelled.

Eleanor skidded to a halt on her bicycle as a rosy-cheeked woman shot through the hedge. 'Sorry, but can you help? They've escaped again, the little rascals!'

From the chequered apron, wellington boots and piglet under her arm, Eleanor deduced the woman was a farmer's wife. She leaned her bicycle against the gate. 'Yes, of course. How many are there?'

'Thirteen, but I've got the runt here.' An indignant grunt emanated from the wriggling pink bundle. 'Hubby's way up on the top field, we'll have to catch them ourselves.'

'No problem.' Eleanor took off her scarf and made a loop at one end. A particularly chunky piglet whom the others seemed to regard as the ringleader ran towards her. She bided her time and looped the scarf around its neck as it barrelled past.

It dragged her a good fifteen feet before she brought it to a standstill. 'Strike one to Eleanor!' She grinned at the farmer's wife. 'Two down, eleven to go.'

The woman laughed. 'Let's shove them in the empty chicken run just inside the gate.'

Many fraught and exhausting minutes later, they secured the remaining piglets and left them squabbling over the chicken feed in the hen run.

The woman brushed down her apron and smiled at Eleanor. 'Goodness, I can't thank you enough! I was so worried they'd get hit by the coal lorry or the milkman, charging about in the road like that.'

'No trouble. I'm Eleanor Swift, by the way.'

'What? Lady Swift!' The woman put her hand in front of her mouth. 'Goodness, I don't get out enough! What must you think of me stopping you and asking for help in rounding up pigs?' She glanced at Eleanor's scarf and shoes and grimaced. 'Please do come into the farmhouse and let me lend you something, although I've nothing fancy.'

Eleanor pulled her uncle's pocket watch out. 'Thank you, but I'm a little late.'

She looked down at her clothes. Saturday morning had dawned with the promise of being one of those rare autumnal days when the English countryside was at its most enchanting. She'd dressed accordingly in light colours. If she'd known she would be rounding up pigs, she wouldn't have bothered.

'Don't worry, I'll swish it off with, er… champagne.' Realising how much of a princess this made her sound, she gave an embarrassed shrug.

The woman laughed. 'Then I won't detain you any longer than it takes to say a most heartfelt thank you from me and my hubby. We're the Atwoods, we own the farm yonder.' She paused. 'Your uncle was a wonderful man, Lady Swift. We owe him so much.'

And with that, she left Eleanor to complete her journey.

As she reached the airfield, she saw Lancelot standing on the roof of a lorry, scouring the roads like a captain on the ship's bridge. He gave her an exaggerated salute, his silk scarf billowing behind him. 'Ahoy there, Sherlock! I thought you'd been abducted by pirates.' He closed up his imaginary telescope with a snap and deftly swung himself down.

'I say!' He held his scarf over his nose. 'Don't like to mention it but there's a certain something dashedly disconcerting to the nostrils about you. New scent, is it?'

Eleanor gave a haughty toss of her red curls. 'Indeed, the latest from Paris, you know. It's called Eau du Ferme.'

'I can think of a better name for it. Truthfully, Sherlock, it could curdle the picnic!'

She slapped his arm. 'That "stink" as you so ungallantly put it is the result of my being a good citizen and helping to round up a bunch of escaped pigs.'

Lancelot held her at arm's length. 'Darling fruit, remember I told you that you are deliciously peculiar?'

She nodded.

'Well, I've changed my mind.'

'Oh.' She failed to keep the disappointment from her voice.

'I've decided instead that you are dashedly and delightfully crazy!' He winked. 'Whoever heard of a lady of the manor rounding up pigs in the street like a labourer? I'll just have to tell Mater. She'll simply curl up and die with horror!'

'You will do no such thing! I happen to be growing rather fond of your mother. She's been an absolute dear to me, even before I saved your misbegotten life. Now, where's this ride in the sky you promised me?'

'Just over there, via the makeshift washing facilities.'

At the far end of the airfield, Lancelot's plane with its dragonfly-blue paint looked too dainty to carry them up into the cloudless blue sky. Especially as the airfield was no more than a rough meadow with a mown strip down the centre for a runway.

Lancelot leaned into the cockpit. 'There...' He held out a bunch of delicate-scented, white yarrow, the tip of each flowering crown still tinged with a blush of pink. She ran her fingers along the tiny leaves.

'Why, thank you, kind sir. A handful of the finest weeds.'

He flicked her nose. 'Honestly, Sherlock, don't you have any romance about you? They're wildflowers, like you. Down to earth and dashedly uncontrollable.'

She sniffed the flowers. Could she really have found a man who liked her for who she was? *Oh, Ellie, best not hope for too much!*

He gestured at the sky. 'Come on, Florence is itching to fly. Poor old girl, she's been cooped up for weeks whilst I sorted out her sticky throttle problem.'

She stared at him. 'Goggles, are you sure it's safe now? Remember the last time you had the same issue?'

He tutted. 'That was a wonky steering linkage, completely different. And I was the one who had to wait for help whilst your inspector fussed over you like a...' He trailed off and looked away.

Eleanor smiled at the memory. Detective Chief Inspector Seldon had helped her solve two murder cases in the past and the detective had certain feelings for her she tried to deny. She shook her head. 'I do believe you're jealous, Lord Fenwick-Langham. Anyway, there will be no one to rescue me this time... except you.'

Lancelot grinned. 'So, you're not baling before we're even airborne? Because, honestly, I've only got one parachute.'

'What?!'

'Joke!' He slapped his leg. 'I haven't got any parachutes.'

Was that another joke?

Sitting in the single passenger seat behind Lancelot, she realised he was absolutely serious about taking her flying. He leaned over and fumbled around behind her. In doing so, his shirt rode up out of his waistband, causing her to catch her breath at the glimpse of his taut, muscular stomach.

'Here you go, helmet and,' he pushed her curls out of the way and stretched a set of goggles over her head, 'one set of bins. Very fetching!'

'Bins?' She peered through them at him.

'You know, it's cockney rhyming slang.'

'How does that work? I can't think what rhymes with goggles to come out as "bins".'

'Nor me.' He grinned, but then waved his finger in her face. 'Now, safety checks and important information. Sit up and listen, Lady Swift.'

She gulped. The enormity of what she was about to do hit her. She was entrusting her life to a man who thought putting his shoes on the wrong feet was hysterical.

'There is only one thing you need to know when flying in a two-seater like Florence.' He lifted the leather flap of her helmet and spoke into her ear. 'No opening the champagne below five hundred feet!'

With that, he clambered out, kissed the plane's nose cone and gave the propeller several sharp turns until the engine sputtered into life.

'All aboard!' he called, now back in the cockpit. She gave him a thumbs up and then gripped her seat as Florence started to move. The plane turned in a wide arc and came to a stop. Lancelot held a hand up and counted down on his fingers. 'Five… Four… Three… Two… One… LIFT OFF!'

Then they were bumping over the rough grass. The far hedge approached with alarming speed. Just when it seemed they would plough straight through it, the nose lifted and they were airborne.

'Oh, my word, that is so beautiful!' Her hands gripped either side of the rear cockpit as she peered over. The hedgerows and stone walls divided the fields into higgledy-piggledy squares, dotted with white, fluffy ewes, making her feel they were flying over a huge, handmade patchwork quilt.

As they cleared the heavily wooded ridge, resplendent in red and gold autumnal colours, she caught her breath.

'Henley Hall!' Lancelot shouted over the drone of the engine. It lay below and to the left, like a delightful doll's house. Next,

Little Buckford appeared, looking for all the world as if it were a model village, with its quaint high street, tiny cricket ground and Norman church. Feeling she could reach out and pick up a row of the Lilliputian red-roofed terraced houses, she let the wind rush through her fingers. She raised her arms out like wings and yelled into the wind.

'Sherlock! SIT STILL! You're like a flailing squid!'

'Sorry!' She sat back in her seat. She'd been up in a plane before, but not one with an open cockpit for the passenger. It was exhilarating and the view was spectacular.

'Langham Manor!' Lancelot shouted over his shoulder.

She gave him a double thumbs up as the huge mansion came into sight, the extensive formal grounds giving the scene the air of an old oil painting. The plane banked, and soon they were flying over a string of hamlets. She traced the winding grey ribbons of the country lanes with her finger, trying to place exactly where they were. Here and there, the movement of a person walking caught her eye. Surely this was a child's toy cupboard come to life? A peep into the secret world of what happens when the door is clicked closed at the end of playtime?

A few minutes later, something glinted far off to the right. Mystified, she stared at it intently. *Ah, the River Thames!* As they reached it, Lancelot turned Florence and followed the river's course. As they flew along it, she could make out clusters of tiny white dots that must have been the many families of royal swans. Six of the famed Oxford University's rowing teams sped past, the water shimmering off the swift blades of their oars. A little further on, a small flotilla of the renowned Salter's tent boats chugged along, the tourists aboard waving up at the plane. Eleanor waved back, feeling every inch the queen enjoying a spectacular birds-eye view of her kingdom.

A few minutes later, he pointed to a cluster of fairy-tale spires on the horizon: 'Oxford town! We'll be there in—'

Suddenly, the plane veered wildly. She braced herself. What was going on?

Lancelot appeared to be wrestling with the controls. 'That field!' He waved frantically. Unable to see, she nodded anyway. But then her stomach lurched up and seemed to hit her throat. Surely they were falling out of the sky? Up front, Lancelot had obviously lost his battle of wills with his errant controls. 'Might... get... bumpy. HOLD ON!'

She looked over the side of the plane and then wished she hadn't as the ground rushed up to meet them.

When the impact came, it was softer than she'd expected. The wheels bumped along the cut grass of the field before a small haystack slowed them enough for the plane to slide gracefully into a lake.

Lancelot cheered as they floated to a stop. 'Best landing ever! Impressive what, Sherlock?'

Eleanor stared at the back of his head. She'd met some dangerous characters on her travels, but this one was in a league of his own. She peered over at the water. 'Will she float?'

'Of course!' They both scrambled out onto the narrow fuselage. He held her hand and looked at her with concern. 'Darling fruit, your hands are shaking! You weren't scared, were you? You always seem so tough, so capable, like nothing ever fazes you.'

She let out a deep breath. 'I'll be fine in a minute. It's just that the plane I took from Cape Town to London to get back to England after my uncle died crashed three times. The first time I thought I'd die from the impact, the second from thirst and the third from wild animals. On none of these occasions was there the luxury of a lake to land on.'

For once, Lancelot looked serious: 'Was it a flying boat?'

'No.'

He grinned. 'Then it would have sunk, anyway.'

She punched him on the arm.

'Ow!' He rubbed the spot. 'You hit hard, for a girl.' He moved out of range. 'Only kidding! Poor old Florence, though, she'll have soggy underparts for a good while, that's for sure.'

She shuffled across to him. 'As will we, you oaf! What are we going to do?'

'Enjoy the picnic?'

Still sitting on top of the plane, and even though she wanted to push his grinning face into the lake for being so flippant about, well, everything, she found his childish delight infectious. They were soon tucking into a delicious feast of scotch eggs, fine cheese and cucumber sandwiches, all washed down with generous amounts of champagne.

She turned her glass in her hand and looked out over the water. For no apparent reason, it reminded her of evenings sitting with her parents, looking out over the small lake at the back of their hut in Peru.

'Lancelot, do you ever feel bad about how much you've got when others have so much less?' She sighed. 'Sorry, I didn't mean to get earnest, but campaigning in Little Buckford and Chipstone has been a real eye-opener.'

He shrugged. 'What's the sense in not enjoying what you have? That strikes me as ungrateful and, if I'm honest, being a martyr doesn't suit you.'

The remark stung. 'I'm not being a martyr.'

'Aren't you?'

Suddenly, he jumped up, waving both arms like a shipwrecked sailor. 'Ahoy!'

Across the field, a small tractor was trundling towards them, a scowling, stocky man at the wheel. He stopped next to the edge of the lake.

''Tis private property, this.'

Lancelot grinned and reached for his wallet. 'Most observant of you! Trouble is,' he winked at the man, 'I was trying to impress the lady, and, like a damned idiot, overdid it. Let me compensate you for the inconvenience of you being so kind as to pull us out. And any damage, of course.'

The farmer's shoulders relaxed as Lancelot pulled several notes out of his wallet. 'Well, it don't appear too much damage done, sir.' He climbed out of his tractor and gave a wry smile. 'One question first, though.'

Lancelot slid from the fuselage into the waist-high water and waded ashore. He nodded as he handed the money over.

The farmer covered one side of his mouth and whispered, 'Was the lady impressed?'

Rising from her seat, Eleanor called out, 'Yes, she was!'

Both men stared in surprise, and then Lancelot's laughter rang out across the Oxfordshire countryside.

The evening light was ebbing as Lancelot tucked his wet jacket around Eleanor's shoulders. By the time they had got themselves and Florence out of the lake, they were both soaked and covered in weed and wet hay. The farmer had towed the plane into a nearby shed and Lancelot had flagged down a coal lorry and repeated his tale of woe in exchange for a lift. From up front, the driver repeatedly turned to peep at them, as they sat on the open tailgate, their legs dangling, water dripping from their socks and stockings.

Eleanor held her battered bouquet of yarrow flowers and one shoe, the other lost in wading ashore. Her limp curls stuck to her coal-dust-streaked face. Lancelot slipped her hand into his and wrapped his fingers round hers, whistling nonchalantly and looking straight ahead. She felt utterly content.

'Sherlock?'

'Mmm?'

'Will you come up with me and Florence again?'

She thought for a moment. 'Only if you stock up on parachutes, lifejackets and spare clothes.' She nestled into his shoulder. 'And most importantly, more champagne.'

CHAPTER 20

Mrs Butters was still fussing as the hall clock struck twelve noon the next day. 'But, my lady, you had a nasty dunk, swimming about in goodness only knows what. Another spoonful couldn't hurt.'

Eleanor stopped fiddling with her Women's League rosette and stared at her housekeeper in the mirror. 'Yes, it could. It could take the rest of the lining off my throat and I need my voice to carry loud and clear at this afternoon's debate.'

'As you wish, my lady. You don't feel feverish at all?'

Eleanor turned and took Mrs Butters by the shoulders. 'Do you realise how much of a blessing you are?'

'Tsk, tsk, I wasn't fishing for compliments.'

'I know. As usual, you were trying to take better care of me than I am myself. Now, wish me luck because I fear I may need it.'

Chipstone High Street seemed to have an air of expectancy to Eleanor's mind. As Clifford stopped the Rolls as near to the Town Hall as possible she stuck her head out of the window and stared at the sizeable crowd gathered outside.

'That's odd. I rather thought our audience would be mostly reporters, and a few retired chaps who have tired of cribbage. Everyone else should be busy getting on with life and yet there's quite a group waiting.'

'There is a lot of uncertainty over events in Whitehall, my lady. The coalition government is causing significant alarm with its very public and repeated disagreements. I suspect the local populace are seeking reassurance that things on their doorstep will be considerably more stable.'

'Well, if they vote for me, they will be.'

'A bold promise. Might one enquire if that is to be the thrust of your message today?'

'Actually no, it isn't. But you'll have to wait like everyone else to find out what it is.' As she stepped out of the car, she muttered, 'And so will I.'

Inside the Town Hall, the air felt thick and stuffy. A movement at the far end of the corridor caught Eleanor's eye. Hoping it was Miss Mann, she was disappointed to find it was Mrs Brody striding towards her.

'Lady Swift, excellent! I wanted to see you. Thursday evening, seven o'clock in the Reading Room, you are invited to our next meeting.'

Eleanor tried to sound non-confrontational. 'Mrs Brody, I truly appreciate you and your ladies' support, but I cannot condone the tactics you used at the last debate. I learned that it was your group who drowned out Mr Blewitt and the other candidates as they tried to address the public? And then incited the crowd to storm the stage? I realise how well-intentioned your group is, but—'

Mrs Brody burst into laughter. 'Can you really be that green that you imagine, as a woman, you can win this election without those sorts of tactics? And worse!'

Eleanor bristled. 'I do not believe the use of underhand tactics will further our cause.'

Mrs Brody folded her arms. 'Do you honestly think that all the other candidates aren't doing this kind of thing all the time? And that this doesn't happen all over the country? Because if you do, then you need our help more than I thought. Besides, my group has a lot more extreme tactics planned for the next debate. And so will your opponents.' She shook her head. 'Next, you'll be suggesting that the best party should win only by fair and square means.'

Eleanor tossed her red curls. 'I wouldn't suggest that, I would declare it. Politics might be a cut-throat game, but I won't stoop to winning unfairly.'

Mrs Brody's exasperation was obvious. She spoke to Eleanor like a small child. 'Don't you realise the outcome is a foregone conclusion unless we intervene? As an independent and a woman, you stand no chance! I invited you to the next Firebrand meeting, not to support you, as you put it, but to drum some realisation into you. The Women's League is a bunch of old women with little or no real concept of how to get a woman candidate elected. Especially with that man Blewitt...'

Lady Langham's words came back to Eleanor: 'What is to become of this country if all the women are slandering and fighting each other in public and whoring and gambling in private like the men?'

She raised her hand and voice. 'Then, Mrs Brody, I'd rather lose. Don't you see that by cheating and dirty-dealing, you are merely aping the men you claim to despise?'

Mrs Brody's eyes flashed. 'So "stooping" to their tactics isn't acceptable?'

Eleanor shook her head this time. 'I'm not passing judgement on some of the radical actions carried out by Mrs Pankhurst and other suffragettes, I know the poor lady is currently in prison on charges of sedition, of all things. I'm merely agreeing with the words of Miss Mann, that, in a rural backwater like Chipstone, such tactics will alienate the general voter. Including a lot of the women we're trying to help.'

Mrs Brody took a step closer. 'You,' she poked Eleanor in the arm, 'are living in a dream world. You titled lot always are. Head in the clouds, the lot of you! Think you can get what you want without getting your hands dirty. Well, I will sully mine by doing whatever it takes. Any stains from fighting for our cause will not stop my conscience sleeping at night.'

Mrs Brody stomped off, then turned back to Eleanor and smiled thinly. 'I see your true colours now, Lady Swift. If you are not with us, you are against us.'

A slight chill ran down Eleanor's back. She remembered Oswald Greaves' parting words. 'You are the enemy!' It seemed no matter what she did, she was indeed making enemies everywhere.

Her eyes darkened. The more good her parents tried to do, it seemed the more enemies they'd made until... She shook her head. It was going to take more than a few vague threats to stop her keeping her promise to herself. *Now, Ellie, you've a debate to win!*

She spun round smartly and collided with the woman standing in front of her.

Miss Mann rubbed her forehead. 'Lady Swift, I do apologise!'

'No, it was my fault. Are you alright?'

'I think so, thank you. The debate is about to start.' Miss Mann hesitated. 'Lady Swift, I owe you an apology.' She paused, obviously struggling with some inner conflict. 'I should never have asked you to stand. For... for I never believed you could win.'

After her encounter with Mrs Brody, Eleanor wasn't prepared for any more nonsense. 'Whatever do you mean, Miss Mann? If that's the case, why on earth did you ask me to stand for the Women's League?'

Miss Mann's hands trembled as she clutched her papers to her chest. 'I am sorry, honestly. We felt we didn't have a choice.' She seemed to gather courage. 'Chipstone isn't a rotten borough, Lady Swift, you can't buy a few key votes and get elected here, not like you can in some areas. You've got to persuade people to vote for you, even if candidates sometimes do use questionable methods to get them to do so.' She darted a look at Eleanor. 'Oh, goodness, I don't mean you! I only meant that the greater proportion of voters in this constituency are working class and they see you as... well, as far from their ken as foreign travel or caviar. And... and the reality is most wives will either vote as their husbands do, or not at all.'

'But you were the one who worked so hard to persuade me!' Eleanor's thoughts whirled. Were Mrs Brody and Miss Mann right? Was she fighting a hopeless battle? She shook her head. 'Please explain yourself. Why, for goodness' sake, did you choose me?'

Miss Mann took a deep breath. 'After Mr Aris' tragic death, we had to field an independent candidate to try and stop that awful man Blewitt getting his anti-women's rights candidate elected. But the truth is, the chance of our candidate, whoever we chose, winning in such a traditional area was always slim to none.' For the first time, she looked Eleanor in the eye. 'But I assure you that isn't a reflection on yourself, Lady Swift. We just wanted to keep whoever Blewitt chose out.'

By now, Eleanor had gone from shock to dismay, to frustration. 'Hold on! If you were all so sure I wouldn't be accepted by the majority of working-class voters, why didn't you choose, say, Mrs Brody, as your candidate instead of me? Maybe she would have had at least a slim chance. She was a supporter of Mr Aris for years, I believe. She's definitely working class and certainly has more than enough to say on the subject of women's rights!'

'What, that woman!' Miss Mann patted her tightly clipped chignon. 'She is banned from even setting foot near an election or the Women's League.'

Eleanor remembered Mrs Aris saying something similar. 'But why ever was that necessary?'

'Why? Because the woman is impossible! She wanted to be our candidate at one point, but even we couldn't accept her. She rowed with every member of every party, especially Mr Aris and

Mr Blewitt. They hated her equally.' Miss Mann looked around and lowered her voice. 'Mr Aris tried to have her Reading Room closed down because she was using them to indoctrinate local women into railing against their situations. He said that was not the usage for which the money had been granted for it to be set up. When Mrs Brody heard he had lodged a formal complaint to the Parish Council, she went round to his house and threw bricks through his windows. She—'

They were interrupted by the call for candidates to take their place in the hall.

Miss Mann flashed her an apologetic smile. 'Good luck, Lady Swift. And don't worry about Mrs Brody and her group, the master-at-arms has put extra security on the door and around the building. Have you your speech prepared?'

Eleanor pulled out a folded card and waved it with more confidence than she felt. 'Perfectly prepared, thank you, Miss Mann.' She turned and took her seat on the stage.

It's showtime, Ellie!

CHAPTER 21

On the raised platform, Eleanor looked out over the crowd of expectant faces, pleased to see that Clifford had found a discreet spot where she couldn't see him watching her intently. Most of them appeared to be men in their late thirties and forties, with a few middle-aged women sat at the back. She sighed to herself, Mrs Brody and Miss Mann's recent words eating away at the last of the confidence her silent pep talk in the intervening minutes had mustered.

She looked along the row of other candidates, catching Carlton's mocking eyes and glanced away, only to meet Duncan Blewitt's scornful look. She reminded herself that one of the men sitting up on stage with her was likely to be Aris' murderer. Suddenly she had an overwhelming urge to flee the building. Flee and forget all about the election and the murder investigation, the two becoming more and more entwined in her mind.

She forced herself to take a deep breath and count to ten.

Come on, Ellie! If you were going to quit, you should have done it before when you had the chance. You're committed now.

She took another deep breath and reached into her pocket for the card she had waved at Miss Mann.

What the...? The card she pulled out wasn't the one she'd written her carefully prepared notes on. One side was blank, whilst on the other in beautiful copperplate lettering were the words: *'Be yourself, everyone else is taken.'* Oscar Wilde.

She gasped. Clifford had hidden this in one of her unfashionable walking shoes when she was going out on her first proper date with

Lancelot months ago. The note had sat on the base of her bedside lamp ever since. He'd obviously switched it surreptitiously for her notes whilst she was in the Rolls. She stared at the quote for a moment, and then mouthed the words, 'Thank you, Clifford.'

On stage a succession of candidates were called to the lectern. The crowd quickly switched from anticipation to boredom as each started speaking. With no chance of a repeat of the disarray at the first debate, the public felt cheated out of their entertainment. Quiet mutterings turned into loud heckling.

The master-at-arms banged his gavel repeatedly.

'Silence! I will have order or I will have the room cleared!' Reluctantly, the crowd complied.

As he announced the next candidate, Eleanor's nerves bubbled up worse than ever. Winning this debate mattered, really mattered. She heard her name called. She stood and walked to the middle of the stage in a daze.

Looking out over the sea of faces, she tried to let her mind relax. *Take a deep breath, Ellie, just be yourself.* She closed her eyes and then opened them. People shuffled in their seats. The master-at-arms glared at her, picked up his gavel and then placed it back down as she started to speak.

'Good afternoon, everyone. Now, I know you are wondering what on earth I'm doing up here, and to tell you the truth,' she paused, 'so am I.'

People turned to their neighbour, sharing a puzzled frown. Eleanor relaxed as her words rolled out. 'You see, as well as being the only woman standing here today, I'm also very much the new girl in town. And do you know when I arrived,' she held her hands up and looked around, 'I wasn't sure at all that I wanted to stay.'

The room tensed. Eleanor nodded slowly. 'You see, I only came back at the death of my uncle, Lord Henley, out of a vague sense of duty.' She hesitated. 'I didn't really know my late uncle, but I'm told he was a wonderful man.' This brought a round of nodding and a murmur of agreement from sections of the crowd.

Encouraged, she continued. 'So, there I was, the long-lost niece, standing on the steps of Henley Hall, remembering that the last time I was there, I was too short to reach the bell pull.' The ladies in the back row patted each other's hands without taking their eyes off her. 'And I have to tell you,' she scanned the rows again, 'I'm actually mighty cross with most of you.'

The outbursts that followed seemed split between confusion and anger.

'Cross with us?'

'What's she on about?'

'The cheek!'

The rap of the master-at-arms' gavel brought the crowd up short. 'Gentlemen, ladies, let Lady Swift continue.' He raised an eyebrow in her direction. 'I, for one, am interested to find out how exactly I have annoyed her.'

She smiled at him. 'Well, I thought I had my plan sorted, you see. Pop over here, do what needed to be done and then escape back to my other life. But,' she sighed, 'I've discovered that I can't bring myself to leave. I have fallen head over heart in love with this beautiful county. And even more so with the incredible community of kind-hearted, genuine folk who live here.' The entire main chamber was silent. Even Greaves looked up from his notebook. Eleanor looked over the sea of faces before continuing. 'Can I be totally honest with you? It's something of a secret, so please keep it to yourselves.' Everyone, including the master-at-arms, leaned forward. Eleanor cupped her mouth and whispered just loud enough to be heard: 'I don't fit in, I'm not one of you.'

Carlton's roar of laughter made everyone jump. The master-at-arms gave him a stern look and waved his gavel in his direction. All eyes were back on Eleanor as she continued. 'You see, I'm the

outsider, the offcomer and yet…' her hands went to her chest '…
you've made me feel like family. And the truth is…' she paused and
swallowed the lump in her throat '…I've never felt that anywhere
else before.'

Several men coughed, whilst several of the ladies pulled out
handkerchiefs and pretended to wipe their noses. Eleanor took
a deep breath. 'And that's why I'm so cross with you all. I can't
leave and yet I can't stay. Not without giving something back. Not
without trying to be a good neighbour and a kind-hearted friend,
because that's what you've been to me. If I did, I really would be
the spoiled princess who inherited the world then, wouldn't I?'

This brought a lot of chuckles and elbow nudging. 'Gentlemen
and ladies, I can only make you one promise. I haven't got a raft
of policies, in fact I have no experience in politics, I've never seen
the Houses of Parliament. And I think I'd look terrible in those
stuffy gowns. Black is a death colour on me!' Laughter rang round
the chamber.

Eleanor lowered her voice, but her words carried easily to the
back of the room. 'I'm not my late uncle, although I believe we
share many similarities, perhaps stubbornness being the most
prominent. However, you've compelled me to want to follow in
his footsteps. I simply have to do something to say thank you for
all that you've done for me since I arrived here. And the best way
I know I can do that is to take your concerns, your problems and
your hopes, to Whitehall. And…' for the first time since coming to
the lectern, she raised her voice '…and do my absolute damnedest
to get them heard whatever it takes!'

A sizeable group in the second and third rows leapt up and
applauded. Soon the rest of the audience were on their feet, cheering
and clapping. Shouts crossed the room.

'Hear, hear!'

'We'll give you a shot, won't we, Ma?'

'Didn't think she had it in her, but she has!'

'Go, Lady Swift!'

Eleanor beamed at the crowd and surprised herself by blowing out a kiss.

At the side of the stage, Duncan Blewitt punched a stack of chairs and spun round, his back to Eleanor. As she turned, Ernest Carlton caught her eye with an appreciative arch of one brow. She took her seat and continued to stare forward, ignoring his whispered, 'Didn't expect you to pull out the emotive card, old girl. I see you're going to take some stopping. But I will…'

CHAPTER 22

'Gracious, Polly! Are you alright?'

Her maid lay where she'd tripped, the newspapers she'd been carrying scattered perilously close to the crackling fire in the room affectionately named the snug. Gladstone lumbered up from where he had been sprawled on the marble hearth and stretched out first one, then the other, of his short, stiff legs as he licked the maid's cheek. Polly looked up. 'I'm sorry, your ladyship, I was so excited. But was that wrong of me?'

Eleanor knelt and lifted the young girl's chin. 'I don't think being excited can ever be wrong, can it?'

Polly scrambled up onto her knees and fiddled with the edge of her apron strap. She whispered, 'You don't, your ladyship, really?'

'No, I mean excitement is a wonderful thing.'

'Isn't it though? I love that fizzy feeling.'

Eleanor laughed. 'Fizzy feeling? Is that what excitement is like for you?'

Polly nodded emphatically. 'When something exciting is happening, I feel full of bubbles growing and fizzing and bubbling up inside me, like Mrs Trotman's special gravy does on the range.'

Eleanor couldn't help but smile. With Gladstone now leaning sideways against her with his head on her shoulder, she shuffled awkwardly into a cross-legged position. She put her arm around the bulldog's neck and stared up at the ceiling. 'Excitement for me is like a hundred fireworks going off with a marching band playing at the same time.'

Polly clapped her hands in delight.

A cough made them both turn to the doorway. Clifford stood holding a silver tray, his face registering his hearty disapproval of the sight before him. The young girl jumped to her feet, her cheeks scarlet.

Eleanor gave him a cheery wave. 'Morning, Clifford. Polly and I were discussing something most important.'

He stepped over the papers and placed the tray on the breakfast table. 'Evidently important enough to be huddled on the floor with members of the staff and Master Gladstone amongst the tatters of the morning papers?'

She winked at Polly. 'Absolutely.'

Clifford shook his head. 'Polly, Mrs Trotman will be waiting for you.'

'Yes, sir! So, sorry, Mr Clifford, sir.' Polly scampered off in the direction of the kitchen.

Eleanor called after her. 'But, Polly, you didn't tell me what you were so excited about?'

Without stopping, her maid shouted over her shoulder, 'It's the newspapers, your ladyship! Everyone loves you as much as we do!'

Clifford ran a white-gloved finger along his starched collar. 'My apologies, my lady. I will speak to Polly.'

Eleanor wiggled out from under Gladstone's bulky form and stood to put her hand on Clifford's arm. 'Please don't. She's trying so hard to get it right and I'd hate to see her delightful little spirit constrained.'

'As you wish.'

'But I'm intrigued by her parting words. Is there a write-up about yesterday's debate?'

Clifford had started collecting the newspapers and matching the right pages to the right publication. He stood up, looking at the crumpled heap in horror. 'No, my lady, there are a great many write-ups and the vast majority are hailing you as a local heroine.'

'What!' Eleanor's mind spun. 'Really? I mean, I just stood there and said what came into my head.' She smiled fondly at him. 'But I think someone not too far away might have engineered that.'

'Master Gladstone has often been observed going through your pockets, my lady.'

'Nice try.'

'Might I interrupt the thread of conversation to thank you for generously sharing your delight at the reception your speech received with an impromptu party for the staff last night. It was greatly appreciated and will, no doubt, be the talk of many long winter evenings.'

'I'm so pleased everyone enjoyed it as much as I did. It was honestly my greatest pleasure to spend it at home, amongst fam—' She gave an embarrassed shrug. 'I will try not to make a habit of it. I say, those sausage meat and herb pastry rolls Mrs Trotman conjured up so quickly were divine. Hot and buttery from the oven. And the Stilton and bacon fellows. Ooh, but the piquant Cheddar and field mushroom, yummy!'

'And you found her homemade rhubarb wine a fine complement?'

She smiled at the memory. 'We all did and the damson rum for afters.'

'Well, the celebration was not only appreciated but also well deserved, it seems. The press have seized upon your frank and self-effacing message with uncharacteristic positivity in the main.'

'Look at this!' She held up the front page of *The County Gazette* and pointed to the photograph of her blowing a kiss to the crowd.

He read out the reporter's opening line: 'The question on everyone's lips isn't is Lady Swift ready for Whitehall, but is Whitehall ready for Lady Swift?' The corners of his mouth twitched. 'Let's hope so, my lady.'

She shook her head and sat down. 'I'm amazed, Clifford, really. It could have gone so wrong. I half expected rotten cabbages to rain onto the stage.'

Clifford cocked an eyebrow. 'Which simply goes to show how very true the words of your speech were, my lady.'

'How so?'

'As you said so honestly, you are the interloper. Cabbages are never harvested before November in Buckinghamshire, every local knows that.'

She laughed and fell back onto the Chesterfield, spilling the tea Clifford had brought with him.

The housekeeper appeared in the doorway as Clifford was mopping up the mess on the tray. 'I am sorry to interrupt you, my lady, but you have visitors.'

'Who is it, Mrs Butters?'

Before the housekeeper could reply, two policemen came in behind her.

Eleanor regarded them without too much concern. She was rather used to the police by now. 'Good morning, Constables? Or is it Sergeants? I'm rubbish at knowing what all your wonderful stripes and buttons mean. Will you join me for some tea whilst we discuss whatever you've come for?'

The taller of the two replied: 'Inspector and Constable, as it happens.' He tapped his shoulder with his gloved finger. 'I'm Inspector Fawks. And this,' he pointed at his companion, 'is Constable Wainfleet. And no, tea will not be appropriate, thank you.'

'I see, well, how can I help?'

'By accompanying us to the police station, Lady Swift.'

Eleanor's smile faded. 'In connection with what, Inspector?'

'In connection, Lady Swift, with the murder of one Ernest Carlton.'

CHAPTER 23

Eleanor shook her head. 'Murder?' Slowly, comprehension dawned. 'Aris. You mean Arnold Aris, surely?'

Inspector Fawks frowned. 'Who's Aris? The deceased's name is Carlton. Ernest Carlton. Who is this Aris character? Have you been drinking?'

Her hand flew to her mouth. 'Carlton! He can't have been murdered. I was sitting next to him only last night.'

The constable spoke for the first time: 'That might be, but this morning, he's as dead as the proverbial doornail.'

Inspector Fawks nodded. 'But then you knew that already, didn't you, Lady Swift, seeing as you murdered him? So, please, don't try and confuse us. Save any theatricals for the judge. Now, you will accompany us to Oxford Police Station for questioning without further delay.'

Eleanor's head was still swimming. 'The one on Blue Boar Street?'

Inspector Fawks smiled grimly. 'Already familiar with it, are we? Not surprised!'

'Oh, thank goodness!' *Perhaps Chief Inspector Seldon will be there, Ellie?*

Inspector Fawks looked inquiringly at Clifford. 'Are you sure your employer hasn't taken any strong substance, illegal or otherwise, this morning?'

Clifford nodded. 'I assure you, gentlemen, that despite appearances to the contrary, Lady Swift has not partaken of any substance more illegal than buttered toast.'

Inspector Fawks seemed unconvinced. 'That may be. Constable, escort Lady Swift to the car.'

Clifford stepped forward. 'Inspector, I can vouch for Lady Swift's recent whereabouts. Perhaps you might wish to take my statement at the station.' He lowered his voice. 'She may succumb to a delayed attack of hysterics.'

Inspector Fawks looked him up and down. 'Perhaps that is a good idea.'

'Especially after that woman bit you last month, Inspector,' said the constable.

Inspector Fawks grimaced and rubbed his elbow. 'Yes, we will need your statement as well. You'll have to make your own way there, however.'

Eleanor threw Clifford a grateful look. As the constable took her arm, she shook his hand off. 'Constable, unhand me! I am coming without a fight so please show some decorum.' The young policeman looked helplessly at his boss.

Inspector Fawks gave a heavy sigh. 'Lady Swift, perhaps on the journey to Oxford I shall instruct you on prisoner protocol?'

As the constable led her out to the waiting police car, she turned to Inspector Fawks. 'By the way, you haven't given me any indication as to why on earth you imagine I had anything to do with poor Mr Carlton's death?'

'Aha, well, you see, in my professional experience most toff… most titled gentry and ladies make a good few enemies, and you're no exception.'

Eleanor stared blankly out of the car window, trying to grapple with her situation. Someone had set her up. *But who?* She groaned. It could be any of their suspects. Or even one of the other candidates who had nothing to do with Aris' death, but who saw the opportunity to get rid of an opponent.

'Oh, this is ridiculous! I don't even know how Carlton died,' she said out loud.

When they arrived in Oxford, the constable showed Eleanor into a small room with a bare wood table and two hard chairs whilst Inspector Fawks disappeared without an explanation.

She was still in shock over the news of the murder of Carlton, but determined not to be browbeaten. She sat down, drumming her fingers on the table. Thankfully it was a short wait. And one that ended with a potential spot of relief as DCI Seldon's tall, athletic frame ducked under the door frame, his broad shoulders straightening as he swept into the room, with Inspector Fawks following in his wake.

He nodded to Eleanor. 'Lady Swift, would you—'

'Like tea? Certainly. With two sugars, if you please.'

He frowned. 'I haven't offered tea.'

'I know and you're quite right. Maybe a stiff coffee is needed?'

'Lady Swift, do you understand why you are here?' Inspector Fawks said, glancing at DCI Seldon, who rolled his eyes but gestured that the policeman should meet Eleanor's request.

Only a few short, but awkwardly silent, minutes later, she took a sip of her coffee, wincing at the strength. 'Now, Inspector Fawks, to answer your question as to my understanding of why I am here, yes, I do. I understand someone has tried to set me up for the death of...' she shook her head, hardly able to believe it '...for the death of Mr Carlton. And that it is the police's job to investigate such unfounded claims.'

DCI Seldon tried to hide a smile, whilst Inspector Fawks frowned. 'Then I need to enlighten you further, Lady Swift. This is a most serious matter. A man is dead at the hand of another and at this point in our inquiries yours is the hand that appears to have been responsible.'

DCI Seldon snorted. 'Fawks, I realise this is your investigation, but I can vouch for Lady Swift. She is much more likely to be solving a murder than committing one.'

Eleanor shot him a grateful smile. 'Thank you. And might I enquire now as to how Mr Carlton was murdered?'

Inspector Fawks shook his head. 'No, Lady Swift, you may not. It is my job to ask the questions. Yours is to answer them. Whilst enjoying your coffee, of course.'

She stared at him. Was he trying to do that good policeman/bad policeman routine she'd read about in those penny dreadfuls? Or was he just a little odd?

Inspector Fawks tapped his pen on the table. 'Now, where were you last night between the hours of eight and nine in the evening?'

She frowned. *At least I now know the time of Carlton's murder.* 'Honestly, I don't remember. I'll have to start a minute-by-minute diary if this kind of thing is going to become a habit.'

DCI Seldon coughed, covering up what sounded suspiciously like a laugh.

Inspector Fawks leaned forward. 'It is more a case of whether murder becomes a habit of yours, Lady Swift.'

DCI Seldon grunted. 'Fawks, if you had been taking notes, you might find as I mentioned earlier, that Lady Swift is more in the habit of solving murders than perpetrating them.'

Inspector Fawks shot DCI Seldon an exasperated look. 'I appreciate that, sir, but I have to follow up my information, as you are aware.' He turned back to Eleanor. 'So, having been involved in murder before, in whatever capacity, you'd understand how to cover your tracks?'

Despite herself, Eleanor had to admit he had a point. She flapped a hand in reply.

Inspector Fawks had taken a notebook from his top pocket and was writing. He looked up. 'So, I'll ask again, where were you last night between the hours of eight and nine in the evening?'

Eleanor tried to remember what she'd been doing, but she rarely took notice of the time, especially when at home. 'I'm sure I was at Henley Hall by that hour, but as to what I was doing, I can't recall.'

'Were you alone, Lady Swift?'

'Well, one is never alone, Inspector, my staff would have been there. They can vouch for me. I do remember I had a delicious late supper with them all in the kitchen. Clifford mentioned it was about two o'clock this morning that we finished celebrating. Then I probably cuddled up with Gladstone and fell into a most happy slumber.'

DCI Seldon turned to inspect the wall minutely for a moment at her description of her evening's activities. He seemed to be trying not to laugh.

Inspector Fawks slapped his pen down on the table. 'Still being flippant then?'

'Sorry?'

He leaned back. 'You say you were alone all evening and yet,' he looked at his notes, 'you now claim to have spent it in the presence of staff. And then the early hours onwards with a certain Gladstone. Is he another member of your staff?' Before she could reply, he fixed her with a severe look. 'Wasting police time is a serious offence. Nearly as serious as murder in my book. Now, who is this Mr Gladstone if he isn't the late, dead, Prime Minister? Your beau, perhaps?'

Despite the seriousness of the situation, she couldn't help smiling. 'I am not usually to be found lying on sofas embracing members of my staff or ex-prime ministers, Inspector.'

DCI Seldon failed again to disguise his laugh as a cough. 'I believe you'll find, Fawks, that Master Gladstone is the late Lord Henley's bulldog. Lady Swift inherited him along with her uncle's estate.' He turned his gaze on her, his eyes smiling. 'I'm sure he performs some useful function, although it mostly seems to consist of hogging the sofa, stealing sausages and crushing the hats of unsuspecting visitors.'

'I see,' Inspector Fawks said tersely, evidently not seeing at all. Eleanor tore her gaze away from DCI Seldon. 'Yes, Inspector. In fact, I believe my butler, Clifford, is probably now somewhere about the building. He will substantiate the facts I have given you.'

'Never mind that.' Inspector Fawks made a note and looked up. 'When we first arrested you, Lady Swift, you mentioned that you thought you were being arrested for the murder of a Mr Aris, not a Mr Carlton?'

DCI Seldon stared at her quizzically and went to speak, but she jumped in, deliberately not looking at him as she was finding his gaze unsettling. 'Well, Inspector, when one murders as many people as I do, how is one to keep up?'

Did you just say that out loud, Ellie? She groaned to herself. Whenever she was in a stressful or dangerous situation, her nerves brought out the glibbest of remarks.

DCI Seldon seemed to be having yet another coughing fit. Once he'd regained his composure, he nodded to Inspector Fawks, whose thin set lips suggested he wasn't amused.

'Tell me about this Mr Aris?'

DCI Seldon interrupted. 'Mr Aris died of a rare food allergy about a week ago, Fawks. I'm currently investigating his death. Although, despite Lady Swift's assertion, we have no firm evidence yet that this was caused by anything other than gross negligence. We're currently deciding whether to press charges.'

Inspector Fawks was still looking at her expectantly. 'I met Mr Aris and his wife at a luncheon at Langham Manor. We didn't really get acquainted. I then visited Mrs Aris after I'd heard her husband had died to, er, offer my condolences.'

'I see.' Fawks' pen scratched across the paper as he mumbled, 'Possibility of collaboration between Mrs Aris and the accused.'

She leaned over the table and jabbed at his words. 'That, Inspector, is misrepresentation. Perhaps you missed your true vocation as a journalist?'

He stopped writing. 'Actually, I did dream of becoming a reporter. And I did enjoy this morning's newspaper coverage of your speech at the debate.'

She shook her head. 'Which one? There were so many?'

'There was a common thread which I found most interesting. The one where every journalist to a man quoted you as saying,' he turned the first sheet of his notebook back over and read, "I will win whatever it takes."'

She tutted. 'That was just hyperbole. For emphasis, Inspector, although I do like to win… a lot.' She caught DCI Seldon nodding. She looked back at Inspector Fawks. 'In fact, I don't remember saying exactly that, anyway. But surely you can't imagine if I had intended to kill Mr Carlton I would have been stupid enough to announce it? Especially at a political debate in front of hundreds of people?'

'She has a point, Fawks,' DCI Seldon said. 'I can vouch that Lady Swift is anything but stupid. If she were to commit a murder, which she wouldn't, of course,' he hastened on, 'she'd be a damned sight more circumspect about it. Now, could I have a brief word with you?'

Inspector Fawks frowned, but nodded. 'Of course, sir.'

He rose and left the room with DCI Seldon. The young constable she'd met earlier stood posted at the door.

Alone with her thoughts, Eleanor wished she'd brought earmuffs to drown them out. The enormity of Carlton being murdered now hit her. This couldn't be happening? How on earth was she not only embroiled in one murder investigation, but now a suspect in another?

Inspector Fawks and DCI Seldon reappeared. Fawks didn't seem thrilled with his brief chat with his superior. He nodded at Eleanor's cup. 'Finished?'

'Yes, thank you, Inspector.'

'Good, as are we.'

'Are you locking me in a cell? For how long?'

'At this point, Lady Swift, I do not have enough evidence to hold you. The lead has proven,' he glanced meaningfully at DCI Seldon, who met his gaze, 'unreliable. Your butler has also substantiated your alibi.'

She went to speak, but he held up a finger. 'You are, however, still under suspicion. My men will be watching you. Good day. Constable Wainfleet will escort you out.'

'Thank you, Inspector.' She rose and left, DCI Seldon looking the other way as she did.

Halfway down the hall, he caught up with her. He waved at the constable.

'I'll escort Lady Swift from here.'

Once the constable had gone, DCI Seldon continued down the stairs with her and led her into a small room. It seemed to be used mostly for storing more hard chairs and a dank-smelling mop and bucket in the corner.

He turned to her. 'I'm sorry you were dragged in here, Lady Swift.'

She smiled at him, struggling not to read too much into his gaze. 'Inspector Fawks was only doing his job, I'm sure. And thank you for your help. I assume your intervention is why I was released?'

He grunted. 'Fawks is a good man, and it's his case. I can't go around pulling rank, it wouldn't go down well, but I did bring certain things to his attention.' He turned his hat in his hands. 'Lady Swift.' She looked up at him and their eyes met, but he quickly dropped his gaze. The sound of booted footsteps and officious voices broke the moment.

DCI Seldon cleared his throat. 'I can't be seen discussing a murder case with a potential suspect like this.'

'Especially in the broom cupboard.'

He smiled. 'But I owe you a debt.'

'I rather thought I owed you one, Inspector?'

He grunted again. 'Not long ago an innocent man would have hung but for your intervention. That's not something I'd want on my conscience so I'm just going to say this: be careful, very careful. Please. Fawks is an excellent detective but doesn't really have any leads as to who killed Carlton yet, but as he was standing in the same election as you are…'

She blinked. *Could she be in danger?*

He was still talking. 'My current investigation into Mr Aris' death has not revealed any connection with that of Mr Carlton. However, it is known to us that there are some very powerful people who would like to see Mr Aris' legacy of tolerance towards women's rights reversed.'

She nodded. 'I'm well aware, Inspector, that some men are intolerant of the concept of women being independent.'

DCI Seldon shook his head. 'Lady Swift, this is not only an issue of bigoted views. Think. MPs are a source of favours, money and power. If you standing stops another succeeding, then a lot of vested interests will be lost. Also, there is some suggestion that Carlton's death was not politically motivated, but more personal. It is too early in the investigation to say either way.'

She let out a long, low whistle. 'He really did seem universally unpopular.'

Seldon stared at her. 'Lady Swift, I know there is no point in my asking, or telling, you to keep away from this investigation.' There was something in his tone Eleanor couldn't place at first. *Was it…?* Then she recognised it. *Concern.* For her. He held her gaze. 'All I can ask you to do, Lady Swift, is to be very, very careful.'

CHAPTER 24

Gladstone trotted by Eleanor's side as she took a stroll around the grounds. It was the morning following her interrogation, and she had woken with a sense of unease, too distracted to notice the vibrant, late-blooming chrysanthemums and dahlias bordering the path.

Two men had been murdered and someone had tried to set her up as the guilty party, for one of them, certainly.

Something was off, though. Passing the police an anonymous tip was just too amateurish. Did the murderer really believe that would be enough to have her convicted? Or did they just want her arrested? Was someone playing a deadly game of cat and mouse? She remembered Blewitt's words outside Mrs Luscombe's shop: 'Stop asking questions about Mr Aris. It is none of your concern and could be bad for your health!'

Feeling no brighter, she was about to round the last corner of the house when she heard Mrs Butters talking to someone whose voice she vaguely recognised.

'Come on, Elsie, you can tell me. Just whisper in my ear.'

'Leave the milk and get on with your rounds. I've nothing to share with you.'

'Extra couple of pints in it for you and the ladies? Or a half-sack of potatoes, they're the best King Edwards I ever saw.'

'Bribery! Be off with you!'

Eleanor held Gladstone's collar as she peeped round the side of the stone wall. Mrs Butters stood hands on hips, glaring at Stanley Wilkes the milkman, who leaned against the kitchen door frame.

He smirked and pulled a notebook from his apron pocket. 'Let's just say today's bits are on the house then.' He ran his hand through his red-brown curls. 'Case you change your mind.'

Mrs Butters kicked his foot out of the doorway. 'I will not change my mind, Mr Wilkes. Get going!'

'Oh, Mr Wilkes, is it now?' His hazel eyes twinkled. 'What happened to Milky?'

The housekeeper folded her arms and pointed at the milk cart. 'I've no idea, he turned into an inconsiderate rogue, trying to fish for a scandal, where,' she jabbed a finger in his chest, 'there isn't one. And make a note in your book, no more milk this week.'

The door slammed in Stanley Wilkes' face.

Once he'd rumbled out of sight, Eleanor turned the handle of the kitchen door.

'Get out!' Mrs Butters came flying onto the step. 'Oh, my lady. Beg pardon, so sorry. I thought it was that rascal again.'

Eleanor held her hands up in mock surrender. 'No, it's me. Mr Wilkes has gone off with several fleas in his ear.'

'Just as well!' The housekeeper glanced at Eleanor shrewdly. 'Would you like tea in the kitchen, my lady? Of course, I shouldn't have presumed.'

'I wouldn't like tea in the kitchen, Mrs Butters. I would love it. I confess, I was secretly hoping for just such an invitation.'

Her housekeeper chuckled. 'There's a thing, fancy the lady of the house needing an invitation to take tea in her own kitchen. Whatever next?'

Gladstone settled in his bed by the range and pressed his nose happily into one of the leather slippers in his collection. Eleanor flopped into the wooden chair Mrs Butters had pulled out for her.

'My lady, you don't seem yourself today. Are you under the weather? If it's a headache, there's probably a storm coming, although the black flies haven't appeared.'

Her housekeeper's kind and easy chatter was what Eleanor had been craving. 'No, no, really I feel great. Well, a little down in the dumps, I suppose, which isn't like me at all.'

'It certainly isn't. But 'tis not surprising with all the er... business lately.'

Eleanor took the tea held out to her. 'Thank you. I'll be fine. I was born with the skin of a rhino.'

Mrs Butters stepped into the pantry and returned with a plate of jam roly-poly and two napkins. She cut three generous slices and placed them on a tray in the top warming oven.

She took the chair next to Eleanor and patted her hand. 'My lady, forgive me for speaking out of turn, but I see things a little differently.'

'Go on.'

The housekeeper scanned Eleanor's face. 'I think there's a good deal of rhinoceros in you. Probably from all the travelling to exotic places you did growing up with your parents and then later on making your own way in the world. But you're also a beautiful young woman, and they dent quite easily. I've seen it afore. And rascals like that Stanley Wilkes trying to gossip about the difficulties you've had are enough to make a much lesser woman lie down and give up.'

The jangling of the doorbell interrupted Eleanor's reply. 'Gracious, I had no idea it was so loud in here!'

'Mr Clifford made most careful adjustments to each of the bells many years back, my lady. They are all a good deal louder in the staff quarters now, including his own office.'

Eleanor smiled over the rim of her teacup. 'You mean the boot room? I've worked out that's his sanctuary.'

Mrs Butters nodded. 'Everyone needs a place to unwind and get some peace.'

'I don't, not this morning. I fancy being heartily distracted from all the nonsense of the last few days.'

Clifford appeared, and Eleanor caught his subtle nod to Mrs Butters. *Dash it!* She was determined to fathom the secret language of her staff, but still, it eluded her. She studied Clifford's face as she asked who was at the door.

'The press, my lady.'

'What! They're here? What on earth do they want?'

Mrs Butters discreetly disappeared into the pantry as Clifford adjusted the seams of his white gloves. 'I would not concern yourself with them, my lady. They will disperse shortly.'

The doorbell rang again, making her jump just as much as before. He made no move to answer it and instead topped up her tea without comment.

'Clifford, there's something you're not telling me, isn't there?'

He placed the teapot back down. 'Regrettably, my lady, it seems that the newspapers have somehow got wind of the fact that you were taken in for questioning regarding the murder of Ernest Carlton.'

Eleanor put her head in her hands. 'What a wretched mess! Why did I ever get involved in this blasted election, or the murder investigation?' She looked up. 'I should have said earlier, thank you for confirming my alibi yesterday.'

He nodded. 'A pleasure, my lady. Although Inspector Fawks remarked that had I seen you carrying a dead body under one arm and a bag of lime under the other, I would no doubt have still corroborated your alibi.'

And you would have too, she thought. She flapped a hand at him. 'Clifford, please sit down and drink some tea.'

'Very good, my lady.'

As if bidden by an unseen force, Mrs Butters reappeared from the pantry. She slid the warmed jam roly-poly from the oven and onto a plate, which she put in the centre of the table. Swirls of hot buttery dough mixed with raspberry jam wafted up. Eleanor stared at it as if it were worth its weight in gold.

Clifford took the chair opposite Eleanor and nodded to Mrs Butters as she poured him a tea before leaving them alone. He coughed and Eleanor started. She stirred her cup. 'Blast! So, I'm trapped in the house until the baying newshounds disperse.'

'Not at all. I imagine the last few hacks will be leaving any minute now.'

She snorted. 'Unlikely, when they think they can get the inside scoop of a would-be female politician suspected of murdering her closest rival. I'm surprised they haven't brought picnic chairs and tents.'

'A certain number did arrive prepared for the duration. I noted several flasks and indeed many a folding stool.'

'Outrageous! How does being a journalist give one the right to barricade an innocent member of the public in their own home?'

'It is, I believe, an unfortunate consequence of the nation's growing desire for a generous dose of scandal with one's morning breakfast tea.'

'Hmm, well now that I'm on the other side of the scandalous charges I shall be more ruthless in boycotting such trash.'

'Another most wise decision, my lady, hence my having relegated this morning's papers to fire-lighting material.'

'Oh, Clifford, what did they say?'

'Nothing of truth or import. I should not let it spoil your roly-poly.'

But Eleanor put her fork down, sweet treat left untouched. 'Come on, enlighten me as to what I'm up against.'

He gave a slight cough. 'Someone pushed this paper through the letterbox this morning.' He retrieved a newspaper from the fireplace. 'I haven't had time to dispose of it yet.'

Eleanor took the copy of *The Common Cause*, smiling at its proud by-line: 'The Organ of the Women's Movement for Reform'.

Then she gasped at the caricature of herself that filled the top half of the front page. She was depicted as flying forwards, her hands handcuffed behind her back as a suffragette kicked her up the rear. She gritted her teeth at the queue of cartoon women waiting in line to give her the same treatment. A signpost pointed to the fictional town she was being dispatched to: 'Disgrace-Upon-Dishonour'.

But what rankled most was the tiara drawn to have flown from her head on the precise trajectory to a heap of rotting vegetables and soiled rags. She looked up at Clifford. 'Not a very creative headline given the cartoon, wouldn't you say? "Promised so much. Delivered only Disgrace. She let women down. She let the country down. She let herself down."'

Eleanor flopped backwards in her chair and crossed her legs.

'Is that enough, my lady?'

'Thank you, Clifford. More than enough. Please burn it with the others.' She took a deep breath. 'Not quite sure how I ended up in this impossible situation, Clifford. Perhaps putting my hand up to try and help was one of the biggest mistakes of my life.'

'I have never been particularly sizist when it comes to making blunders, my lady.'

Despite the anxiety burning in her chest, she smiled at this, but it quickly faded. Instead she dug into her slice of roly-poly and felt better immediately. 'Can you believe that Carlton is dead? Having one suspect removed feels like a most hollow celebration. Especially as we still don't know if Carlton was responsible for Aris' death and, if so, then there is a second murderer running amok in the streets of Chipstone!' She rubbed her temples and groaned. 'This murder investigation is getting away from us, Clifford. I lay awake pretty much all night, going over everything we've learned, and yet I failed to come up with anything.'

Clifford coughed. 'We may have hit a temporary roadblock in our investigation, my lady. However, a thought struck me yesterday.

I believe that the anonymous phone call was not made with the belief that you would be convicted of murdering Mr Carlton.'

'But to stop me succeeding in the election?'

'Possibly. And possibly not by Mr Aris, or Mr Carlton's murderer. Perhaps it was an opportunist amongst your opponents who saw the chance to discredit you further?'

She nodded. 'I had the exact same thought. That oaf Blewitt sprung to mind!'

'For someone shrewd enough to engineer Mr Aris' demise, that was a most amateur tactic. Unless it was intended to scare you off investigating Mr Aris, or Mr Carlton's demise any further? In which case that is to our advantage.'

Eleanor tilted her head. 'How so?'

'To paraphrase the notable strategist, Napoleon Bonaparte, as Mr Greaves did: "Never interrupt your enemy when he is making a mistake." If the murderer believes they have succeeded in scaring you from investigating further, then we may seize the advantage.'

The doorbell jangled a third time. Clifford moved towards the hallway to answer it.

She frowned. 'What are you doing? Don't let the blighters in, for goodness' sake.'

He stooped. 'That will be a genuine visitor, my lady. I believe the reporters will have gone by now.'

She spread her hands. 'I don't see how you can be so sure?'

'My lady, I sent Silas out to deal with them.' And with that, he left.

She shook her head. Since arriving at the Hall, she'd tried to get a glimpse of the mythical gamekeeper-cum-security guard, but had yet to succeed. She toyed with her plate until he returned.

'The police again?'

'No, my lady. It is Miss Mann. She says she has a most important message.'

'How marvellous! Alright, show her into the drawing room.'

She took a moment to finish her tea and gulp down the rest of her slice of roly-poly for fortification. Finding it rather reviving, she further fortified herself with the second, but reluctantly tore herself away from the third.

In the drawing room, Miss Mann sat on the edge of the sofa, knees together, feet pointing straight ahead. Eleanor noticed that the woman had pulled her hair back so tightly that her face looked extra pinched and severe. She slapped on a smile. 'Miss Mann, so kind of you to call.'

Miss Mann jumped. 'Yes, well, good morning, Lady Swift. I hope your butler passed on that I... I have a... a most important message to deliver to you.' She seemed agitated, even for her. 'I rather expected you might have anticipated my visit this morning.' She clasped the handbag on her lap tightly. 'Lady Swift, the negative publicity of the last twenty-four hours has threatened to totally discredit the Women's League. And in light of your... your... alleged involvement in the case of...' Eleanor was afraid Miss Mann would collapse from nerves before she could finish, but somehow the woman regained enough composure '... of Mr Carlton's m-m-murder,' she swallowed, 'it is my sad duty to tell you the Women's League will no longer be backing your candidacy.' She rose. 'You are obliged forthwith to refrain from activities which might suggest that you are still associated with the League. It means you will return all party property such as rosettes, campaigning literature, policy paperwork and manifestos immediately.'

It was all so ludicrous that Eleanor couldn't find it in herself to be angry, but the sting of rejection still hit her hard. Her shoulders sagged momentarily, but she quickly recovered enough to pretend otherwise. 'Miss Mann, I am sorry you feel that way. Mostly for the women I felt we could help, acting together as a united front. However, I see you have made your decision.'

She rang the bell. Clifford materialised.

'Ah, Clifford, Miss Mann is leaving. Make sure she is given all the political bumpf to take with her, will you?'

'It is waiting ready in the hall, my lady.'

'Good show, Clifford! Please show Miss Mann the door, would you? My jam roly-poly's going cold.'

CHAPTER 25

As Clifford returned from showing Miss Mann out, Eleanor was just finishing her third piece of jam roly-poly, back in the kitchen.

'Argh! Clifford, I could scream!'

He coughed gently. 'It is, my lady, very frustrating, but, in Miss Mann's defence, it is hard to see what other choice she had.' He coughed again.

Eleanor put down her spoon and threw her head up to the ceiling. 'Clifford, I fear your irritating quirk might just tip me over the edge this afternoon.' At his silence, she spun round and stopped in surprise at the items he held out to her. 'Ah, now there's an excellent idea!'

'Good shot, my lady.' Clifford applauded from the sidelines.

Eleanor whacked the next tennis ball at the opposite wall of the court even harder than she had the first couple of dozen.

Clifford clapped again.

She reached for another ball but jerked upright at the sound of breaking glass. 'Crikey, was that me?'

'Most likely, my lady. But Joseph is probably in the herb garden, not the main greenhouse. It is unlikely you have actually speared him with a shard of glass.'

Eleanor put her hand to her mouth. 'Well, who builds a tennis court near a greenhouse, anyway?'

'Perhaps someone who intends to play the more traditional game of hitting the ball over the net and keeping it within the court, my lady?'

His wry smile made her relax. 'Thank you, Clifford. It's amazing what a few minutes of venting one's anger on inanimate objects can do. Ah, I feel much better!'

'Good. Perhaps a little restorative would hasten your return to form, my lady?'

'Yes, but please don't traipse all the way back to the house on my account.' She flopped onto the white bench on the side of the court, her legs stuck out in front of her. Intrigued, she watched Clifford climb the steps of the tall white umpire chair and lift the seat. He retrieved a tweed satchel affair that had all the hallmarks of being a gentleman's binocular case. Back beside her, he unstrapped the lid to reveal two crystal-cut glasses and a decanter of Oloroso sherry. Her mouth dropped open.

Clifford hovered at the end of the bench. Eleanor slapped her hand against the seat. 'Oh, for goodness' sake, sit down, Clifford! This is no time for discretion and aplomb, we need to catch a murderer.'

With a filled glass, she sighed. 'You anticipated a lot of all this nasty business, didn't you?'

He stared straight ahead. 'Your uncle, even though he himself never meddled, always said that the only rule in politics is that there are no rules, my lady.'

'Yet you supported my decision to stand. Indeed, you positively set it up.' She stole a sideways look at his face.

'My lady, I promised your uncle to assist you in whatever way I could. If you will forgive my early observation, given your previous adventures, including those of the heart, I knew the job was never going to be a straightforward one.'

She smiled at this. 'And a fine job you do, having accurately predicted I would require a bucket of tennis balls and a stiff sherry. I say, that is rather good! It's like walnuts and figs with a dash of exquisite marmalade.'

'Your uncle always maintained that due to its complex nose, one could never begin to be truly acquainted with an Oloroso until the fourth glass.'

Eleanor snorted. 'Well, I hope there is plenty more hidden in peculiar spots around the grounds because I fear today I shall require a cellar's worth to raise my spirits.'

Clifford continued to stare straight ahead. Eventually, she broke the silence. 'You know when a situation has galloped away from you? That's what this is like. Sitting here, I can't work out why I ever imagined it would be a good idea to stand for this stupid by-election. What on earth was I thinking of?' She spun her racket on its tip until it clattered to the ground.

'Maybe you saw an opportunity to find your place in the town and village you wished to call home and to help others into the bargain?'

'Am I really that open a book?'

He said nothing, but his eyes twinkled. She bent down and picked up her racquet. 'Oh, dash it, Clifford, what a wretched mess this investigation of ours is in as well! Called in for questioning over the murder of one of our own chief suspects and now shamed in the national press.'

'And caricatured most unbecomingly.'

'That too. I've made ridiculously rash promises in public...'

'Loudly and proudly, my lady.'

'Yes, exactly and... and I've been disowned by the very people I was trying to help. I'm a laughing stock.' From the corner of her eye she caught him nodding. 'Clifford!'

He turned to face her. 'It has been a most difficult road. It is perhaps minor consolation, but there is a local expression which one might deem rather fitting.'

'Try me. I'll take anything that sucks the salt out of my wounds at the moment.'

'"Folks give up the poke long afore the memory croaks."'

Eleanor stared at him. 'Is the sherry stronger than I realised? What are you on about?'

'It means that whilst the fool is still licking his wounds, everyone else has moved on to laughing at the next poor hapless soul who makes a spectacle of themselves.'

A rumble of laughter rolled up from her stomach. 'Fool? Priceless! What's happened to your usual diplomacy?'

'Forgive me, my lady. I didn't mean to imply that...'

'That was no implication, you were spot on.'

He uncorked the sherry and poured her another measure. 'There really would be no shame in bowing out gracefully, my lady. Well, bowing out. No one would expect you to keep standing for election in these circumstances, especially as you now have no group to back you. And as to the investigation of Mr Aris, that seems to have reached rather a – if you will excuse a pun intended to lighten a gloomy subject – rather a dead end. And, as you accurately state, the main suspect in the murder of Mr Carlton at the moment seems to be yourself, my lady. Therefore, I feel no one would censure you for bowing out of both the election and the murder investigation.'

'True. Thank you. I agree, it's the only sensible option. I've done my best in both matters.'

She peered through the dark amber liquid in her glass, watching his reaction. He had stiffened at her words.

'You mean?'

'Mmm, yes. I shall give it all up.'

'But, my lady, are you sure?'

Eleanor slapped her leg. 'Ha! Finally, I'm beginning to recognise when you're goading me, Clifford. You're going to have to raise your game. You laid it all on so thick about how ghastly things are, I started to believe you.'

'I do believe they are that bad, my lady.'

'I know, but you had an alternative motive which,' she took a generous sip of sherry, 'is why I should be certified.'

'Certified, my lady?'

'Yes, certified as truly mad for deciding to carry on against such odds.'

Clifford's shoulders relaxed. 'Spoken like a true Henley – and Swift! Your uncle – and your parents – would be proud, my lady!'

Eleanor swallowed the lump in her throat. Before she could reply, a familiar sound rang out.

Clifford turned towards the Hall. 'Ah, the gong! Perhaps you would like to save Mrs Trotman's jugged hare from drying to a shadow of its full glory and celebrate over luncheon?'

Mrs Butters met them at the head of the steps.

'Perhaps we shouldn't have presumed your appetite was up to a substantial meal, my lady?'

Eleanor patted her housekeeper's shoulder. 'Nonsense! I'm famished. I'll be straight there.'

She sprinted up to her bedroom and changed in double-quick time. Opening the top drawer of her dressing table to grab a bracelet, she groaned in annoyance at the sight of two or three leaflets from the Women's League. 'Blast, I thought Clifford had returned all this bumf to Miss Mann!' In consideration, she realised she couldn't really blame Clifford for not searching her bedroom to make sure she hadn't secreted any away. She grabbed the bracelet from under the leaflets and slammed the drawer shut. She could dispose of the leaflets later. At the moment luncheon beckoned and she was famished.

'Ah, Mrs Trotman!' She smiled at the cook, who was putting the finishing touches to the serving table since Clifford had been otherwise engaged. 'Where is Polly?' The door crept open a crack and her maid jittered in and stood fiddling with her apron strap. Eleanor clapped her hands. 'Just before I devour this amazing meal you have all worked so hard on, I would like you to join me in a toast. Clifford, would you conjure up something suitable to toast with?'

Once everyone had a glass, she continued. 'You see, I have had an eureka moment, thanks to a disgracefully rude newspaper, an unexpected visitor and Clifford's shocking lack of diplomacy.'

Mrs Butters and Mrs Trotman gasped. Polly stared round, confusion written on her face.

'You probably already know that our efforts to clear Mrs Pitkin's name have gone drastically awry. And, at the same time, my attempts to stand as the first woman MP for Chipstone have suffered a similarly drastic setback.' She turned to her cook. 'Well, Mrs Trotman, please assure Mrs Pitkin that we shall now redouble our efforts on her behalf.' Eleanor raised her glass, and the staff followed, everyone taking a sip. She raised her glass again. 'And let me assure you that I have decided not to creep away with my tail between my legs in this election either. With, or without the Women's League, there are women who need someone to represent them in this area, so I am going to continue standing!'

Clifford winced and covered his ears at the women's resounding cheers.

Mrs Trotman at last lowered her glass. 'So, what do you do next, my lady? I mean, how do you clear Martha of murder, when you yourself have been accused of a similar deed, and, at the same time, win an election?'

'It will be a very poor dessert to follow this amazing jugged hare. However, Clifford and I shall take a drive and see if we can't find out a way to solve this wretched mess.'

CHAPTER 26

Eleanor peered in the side mirror of the Rolls as it eased along the outskirts of Chipstone. 'Oh, Clifford, I look ridiculous! Whose idea was it to go in disguise again, remind me?'

'I really couldn't say, my lady.'

'Dash it!' She adjusted the elaborately wound scarf hiding her recognisable red curls and let the heavily tinted sunglasses drop into her lap. 'So, it was mine. But we can't risk newspaper photographers taking pictures of me—'

'Returning to the scene of your heinous crime?' Clifford stopped the car and gestured to the red-painted front door of the end terrace house.

As Eleanor stepped out of the Rolls and put her hand on the gate, the bay window curtains twitched. She reached the front door and lifted the knocker. Before she could let it fall, the heavy steel plate embossed with 'LETTERS' just below flipped up and two dark eyes framed by thick brown hair peered out: 'Go away!'

Eleanor was taken back. Clifford called over Eleanor's shoulder: 'Forgive our unannounced intrusion, madam, we are here to help.'

'I don't need no help.'

'But tragically, Mr Carlton did,' Eleanor replied. 'You have my deepest sympathies.'

The eyes widened. 'What are you suggesting? That I didn't do me duty as his housekeeper? Not that it's any of your business but I couldn't have done him any good, he was long gone when I found him, poor soul.' The door flung open and a pinched woman in her late fifties pointed towards the garden gate. 'Now, get going!' Anger hardened her already careworn features.

Clifford softened his voice. 'The police are very trying in these matters, aren't they? We do understand.'

The woman pulled a wool blanket around her shoulders tighter. 'What's the police got to do with it? They're not popular in these parts. No idea what they're doing neither, too busy stomping dirt and leaves through the house!'

Eleanor pulled her glasses off. 'I'm so sorry, I don't know your name but…'

'Oh, but I know yours alright! Lady Swift herself on the doorstep. Fancy that! I've been cheering for you and all you're doing to help us women. What an honour to have you here.' The woman peered round Eleanor. 'And Mr Clifford too.'

'Good afternoon, madam.'

She turned back to Eleanor. 'You're taking a risk coming here, ain't ya, after the papers said you were the one who did in poor Mr Carlton?'

Eleanor dropped her voice. 'That is precisely why we are here. I have been framed!'

Clifford stepped forward. 'Mrs Eltham, you may not be aware, but there is a plot to stop Lady Swift standing for election. And we believe there may be a connection with Mr Carlton's most tragic demise.'

Mrs Eltham gasped. 'Why didn't you say why you was here first off?' Her eyes darted up and down the street. 'Get inside quick, afore those newspaper fellas get back from scoffing pints down at the alehouse in the next road.'

'Thank you.' Eleanor hurried in. As Clifford joined them, she noticed the hallway was more tastefully decorated than she'd have expected for a man like Carlton. He'd seemed so guarded and calculating. She'd pictured his home as far more clinical and impersonal. Cream and mulberry wallpaper set off the rich plum of the two-seat button-backed loveseat below a painting of wild stallions prancing on some faraway plain.

'Best to come through to the parlour.' Mrs Eltham led them across the polished wooden boards into a room where the same theme ran throughout the surprising number of soft furnishings. A large mirror above the mantelpiece reflected the weak afternoon sun dancing through a fancy cut-glass light fitting.

Eleanor sat whilst Clifford hesitantly took the offered place on the settee.

Eleanor gave her warmest smile. 'How long had you been Mr Carlton's housekeeper, Mrs Eltham?'

'Six, no, seven years. He was a good enough employer, but a right old fusspot about having everything just so, especially with his food. Mr Pernickety, I called him, and he was getting worse. I told him recently he needed to get someone else to do his meals – I've no time for all that mucking about, not in the hours I'm here.'

Thinking that didn't surprise her after their encounter at his office, Eleanor found a gap in Mrs Eltham's monologue to jump in with another question: 'You said the police came. Did Inspector Fawks take your statement?'

The housekeeper nodded. 'The arrogance of that man! I was sitting there, thinking he should be the one on the floor with the back of his head bashed in. He talked to me like I was a lump of the dirt I could see caked to the bottom of his boots.' She sniffed. 'Which I then had to get on me knees and clean up, mind.'

Clifford made sympathetic 'tsk' noises before speaking. 'You probably didn't feel disposed to tell him much at all after that?'

'Spot on, Mr Clifford, I didn't. I clammed up and said just enough to do right by Mr Carlton. It's none of the police's business who he might have owed money to, or if he had a lady friend, or anything else that inspector wanted to poke his nose into. He thought I was dumb, so I played dumb.'

'I'm sure Mr Carlton would have appreciated your discretion,' Clifford said.

Eleanor tried to pick her words carefully. 'I understood Mr Carlton was a bachelor? Forgive me, but I had imagined a more… masculine decor?'

''Tis only the rooms he "entertained" in that are done up so fancy. I'm no gossip, but let's just say, he found the ladies were more relaxed when things were painted up nicely.'

'Ah!' Eleanor said.

'But 'twasn't my place to say anything. Mind, I almost left him a few times. Got so bad I worried the police would come round, thinking this was one of those houses.' She tapped her nose.

'The road to find true love can indeed be long and winding,' Clifford said.

Mrs Eltham snorted. ''Tweren't love he was after though, was it? Otherwise he'd have had one lady friend at a time, not a different one depending on the day of the week.' She spread her hands. 'Well, some men are made that way, it seems. And women find them irresistible, though I can't see why. No matter what class they come from.'

'Am I right in thinking you do not live in?' Clifford asked.

'You are. That's why I wasn't here when it happened.' She pulled a handkerchief from her pocket and patted the corners of her lips. 'I got here at five-and-ten past nine that evening to set his supper warming, turn his bed down, lay out the breakfast things, same as usual. If he weren't entertaining, of course, which he'd said he wasn't.' She frowned. 'A woman came round that evening, though.'

Eleanor stopped looking around the room. 'A woman, you say? Can you describe her?'

Mrs Eltham shook her head. 'I didn't see her, just knows there was one here. Could smell the perfume.'

Eleanor glanced at the door out into the hallway. 'Where exactly did they find poor Mr Carlton? Are you able to tell us what you saw, if it won't upset you too much?'

'If it'll help you find whoever did it, you best come see for yourself.'

Eleanor nodded. Mrs Eltham slipped a trembling arm through hers: 'It weren't pretty, Lady Swift.'

At the furthest end of the hallway, the housekeeper paused and gestured to a white wooden door: 'He was in his office, although he called it his "study". He weren't ever studying anything, so it was always his office to me.'

'May I?' Eleanor asked with one hand on the door.

'Go ahead. 'Tis all cleaned up now. Not that the police did a good enough job. What a picture, me on my knees, scrubbing away the last of my employer with a bucket and brush! Poor soul, lying in the middle of the floor as if he was on his way out when he was walloped.'

Eleanor felt Mrs Eltham's arm slide out of hers as she stepped through the doorway into a medium-sized room. It was closer to the plain white walls and inexpensive shelving of the office they had previously interviewed Carlton in. Near the fireplace, a simple wooden desk sat facing the door, a square-legged chair tucked underneath.

Against one wall, a wooden cupboard that looked suspiciously like an old wardrobe leaned wearily. On the opposite wall a repurposed baize card table top hung, liberally pinned with a selection of maps. She scanned the sash window. 'Might the rogue have come through there, do you suppose?'

The housekeeper waved a hand. 'He'd have had a heck of a job! It's been latched and painted shut for all the years I've worked here. Must have come in the back door, I reckon. Or Mr Carlton let him in the front, but no one in the street saw anyone. Police were up and down, asking them when I could have told them in five minutes, as we was all talking about it over the fences.'

'Did they take anything away with them?'

'Only Mr Carlton himself. Truth is, they left more than they took, dratted fingerprint powder on everything and mud all over the floors.'

'Do you happen to know if they found any fingerprints?'

'Well, they took mine, so as to compare them with summat, so I reckon they did. That Fawks said he thought the killer would have worn gloves, though, seeing as the modern criminal knows about fingerprints and suchlike nowadays.'

'Did you notice if anything was missing?'

'No, the police asked me that, must have been a dozen times. They took Mr Carlton's cricketing trophy, that's the only thing missing now. They said how that was what the killer hit him with. On the back of the head.' She held her handkerchief to her nose.

As Eleanor hesitated, Mrs Eltham waved her hand – 'Oh, go ahead, rootle in whatever you need to! Ain't going to do Mr Carlton no harm now.'

Eleanor stole a peek at Clifford, who gave her the slightest of nods in return.

He cleared his throat. 'Mrs Eltham, might I trouble you to show me the back door? Perhaps we can find something the police didn't see.'

As their footsteps moved away, Eleanor did a slow turn, taking in the sparsely furnished room. The trouble was, she had no real idea what she was looking for. The desk drawers revealed nothing more than the usual letter-writing paraphernalia and an empty hip flask. Equally, the cupboard contained a few stationery items and little else. She tapped the back, then squeezed her hand behind to feel for anything hidden.

Nothing.

There were maps hanging on the wall, various scales and sections of the area around Chipstone. No cryptic notes had been scrawled on the back, however, or black crosses showing the location of buried treasure. She shook her head.

Come on, Ellie, you're not in a penny dreadful!

The trays on the mantelpiece held only an unpaid tailor's bill, four weeks of newspapers marked IN ARREARS, and a series of invitations to dinners, all of which had already expired. An edge of paper caught her eye behind the coach clock. She pulled it out to reveal a newspaper article on the urgent need for more housing, carefully cut from *The Times* on 22 October.

She frowned. Why had he cut out and kept that particular article? She thought back to Lady Farrington's revelation that Aris was helping them secure a housing project on their land. What was the connection? She shrugged, folded the cutting and slipped it in her pocket before continuing her search. Carlton had certainly kept all his cards pressed tight to his chest that day in his office.

Trying to get into the mind of the victim, she pulled out the chair and sat at the desk. There was no sign of a struggle in the room, so it seemed certain Carlton knew his killer. He had almost certainly invited him in and was then struck when he turned his back on his visitor.

She held the sides of the chair and shuffled it back under the desk, then yelped as her finger caught on something sticking out. A blooming bubble of blood on her finger made her shake her head angrily.

Ouch! Why on earth wouldn't Carlton have fixed that? He'd have no fingers left!

Dropping to her knees, she leaned the chair on its two back legs and let out a quiet whistle.

Underneath the solid seat, she saw what had snagged her finger: two tiny brass hooks had been screwed into the side supports, one being bent at the end. The edge of a metal hinge was just visible. Eleanor swung each hook down and then gasped.

*

'Tea would be lovely, Mrs Eltham, so kind!' Clifford's voice echoed along the corridor towards her.

'Clifford!' she hissed at the first sign of his meticulously shined shoe appearing in the doorway. 'Look!' She held up a white linen napkin and peeled the folds back.

'Four squares of... chocolate fudge!'

'From the dinner where Aris died, do you suppose?'

'Indeed, it would seem we have found the missing dessert.' Spotting the gash to her finger, Clifford handed her a clean handkerchief.

'Thank you.' Eleanor wound it round her cut finger, putting the fudge on the desk, her brow furrowed. 'But it makes no sense. If Carlton killed Aris, why would he have kept the evidence? That would be the work of a madman who wanted to get caught!'

'And Mr Carlton struck me as being exceptionally shrewd, my lady.'

'He can't have stolen it to eat. He has a few unpaid bills, but I don't believe he was so short of money he was stealing food.'

'Particularly as he hadn't eaten it.' Clifford pursed his lips. 'Who else would be interested in the evidence, apart from the police—'

'And the killer.'

He arched one brow. 'And, perhaps, someone who wanted to blackmail the killer?'

'Clifford, you clever bean! He was keeping these hidden to blackmail Aris' murderer.' She squeezed her eyes closed. 'Which almost certainly means Aris' murderer also murdered Carlton.'

Clifford quickly placed the handkerchief containing the fudge in his pocket as the clink of cups heralded Mrs Eltham's return.

'Sorry, there's no biscuits or cake,' she set the tray on the desk, 'but Mr Carlton wouldn't have anything sweet in the house. Said he didn't know why folk eat sugary things, it was likely to be the death of them...'

CHAPTER 27

Eleanor gasped. 'Ladies, it looks simply… amazing!'

They all stared at the Rolls, festooned with colourful posters and looping garlands. She read the poster flanking the passenger door. 'Lady Swift. One Promise. The Truth!' She pulled them into a collective hug. 'Golly, I'm so grateful!'

Mrs Butters patted Eleanor's arm. 'Oh, 'tis our pleasure, my lady. The garlands though, they were Polly's idea.'

The young maid's words tumbled over each other. 'Seeing as I couldn't do the posters 'cos I don't spell too well.' She swallowed hard. 'I remember you told us about the town high up in the beautiful mountains, where all the houses looked like tiny castles and everyone came out to welcome you like a princess. And… and all the people and the donkeys and the carts were covered in strings of rainbow flowers…' She tailed off, her face streaked with tears.

Eleanor and the ladies were all choked and looked to Clifford for help.

'I think, Polly, her ladyship would say you have made the exact strings of flowers she described to you. Well done!'

That finished Eleanor off completely and she dived into the boot of the Rolls on the pretext of sorting through the campaigning materials. After a moment, Clifford's legs popped into her peripheral view and a clean handkerchief.

'Thank you,' she mumbled.

'To business, my lady. Shall we say five minutes?'

'Better make it fifteen.'

*

Even the outskirts of Chipstone seemed busy as Clifford eased the Rolls towards the high street. In the back seat, Mrs Trotman, Mrs Butters and Polly nudged each other and patted their hats, unaccustomed as they were to riding in the car. Gladstone had commandeered the right-side seat and delighted in poking his nose out of the window so the wind ruffled his jowls.

'Looks like everyone is up and busy already,' Eleanor mused.

Clifford nodded. 'That should guarantee an excellent audience.'

He pulled up next to the main square alongside the Town Hall. He looked across at her. 'Ready?'

'Not a bit.' She took a deep breath. 'Right, so we're all clear on what we're doing? We'll set up the campaign stand here. Ladies, you'll distribute as many flyers to people as you can, please. Agreed?'

'Agreed!' they chorused. Gladstone added an excited woof and licked Polly's cheek.

Clifford erected an ingenious pop-up table-cum-booth whilst the ladies busied themselves taking boxes of leaflets from the boot. They then strung more posters and garlands from each corner. As they finished, Mrs Butters handed Eleanor an emerald-green silk rosette.

She took it and stared at the intricately embroidered lettering. 'Lady Swift. Let the truth be told,' she read aloud. 'Gracious, Mrs Butters, I don't know what to say!'

'A pleasure, my lady. There's one for each of us. Master Gladstone, too. Ours has only got your name, on account of running out of time. And there's a box of green ribbons and pins for all the folk who come and say they'll support you. I only hope there's enough.'

Eleanor looked across at the rest of her staff, all standing behind the booth, regaled in their rosettes. Mrs Trotman shook her head at Polly's and re-pinned it the right way up.

'But where did you find this beautiful green silk at such short notice? It is my absolute favourite colour!'

Mrs Butters giggled. 'Remember the dress you tore on your second day at the Hall? You said you'd been scrambling through a hedge to catch a certain young gentleman pilot in a field.'

'Oh, yes… Lancelot.'

The housekeeper winked. 'Well, the fabric was too beautiful to put in the rag box. So, here we are.'

Two hours later, as the Town Hall clock struck eleven, Clifford appeared at Eleanor's side. 'We have had a most positive response, wouldn't you say, my lady?'

'I'm staggered. It's been a tremendous surprise.'

'If I might make the suggestion, however, that you and I need to slip away and catch up with our suspects.'

'Clifford! You've found out more information?'

'Indeed, two interesting morsels, in fact, but I was going to tell you over luncheon. Since the topic has arisen, I have discovered that the business practice of Mr Aris and Mr Peel did not separate on amicable terms. Succinctly, it would appear Mr Aris suddenly extracted himself from their partnership and took all the best clients with him. Mr Peel is precariously close to bankruptcy.'

Eleanor gave a long, low whistle. 'Gracious! Well, there's a motive for killing Aris but we have nothing linking him to Carlton's death. We definitely need another talk with him, though. And the other piece of information?'

'You can thank Mrs Trotman for this snippet. It transpires that some months ago at Chipstone Market, Mr Carlton manned a stall promoting the Labour Party. Suddenly, out of nowhere, Mr Stanley Morris appeared and heated words were exchanged. There were several witnesses.'

Eleanor frowned. 'Probably about his wife's affair. Is there a man in this town whose wife hasn't fallen for Carlton's supposed charms?'

Clifford shook his head. 'Possibly not. However, the exchange quickly turned to punches being thrown. The police were called and Mr Morris was ejected from the market on threat of being charged with disturbing the peace.'

'Mmm, I believe as well as Mr Peel, we need to speak to Mr Morris.'

'I agree wholeheartedly, my lady. Might I suggest the Reading Room as the starting point? Mr Morris is always there at this hour.'

She nodded. 'Come on, things are hotting up!'

The normally silent Reading Room had more of a hubbub than Eleanor expected. A different woman to the one she'd met previously sat behind the small, wooden desk, animatedly discussing something in a magazine with two others. Four more women sat in a huddle around one end of the central bench-style table, clearly gossiping instead of reading. A gawky teenage boy in spectacles and short breeches ran his finger along the books in the small science section.

Eleanor nodded towards the back room, where one long leg poked out from behind a table-top book display.

Clifford nodded back and whispered, 'My lady, have you formulated a plan, perchance?'

'No, but time's running out and the killer's running rings around us, and the police. If we're to save Mrs Pitkin from the workhouse, or worse, we need to up our game. The gloves, Clifford, are well and truly off!' She marched under the arched doorway, deliberately knocking into Stanley Morris' legs.

'Mr Morris, I do apologise, how clumsy of me!'

He sighed, but held out his hand to her. 'It is of no consequence to me, Lady Swift. Are you alright?'

'Absolutely!'

'Then I shall appreciate being left to my reading, good afternoon.'
He raised the papers he held and peered at them, blinking through
his thick glasses.

Think, Ellie! She stole a look at the title of the typed papers.

'Clifford!' she called. 'Oh sorry, quieter, yes. Clifford!' she
repeated at the same volume, 'please find me the Parish Council
Meeting Minutes from last week and the week before. Thank you.'

From behind his papers, Morris let out another sigh. 'Lady
Swift, I am reading the Parish Council Minutes.'

'What a coincidence!'

'Is it?'

She took the chair next to him, ignoring his look of exasperation. 'I think it is so important to be aware of all the views of one's
constituents. I do find it quite time-consuming though, don't you?'

'Only when I am constantly interrupted.'

'Couldn't agree more! So, what have our good folk been discussing of late?'

Morris stared at her with obvious irritation. She slid one of the
back papers out of the sheaf he held. 'Oh, look, see, there I knew
that would come up. The ladies of the Women's Institute have
asked for a... a reduced hire fee for the council meeting room. That
seems fair, wouldn't you say? Isn't your good lady wife a member
of the Women's Institute?'

'She was.'

'Was? Oh dear, she must be frightfully busy! I've never seen her
at any of our political debates. Unless of course I've missed her in
the audience?'

'You have not.'

'Right. But I'm sure she wholeheartedly supports your important
work as a politician?'.

Morris snorted. 'Lady Swift, I have not installed myself in this
seat in the very public Reading Room to discuss my personal life,
thank you.'

'Oh gracious, I do apologise! Perhaps I've touched upon a most painful nerve, forgive me. Mrs Morris is clearly a thoroughly modern woman and makes her own choices.'

'Indeed!'

She leaned in. 'Must be dashedly awkward for you, though?'

Morris stiffened.

'Well, I mean if your wife is voting for the other side, as it were. Now that I think about it, I did hear that she favoured some of the Labour Party's policies.' She tapped her forehead. 'Now, where did I hear that?'

Morris slapped the papers down into his lap. 'I imagine, Lady Swift, it was in the public bar frequented by tradesmen. Or, perhaps, in the tea rooms frequented by housewives with too much time and too little to do, or indeed, perhaps in the gutter!'

'Mr Morris, I fear I've upset you.'

'Of course, you have, you infernal snoop!' he said, getting angry. 'You clearly know already that,' he lowered his voice to a fierce whisper, 'that my wife and Ernest Carlton had a… liaison.' His face flushed.

Eleanor felt guilty, but reminded herself again, an innocent woman's future hung on finding the truth. 'Honestly, Mr Morris, I had no intention of rubbing salt in your wound. That can't have been easy for you. Would it be indiscreet of me to say that now Mr Carlton is dead, perhaps you have a chance of repairing your marriage?'

'Yes, it would.'

'Yes, of course it would. Most insensitive!'

'She wasn't the only one, you know. That should make it better, I suppose, but it doesn't. Carlton was a blaggard, a womaniser. A despicable wretch who used women. And he used MY wife!'

'A small consolation, I'm sure, but I commend you on your self-composure. You sat through all those debates on the stage with Carlton knowing what he had done. Gracious, you must have wanted to reach over and strangle him!'

'Every time I clapped eyes on his stupid, smug face.' He stared at her. 'Was he strangled then?'

'I've no idea. I thought you might know? Where were you on Sunday night, around nine or ten?'

Morris gave an uneasy laugh. 'You're not very subtle. And the police have already asked me that. For your information, and to ensure you keep your nose firmly out of any further part of my business, I did not kill Ernest Carlton!'

'Any idea who might have killed him then?'

He leaned forward, his face close to hers. 'Maybe *you* did, Lady Swift? The police, at least, seem to think so. But,' he uncrossed his long legs and stood up, 'when you find out, be sure to let me know. I'd like to shake his or her,' he shot her a pointed look, 'hand.' He dropped the papers in her lap and strode out, knocking Clifford's shoulder on the way past.

'Mr Clifford.'

'Mr Morris.'

CHAPTER 28

As they turned into the road where Vernon Peel's office was situated, Clifford pointed through the windscreen of the Rolls at the man himself hurrying along the pavement. He appeared to be consulting his pocket watch every few steps.

'I would guess, my lady, that Mr Peel has an appointment shortly. Perhaps we should catch him whilst we can?'

'Absolutely!'

Clifford eased the car to a stop outside the brick-fronted Georgian office. Eleanor leaped out and went to open the dark grey door. It was locked.

'What on earth?'

Clifford frowned. 'Most irregular that a law practice would not be open for business at almost twelve o'clock.'

At that moment, their quarry scurried round the corner, his cheeks the colour of aubergine.

'Good gracious, Mr Peel, are you alright?'

'What? Yes, just very late. Excuse me.' He pushed past her.

'It would appear your secretary is also late, Mr Peel.' Eleanor nodded at the locked door.

The barrister pulled out a key chain and fought with the lock. 'My secretary is er... temporarily seconded elsewhere.'

Eleanor shot Clifford a look. The lock defeated, Peel burst through the door but stopped in dismay at an envelope lying face down on the mat, a red seal visible. Without stooping to pick it up, he flopped into the secretary's chair and groaned.

Eleanor followed him inside. She took the letter and placed it on the desk in front of him. 'Gracious, is it bad news?'

Peel sat with his head in his hands. 'The worst,' he mumbled between his fingers. 'What to do, oh goodness, whatever to do now?'

Eleanor sat on the edge of the desk. 'Are you in trouble, Mr Peel?'

'No, no, not at all.' He jerked upright. 'Staring insolvency in the face, that's all.' His shoulders shook as he sobbed quietly.

Eleanor nodded at Clifford, who took a quick look around the outer office they were in. He opened the top drawer of the only piece of furniture, a bureau, and produced a bottle of brandy and a glass. Placing a generous measure in front of the distraught man, he added a clean handkerchief next to it. Peel grabbed the drink and quaffed half of it in one gulp. Spluttering, he looked up and shook his head: 'Forgive my lack of composure. Since Aris left the partnership, times have been harder than I ever expected.'

Eleanor topped up his glass and asked gently, 'Your secretary hasn't been seconded to another practice, has she?'

Peel shook his head. 'I had to let her go. And how I shall honour her last salary packet I've no idea.' He sighed. 'Aris ruined me when he left with all our best clients. All our clients, in truth.' He stared at the brandy glass in his hand. 'I've tried, but I simply can't make a go of it on my own.'

'Why did Aris leave?' Eleanor asked softly.

'Greed! He wasn't content with his half of the profits, he wanted it all. That was his approach to everything in life. He'd find a patsy to do the donkey work and then stride off with the golden prize when the time was right.'

Eleanor chewed her bottom lip. 'Mr Peel, I've also recently been set up as a patsy or a donkey or whatever it is. I know just how awful that is.'

Peel put his glass down and nodded slowly.

'Did you hope that Aris might reverse his decision and come back?'

He nodded again. 'It was probably a vague and hopeless bit of blind optimism, but I hoped he might tire of having to do all the basic legwork that I always did. I foolishly imagined he had valued something in our working relationship.'

'So, when he died…'

'My hopes of that happening died with him. I've been trying to plough on, most unsuccessfully it appears.'

Clifford cleared his throat.

Eleanor rose. 'Mr Peel, we are truly sorry about your situation. If the opportunity arises to suggest your name to anyone in need of your services, rest assured I will send them directly to you. After that, you must prove your own value, which I am sure you are capable of. Remember, Mr Peel, circumstances do not make the man, they reveal him. I forget who said that, but I am finding it very true.'

Peel rose and held out his hand. 'Thank you. You've made me feel more optimistic. I appreciate your time.'

'And I yours.'

As they turned to the door, Peel called them back: 'Wait! Please.'

Eleanor stepped back to the desk. 'Is there something you need right now?'

'No, Lady Swift. I have something you need right now. You made me realise the right thing for me to do. Please, both of you, take a seat.'

'Happily, Mr Peel.' She smiled and shot Clifford a puzzled look.

Peel took a deep breath. 'I have never broken client confidentiality in all my years in practice but what's the point of upholding the oath when it would merely allow for more injustice?'

'Absolutely, Mr Peel.' Eleanor smiled encouragingly for him to continue.

'Ernest Lucius Carlton was a reasonably wealthy man, despite all his attempts to play the working man's colleague and thus win votes under the banner of the Labour Party.'

'We had deduced something along those lines,' Eleanor said.

'But perhaps what you haven't been able to deduce is where Carlton's father got all the money that he bequeathed to Ernest?'

Eleanor and Clifford shook their heads in unison.

'Land! Acres and acres of land. All purchased from bankrupt farmers in a four-year run of terrible harvests between 1875 and 1879. With cheap cereal crops imported from America, our farms perished as quickly as their own crops. Carlton Senior was a shrewd man, you see. He concluded that if marine cargo could be developed so quickly, so would public transport. And then, people could move out from London, which would mean great tracts of housing would be required, so he was the first to swoop in and profit, paying little more than enough to keep the poor souls from the workhouse.'

Clifford steepled his fingers. 'Only he passed away before he could realise his investment?'

'Indeed. He left it all to his only son, Ernest.'

'But with the Addison Act of last year…' Eleanor slapped Peel's desk. 'Carlton should have been in the prime position of owning the perfect land for selling on for council housing.'

'Should have been, my lady?' Clifford said. 'So, it is Lord Farrington's land, not Mr Carlton's, that is listed in the contract for said housing? And the man who orchestrated that was…'

'Aris,' Peel said wearily. 'He persuaded the planning committee that the Farringtons' land was a more appropriate siting for a number of reasons, all of which are spurious.'

'And, as an honest man, you told the planning committee this?'

A flicker of comfort brushed Peel's face. 'Thank you, yes, I did. That is the real reason Aris quit our partnership. Anyway, that is not the matter in hand now. You see, Aris relied on the less-trained eyes of the planning committee members. He used his expertise of property law to bamboozle them. The odd palm will have been greased as well, I'm sure. That was another of Aris' specialities.'

Eleanor's mind was whirling. Peel obviously had a motive to kill Aris. Or perhaps, if he really did hope Aris would return to his business, a motive to keep him alive. *But Carlton?*

She tried to keep her voice light. 'Despite all this, Mr Aris seemed quite popular. Mr Carlton, on the other hand, didn't seem popular at all. No one has said a positive word about him. Did you feel the same way, Mr Peel?'

Vernon Peel gave a soft titter. 'Lady Swift, I have stood in court for over twenty years and listened to hundreds of cases. If I had murdered Carlton, I could cover my tracks better than most. However, I barely have the fight to keep my business from sinking. I had no argument with Carlton, except perhaps a small, silent envy of the man who seemed imbued with a charm and poise that I have lacked my whole life. Fortunately, on Sunday evening I was in Oxford. I'm sure I could find some witnesses.' He shrugged. 'Hawking my sorry self around the inns and hostelries, trying to pick up enough business to stay afloat. It was far enough away that I could offer lower rates without my clients in Chipstone knowing, you see.'

'I do see, entirely,' Eleanor said gently, making a mental note to find out if Abigail could confirm his alibi had been checked by the police. 'Your efforts to turn things around are admirable. I sincerely hope you are rewarded.'

Peel rubbed his face with his hands and pushed the glass away from him. He smiled weakly. 'Please dispose of the rest of the brandy. The answer to my problems does not lie at the bottom of a bottle.'

'That's the spirit!' Eleanor shook his hand warmly and nodded for Clifford to scoop up the bottle on their way out.

As they reached the office door, Peel called out, 'Lady Swift, you asked me if I had reason to kill Mr Carlton. However, you did not ask me the same question about Mr Aris?'

She smiled at him. 'That, Mr Peel, is because I know you did.'

*

Outside, Eleanor took a deep breath. 'Clifford, that was horribly awkward. Poor chap! Did you believe him when he said he hoped Aris might come back to him?'

'I did, my lady. Although, if he was lying—'

'Exactly. As for Carlton, we have no known motive for why Peel might have wanted him dead. However, Peel's revelation about Aris pulling the carpet out from under Carlton in that land deal gives Carlton a strong motive to kill Aris.'

Clifford nodded. 'Indeed, my lady. It would have cost Mr Carlton a small fortune. And given the existing animosity of the two men towards each other, I believe Mr Carlton would also have taken it very personally.'

'So logically as he had the means, opportunity—'

'And strongest motive.'

Eleanor nodded slowly. 'Carlton killed Aris.'

In the Rolls, Eleanor sat back in her seat. As it pulled smoothly away, she closed her eyes and let out a weary sigh. 'Carlton didn't kill Aris, did he, Clifford?'

Clifford shook his head. 'No, my lady, he didn't.'

CHAPTER 29

Clifford stepped into the morning room, carrying a refilled pot of coffee: 'They have arrived, my lady.'

Eleanor paused with a piece of fried bread halfway to her mouth. 'Who has arrived? I've no time for visitors today!'

'Not who, my lady, but what. Mr Rigby has just dropped the boxes off personally.'

'The printer? Gracious, now that is what I call service! We could have collected them when we got to Chipstone.'

'Being Thursday, I am minded to think that Mr Rigby wanted to ensure he could be at church on time. He is the stand-in organist at St Winifred's and rather protective of any opportunity he gets to play midweek.'

'I see. I'm also mindful it is Thursday and greatly appreciate you swapping your day off. Thank you, Clifford. Now, we'd better get the show on the road.'

'The ladies are ready and waiting, my lady. I might add that Master Gladstone is making something of a protest at being left with Joseph today.'

Eleanor smiled at this. 'I do love a dog who knows his own mind! I'll play an extra-long game of ball on our return by way of apology.'

Before Clifford could reply, the ringing of the telephone interrupted them.

A moment later, he reappeared: 'Chief Inspector Seldon for you, my lady.'

'Excellent! Maybe there's a development in the case.'

There was. But not the sort she'd been hoping for. 'Manslaughter? Surely not?'

DCI Seldon's gruff voice came down the line. 'I am well aware that you have an interest in this case, Lady Swift. And given that you have been proven right on occasion and that you have, I personally believe, been wrongly suspected of Mr Carlton's murder, I'm passing on this information strictly in confidence.'

Eleanor couldn't but feel elated for a moment. Not only because the Inspector believed she had nothing to do with Carlton's murder, but because he was treating her with respect. As an equal. He was taking her seriously, something Lancelot, for all his wonderful qualities, ever did. Again, she wondered what life would be like if she and the Inspector…

She was jolted back to the present by DCI Seldon's next words: 'Mrs Pitkin has disappeared.'

'Disappeared?'

'After charges of manslaughter were filed against her, my men went to the address she had given us, but she wasn't there. Do you know where she is, Lady Swift?'

Eleanor hesitated. She didn't want to obstruct the police, but in her mind, she knew Mrs Pitkin to be innocent.

'Look, Inspector, you've been straight with me, so I'll return the favour. I do know where Mrs Pitkin is, but in her present state for the police to turn up and cart her off to jail is the last thing she needs. I… I don't have any actual evidence, you know, you could use in court, but I know she's innocent.'

Briefly, she told DCI Seldon all that she and Clifford had discovered. After she'd finished, there was a brief pause before the Inspector came back on. 'Lady Swift, as I said at the police station, there is no point in my telling you to desist from your investigations, as I've learned in the past. I've also learned you have an irritating knack of being right, and even though the evidence you've recounted is far from conclusive, I'm willing to play ball. For now.'

Eleanor was amazed. 'That's very... compassionate of you, Inspector.'

DCI Seldon grunted. 'My... my mother was falsely accused of theft and dismissed from service when I was ten. Back in the 1890s, times were even harder and the word of an employer, especially a titled one, against a servant always prevailed, so I understand Mrs Pitkin's position. Times have changed, but she would have no chance against the word of Lady Farrington, with her husband being the Earl of Winslow, as you say. And, yes, my hands would be tied.'

Eleanor was amazed the Inspector had told her about his mother. He was such a private individual. *And the 1890s?* That would make him somewhere between thirty and forty. She shook her head. *Focus, Ellie, this isn't about you.* 'So, what can we do? I can't refuse to tell you where Mrs Pitkin is, but—'

'Lady Swift, let's both pretend this phone call never happened. But between us, I'll hold you responsible for Mrs Pitkin. I'll have to put out a warrant for her arrest, but I can delay that for twenty-four hours at most.'

Eleanor breathed a sigh of relief. 'Thank you, Inspector, I really appreciate that.'

She put the phone down and hurried to the kitchen. The ladies were all there, busy with chores. 'Mrs Trotman, I'm so sorry to interrupt, but something urgent has arisen...'

As they reached Chipstone, Eleanor glanced sideways at Clifford.

'Come on then, spill the beans! What tortures have you got lined up for me?'

'Tortures, my lady?'

Mrs Butters and Mrs Trotman pretended to be busy looking out of the window.

'You know what I mean. You insisted I needed to "increase my efforts" in the final days leading up to the last debate. However, I feel we must go over everything we know about the Aris and Carlton murders thoroughly. There must be something we're missing.'

Clifford nodded. 'I was not suggesting you had been slacking. Merely that as you are now standing without the support of the Women's League, you need to reach as many people as quickly as possible with your message. And that we can then reconvene and discuss the case.'

She nodded back. 'Agreed. Although, we've got one day at best, it seems. We'll get this out of the way as swiftly as possible and afterwards put our minds to getting a breakthrough in our investigations. So, come on, what have you arranged?'

He cleared his throat. 'An address to the Women's Institute, which the Women's League will also attend, I'm afraid.' He hurried on at her look. 'Then a brief policy discussion with the members of the Shopkeepers' Union, followed by a question-and-answer session at the Reading Room.'

She groaned. 'That sounds hideous! I didn't hear the word "elevenses", "lunch" or "fruitcake" in any of it.'

Mrs Trotman patted Eleanor's shoulder from the back seat. 'Not to fret, my lady, Butters and I packed a splendid picnic to keep your strength up.'

Eleanor turned to her three loyal staff. 'Thank you, ladies. And thank you for coming along today. I would be lost without your support.'

''Tis our pleasure,' Mrs Trotman said. 'And I can't thank you enough for all you are doing for poor Martha.'

Eleanor smiled over her shoulder. 'You don't have to thank me, Mrs Trotman. I should not sleep in my bed if anything happened to that poor woman on account of these false accusations that have been brought against her. Now, Alfie and his gang should be along any minute. If you and Mrs Butters organise the search party, once Clifford and I are finished, if you haven't found her, we will join you.' She tried to sound more optimistic than she felt. Mrs Trotman had sent word to her sister where Mrs Pitkin had been staying, but she had found the cook's room empty and her belongings gone. *Had she somehow heard that she was going to be charged with manslaughter, or had she just decided she'd been enough of a burden and decided to…?* She shook her head. *There's no point in thinking like that, Ellie.*

Outside the closed Town Hall, the ladies tumbled from the Rolls. Eleanor stared up and down the road. 'Clifford, are you sure the troops know what time to be here?'

At that precise moment, a herd of boys in short trousers, hand-me-down jumpers and caps ran out of the narrow passageway alongside the Town Hall.

Eleanor clapped her hands. 'Captain Alfie, Sergeant Billy, how splendid to see you all!'

'Mornin', miss.' Alfie pulled off his cap, which prompted the others to do the same. At his salute, they shuffled into a semblance of a line and waited expectantly.

Despite the potential seriousness of the situation, Eleanor couldn't help but smile at the boys' excitement. 'First of all, thank you all so much for coming. Your usual payment is ready and waiting in the form of pennies and meat pies.' Alfie dug Billy in the ribs and grinned.

She took a deep breath. 'If you'll wait a moment for instructions.' She turned to her staff. 'I suppose I had better get off to meet with the Women's Institute, though quite what I'm going to say, I've no idea. Clifford, are you alright helping the ladies organise things this end?'

'Indeed, my lady. And then I shall collect you in thirty minutes and deliver you to the Shopkeepers' Union meeting.'

'So kind!' She turned to the ladies: 'And good luck with the search.'

Almost two hours later, Eleanor was seriously flagging.

'Just the Reading Room left, my lady.' Clifford eased the Rolls to a stop. 'Word is that you are making quite the impression this morning. My congratulations.'

She ran her finger along the intricate pattern of the inlaid dashboard. 'It's hard to stay focussed and say anything sensible with this murder business going on. How can I concentrate on answering questions about how many stalls to allow at the town fair or whether out-of-county pork is allowed at the market?'

Clifford nodded. 'An interesting question. Might one ask how you responded?'

'Apparently, rather amusingly. All I said was "only if the crackling went as crispy as our home-grown pigs".'

His lips twitched.

'I don't see what's so funny about that. I've no idea what they were on about or why they think it's important. Two men have died in their town and yet everyone is carrying on as if nothing has happened.'

'Perhaps because life does carry on, my lady.'

'I know.' She looked round at the flint-and-stone houses with their smartly-painted front gates and neat hedges that finished where the top end of the high street started. 'Who would have guessed these sleepy villages and market towns are such hotbeds of political intrigue, murder and vice? Actually, most of the Women's Institute meeting was taken up discussing the question of Mrs Pankhurst being given a six months jail sentence for sedition. Many of the women were sympathetic, but most thought she'd gone too far. I think Miss Mann may have been right when she said this area is fifty years behind London.'

'Indeed, my lady. I am not sure how much murder and vice take place in the Reading Room, but I believe your audience await you. Afterwards we'll head back to the Hall. The ladies should be back there by then.'

'And hopefully, they'll have located Mrs Pitkin. There's no news?'

He shook his head. 'Perhaps there will be better news at Henley Hall.'

Eleanor nodded, but in her heart she wasn't so sure.

Back at the Hall after a light tea, Clifford and Eleanor retired to the morning room. There had, indeed, been no news of Mrs Pitkin, but Mrs Trotman had assured them that they had enough people looking already. Clifford had agreed, suggesting their time could be better spent trying to get a breakthrough in the case rather than join the search party as originally intended.

Eleanor took out her notebook and turned to the list of those who attended the dinner the night of Aris' death.

'Right, Clifford, it's essential we make some serious progress. If, and I say if, these murders are politically motivated, the last debate is tomorrow and then the election early next week. It's possible the murderer may strike again.' She didn't need to say any more, Clifford's serious expression said it all. Eleanor hurried on: 'And we still haven't located Mrs Pitkin. We must find her before… anyway, we simply must find her.'

'The ladies will find her, my lady, have no doubt. The best thing we can do is to find Mr Aris' killer.'

'And in the process, hopefully find Carlton's killer.'

'Indeed, my lady. And I can open the proceedings with interesting news. I received additional information which appears to clear three parties of Mr Carlton's murder.'

'Oh, what?'

'That was Miss Abigail on the phone just now. She sent word that the police have ruled out Mr Morris in connection with Mr Carlton's death. It seems he was seen at the time of the murder by at least a hundred people at a very public exposition of seventeenth-century painters. He was there in his capacity as Chairman of the Arts Committee for Buckinghamshire.'

Eleanor gave an exaggerated yawn. 'My idea of absolute torture.'

'But not Mr Morris and, fortunately for him, it means his alibi appears to be watertight. All the more so as he was over forty miles away in Stony Stratford. And Miss Abigail's second snippet of insider information concerns our communist friend Mr Greaves.'

Eleanor looked at him expectantly. 'Another alibi?'

Clifford nodded. 'Mr Greaves was at the Chipstone Working Men's Club at the time of Mr Carlton's death.'

'And he has sufficient witnesses, does he? Because,' she bit her lip, 'isn't that close to Carlton's home?'

'Indeed. However, Mr Greaves is known to a great many members of the club. Over a dozen confirmed he didn't leave the premises between his arrival at 7.30 p.m. and closing time when the barman swept him out into the street, well after Mr Carlton's demise. And thirdly, the night of Carlton's murder, Lord and Lady Farrington were attending a twenty-first birthday ball at Templey Court, near Windsor. It was in all the society papers.'

'Oh dear, all of our chief suspects seem to have been ruled out! So, let's see where we are. We are running desperately short of time, so let's go down the list ruthlessly and stick mainly to Aris' death. I still think we're right to assume Aris and Carlton were murdered by the same person, so let's see who we end up with. Agreed?'

'Agreed, my lady.'

She scoured the list of names, reading out the notes aloud:

'*"Lord Farrington – no known motive – needed Aris' support for a housing project on his land – possible bankruptcy if not?"* Nothing new to add to him except him and his wife have an alibi for the time of

Carlton's murder. Mind you, with their money and connections, I wouldn't have thought it difficult to get someone to do the actual killing for them. Even so, why would he murder Carlton?'

'Perhaps, my lady, to exact revenge if he suspected Mr Carlton of killing Mr Aris? Or, indeed, if he feared, now Mr Aris was dead, that the land deal might swing back in favour of Carlton's land. Unless, that is, Mr Carlton was taken out of the proceedings, as it were?'

'Brilliant, Clifford! That just leaves the mystery of Lady Farrington.' Eleanor tapped the pen on her chin. 'It's possible that she was protecting the person Carlton was blackmailing about the fudge, assuming they both knew who killed Aris?'

Clifford nodded. 'True, my lady.'

She shook her head in frustration. 'Still, they officially have an alibi for one of the murders, so they're both out at this point. We have to be ruthless, as I said.' She carried on down the list.

' "*Oswald Greaves. Aris tried to get him imprisoned and his party banned.*" Again, nothing new in relation to his motive for Aris' murder, but he does have an alibi for Carlton's, so for the moment he's out.

' "*Ernest Carlton – lost to Aris three times. Could be dumped by his party if lost again. Also fell out with Aris over a woman.*" Well, along with Aris' ex-law partner Peel's revelations, Carlton certainly had enough reasons to kill Aris. Only trouble is, he's now dead. And the most likely scenario seems to be he was trying to blackmail Aris' actual murderer, with the clean fudge we found under his desk as collateral, and it went wrong. So again, he's out.

' "*Arnold Aris. Dead (poisoned by peanuts).*" Unless it was suicide, and he then came back from the grave and murdered Carlton, I think we can move on. Although, I hadn't thought that it could have been suicide on Aris' part?'

Clifford nodded. 'Neither had I. Most interesting, but for the moment, I fear we will have to stick to the notion that Mr Aris' death was not voluntary.'

'Again, agreed. Who's next? *"Miss Mann – no known motive. Aris'
main supporter of Women's League and women's rights in the area."*
Well, she has no motive we can find out for Aris' death. Equally,
however, she has no alibi that I know of for the time of Carlton's
death and she did dislike the fellow. Mind you, most of Chipstone
and beyond disliked Ernest Carlton, so if that were a motive, we'd
have more suspects than I could fit in my notebook.'

'True, my lady.'

'Now, *"Stanley Morris – no known motive."* Well, he may have had
no motive in Aris' case, but he certainly did in Carlton's. However,
fortunately for him, and unfortunately for us, he has an alibi for
Carlton's death, so he's out.

'*"Duncan Blewitt – head of cabal that wants to put anti-women's
rights candidate in seat Aris held. No known motive."* She sighed.
'He's the opposite of Morris, really. No known motive for wanting
Carlton dead, unless he was going to kill all the candidates one
by one until there were none left, but a powerful motive to want
Aris dead. And no alibi we know of at the moment for the time of
Carlton's death. He's a keeper. And, yes, we need to interview him
sharpish – I shouldn't have put it off.

'"In delay there lies no plenty," as Shakespeare put it.'

'Fair point. Anyway, let's move on. We're not counting Lord and
Lady Langham as we know, that leaves… *"Vernon Peel – no known
motive but definitely hiding something."* Well, that's wrong now!
We know that Aris ruined Peel's business, and revenge is a definite
motive for murder in my book. Peel might have said he wanted
Aris back, but he would say that wouldn't he, if he murdered Aris?'

'True, my lady. And he has no proven alibi for the time of
Carlton's death, even though it must be said he also has no motive
we know of. Unless, that is, you count envy of Mr Carlton's "charm
and poise" as Mr Peel put it as a possible motive?'

She shrugged. 'Probably not, but no matter, he's a keeper as
well.' She ran down the page and copied several names to a fresh

sheet. 'Right, if our murderer killed both Aris and Carlton, and didn't use a hitman, then our possible culprits are… Miss Mann… Duncan Blewitt… and Vernon Peel. Unfortunately, none of them have a motive for both murders. In fact, some of them don't even have a motive for one.'

Clifford digested the information for a moment. 'And if we allow that Mr Aris and Mr Carlton's killers may be different people?'

'Well, theoretically, everyone at the table the night Aris died. I admit, the first list we've ended up with doesn't look quite right.'

Clifford nodded slowly.' I agree. However, given the situation we find ourselves in, I propose we concentrate on our first list.'

Eleanor nodded. 'It's no good, Clifford, I've been putting it off. He's such a nasty piece of work, but we need to interview Blewitt.' She shuddered and rubbed her arms. 'I'm not looking forward to that. And then we must find out what Lady Farrington is up to. Alibi or no, I'm sure she is the key to all this. Somehow, I'm going to have to call her bluff.'

CHAPTER 30

The following morning Clifford drove Eleanor back to Chipstone, leaving the ladies to catch up on housework until they returned and collected them for the afternoon's campaigning and searching. The day before had turned up no trace of Mrs Pitkin. Mrs Trotman put on a brave show, but Eleanor noted Mrs Butters with her arm around her in the kitchen afterwards.

This morning Gladstone was in his bed by the range, doggedly watching over his now-burgeoning leather slipper collection. He'd stolen every pair he could find as part of his protest at being left behind the day before. After playing tug with him for five minutes, Eleanor had abandoned trying to rescue the right one of her favourite pair and left him to it.

On the way into town, Clifford spoke up: 'Excuse my suggesting it, my lady, but before we accost Mr Blewitt with a raft of impromptu questions, perhaps a well-thought-out plan might be in order? If he is the perpetrator of one or both murders, I feel prudence is our essential companion this morning.'

'Well, where is she then? Have you hidden her in the boot?' She opened the glovebox. 'Or in here, perhaps?'

'Most droll!'

'Lighten up, Clifford. I need to be in good spirits to deal with blasted Blewitt shortly.'

'My lady, I promised your late uncle...'

'I know, that you would do your utmost to keep me safe. And an admirable job you do, one I greatly appreciate. Perhaps it might ease your concerns if we remember that I did navigate my own way around the world, mostly alone. It's not easy to outrun anyone with ill intentions whilst climbing the Himalayas on a bicycle, they're really rather steep, but I managed it. On one or two occasions, actually.'

'Point taken.' Clifford slowed and doffed his hat to Mrs Atwood as she crossed the road with a herd of squealing pigs, a collie snapping with excitement at their trotters.

Eleanor smiled and waved at the woman, but leaned across to Clifford and muttered, 'Why do farmers keep sheepdogs to round up their livestock? I love dogs, but sheepdogs seem eminently untrustworthy to me.'

'Perhaps, the same reason voters still elect politicians? No one has yet found a more satisfactory solution?'

She laughed. 'Excellent point!'

The Georgian façade gave the Eagle Hotel an imposing air. Through the tall archway a glimpse of the original black-timbered stables and outbuildings that leaned at various and precarious angles showed its true sixteenth-century origins.

Eleanor walked up the foot-worn steps of the main entrance, thinking the last time she'd met someone here, they'd tried to kill her. It had been some time ago, when she and Clifford had been trying to prove Lancelot innocent of a murder charge. She shuddered at the memory. Maybe Clifford had been right about needing more of a plan. She paused with her hand on the brass rail. All she had gleaned about Blewitt so far was that he was unspeakably rude. He was an avid anti-women's rights supporter too. And, judging by his straining buttons, he enjoyed the company of ale and pies more than was healthy.

The door was opened by a fresh-faced young man in a smart waiter's uniform that fell short of fitting his gangly frame by about two inches.

'Welcome to The Eagle, Lady Swift.'

'Thank you. Is Mr Duncan Blewitt…?'

The waiter nodded. 'Partaking of luncheon in the non-residents' dining room, alone.'

'Not for long,' she said grimly. 'Ah, Clifford. This way, I believe.'

Inside the dining room, burgundy flock wallpaper and an over-enthusiastic array of brass ornaments gave a warm, familiar welcome. One echoed by the serving girl who directed her to a table in the corner where the heavy frame of the man she'd come to interview sat hunched over a plate.

Duncan Blewitt seemed unaffected by the genial ambience.

'What do you want?' he grumbled as he speared a chunk of kidney in his pie. His flaccid jowls wobbled as he chewed it vigorously. He nodded behind her: 'Mr Clifford.'

'Good afternoon to you too.' Eleanor smiled sweetly. 'I do apologise for interrupting your rather fine-looking luncheon, but I have a burning question.'

He glared at her with small, angry eyes. 'Lady Swift, your unwanted curiosity can catch fire as far as I am concerned.'

'Do you know, I think you and I started out badly. That day we bumped into each other, we got off on the wrong foot.'

'I have no desire to rectify the situation. I do, however, wish to eat my luncheon.'

'Oh gracious, please don't let Clifford and I stop you!'

'I shan't.' His fork scraped against the plate as he jabbed an enormous section of gravy-drenched flaky pastry.

Eleanor slid into a chair opposite Blewitt, ignoring his ineffectual complaint, which was muffled by another large mouthful of pie.

She looked him directly in the eyes. 'Why did you threaten me?'

'Slanderous talk, that! I should be careful if I were you.' He laughed without humour. 'Or perhaps you're going to take that as a threat as well? That's the problem with women, you can't talk to them like real people. Everything is interpreted and instantly twisted.'

Eleanor tamped down her anger. 'That's a very large brush you are tarring all of womankind with.'

'Nothing they don't deserve. If you have interrupted my food to blather on about how life is unfair and you should be treated equally, please stop using up air pointlessly. I have no interest in the so-called plight of women.'

'Well, I shan't take up any more of your time then. Although actually, I only popped in to reassure you that your secret is safe with us.'

Blewitt jerked and paused in chewing a large mouthful. He stared at her as he swallowed. 'I don't have any secrets.'

'Oh, how strange, because isn't there a saying about everyone having a skeleton in the closet? But anyway, that's a weight off my chest because I'm actually not that wonderful at keeping secrets, they do seem to slip out before I can catch my tongue. So, I'm relieved that I can chatter on to all and sundry about the time you spent,' she paused for a moment, 'detained at His Majesty's pleasure for owning a house of ill repute.'

Blewitt choked violently. Clifford stepped round and patted Blewitt's back until his purple cheeks receded to angry red.

Still panting, Blewitt waved Clifford away. 'How the devil,' he glanced around and lowered his voice, 'did you find that out?'

Eleanor shrugged. 'That's on a need-to-know basis, Mr Blewitt. You don't deny it, then?'

He glowered at her. 'There's no point, is there? What I'm interested in is that that piece of information, which is not for public consumption, doesn't go any further.'

Eleanor sat back and removed her gloves. 'Well, that's not going to be easy, is it, Mr Blewitt? I mean, us women are such twittering birds, spreading rumours far and wide, there's no stopping us. It's in our nature, you might say.'

Blewitt took another mouthful of pie and chewed it thoughtfully. Eleanor hid a shudder. He washed it down with a gulp of ale and leaned back in his seat.

'So, Lady Swift, I see you are a businesswoman, after all. What do you want?'

'Who killed Aris and Carlton?'

That seemed to knock all the bluster out of Blewitt. He stared at her for a moment before shaking his head. 'Why should I have any idea about who it was?'

'Only that the list of suspects has markedly fallen in the last twenty-four hours, leaving just three.'

He sighed. 'And I assume my name is amongst them?'

Eleanor nodded. 'But please don't ask whereabouts in the list you are, because that's not fair on the others. Not very sporting, like politics, I'm learning. Now, Mr Blewitt, to save you from making a gross faux pas and to salvage what is left of your luncheon before it cools any further, we could stop playing games?'

'Alright,' he snapped. 'If I tell you what I know about Aris and Carlton, you'll swear not to mention that indiscretion to anyone? But understand this: I've no idea who killed either of them, and it certainly wasn't me.'

Eleanor shrugged. 'I promise on the word of a lady, if that's worth anything to you, Mr Blewitt, that I won't divulge your little secret. If, that is, you tell Clifford and I what you know about anything that could have got Aris or Carlton killed. But,' she held up a finger, 'I don't promise to remove you from my shortlist of suspects. Clear?'

Blewitt ran his tongue over his teeth, causing Eleanor to shudder openly this time. He took another swig of ale and leaned forward. 'It suited me for certain parties who back my,' he looked at Eleanor without embarrassment, 'campaign to rid the country of this poisonous women's rights nonsense, to believe that Aris and I were enemies. And, on the subject of women's rights, whatever that ridiculous phrase means, it was true. However, behind-the-scenes, Aris and I shared certain business interests.'

'And if these certain parties had known that you were in bed, as it were, with Mr Aris, they would have felt betrayed, given Mr Aris' support for the Women's League?'

'I see you really do understand how business works, Lady Swift. Anyway, that is the reason I didn't kill Aris, whether or not I'm on your blasted shortlist. Because that stupid cook couldn't follow instructions and poisoned Aris, the whole wretched deal is in jeopardy.'

Eleanor feigned a yawn. 'Yes, yes. You were in on the deal over the Farringtons' land being sold for the new housing the council needs to build.'

Blewitt ran his hand along his mouth. Beads of perspiration shone on his heavily-lined forehead. 'How... how could you possibly have found that out?'

'I didn't. You just told me.'

'You...!' He glowered at her. 'Lady Swift, I am happy to report you are not improving my opinion of the way women conduct themselves.'

'As you wish. But you're in a bit of a tight spot, aren't you? Have you confessed the truth to the police? That you wouldn't have killed Aris because there was a small fortune riding on his orchestrating the whole deal?'

Blewitt scowled. 'No, I haven't told them.'

'And what about Carlton's murder, how is your alibi holding up there?'

Blewitt turned his fork in his hand. 'You can't hold up something that isn't there. I was home alone at the time and I live about four streets away from where he was murdered.'

Eleanor turned and waved at the waitress polishing cutlery by the serving table. She rose as the girl appeared at her elbow. 'Another steak and kidney pie with all the trimmings for Mr Blewitt, please. And a hearty brandy to go with it. I shall pay on my way out.'

'Bon appetit!' she called over her shoulder as Clifford held the door out to the hotel lobby open.

'Truth or lies, do you think?' she asked as she stepped into the Rolls.

'Given the significant disclosures Mr Blewitt made, I am inclined to believe him. His business reputation would not survive it becoming knowledge amongst his backers that he was in any association with Mr Aris.'

'But he can't defend his whereabouts on the night of Carlton's murder?'

'Which he readily admitted to, rather than make something up. A man in his position could find a person of unquestionable character to vouch for him being somewhere he wasn't with ease.'

'So, either he did just lay all his cards on the table and he's entirely innocent or he's risking the biggest bluff of his life.'

'And,' Clifford added, pulling out behind a coal lorry, 'we still don't have a motive for him killing Mr Carlton.'

Eleanor shook her head. 'Don't we? Blewitt has just told us that he was in cahoots with Aris over this land deal. With Aris out of the way, Carlton was free to make sure the council housing was built on *his* land, not Lord Farrington's. Which means not only Lord Farrington and Aris, but also it seems, Blewitt, would lose out financially big time. And if Mr Blewitt likes his money half as much as he likes his pies, then it's a wonder Carlton survived this long!'

CHAPTER 31

'You might have telephoned instead.' Lady Farrington's voice was as cold as the ice-white silk of her dress as she appeared in the doorway of the cavernous reception room Eleanor had been shown into.

'Yes, I might have, but face to face seemed a better choice,' Eleanor said.

'Well, it was not a better choice. Alexander is home. I cannot speak with you about the matter we discussed before. Not now.'

Eleanor rose and smiled. 'No problem, I thought you would prefer to speak to me now rather than the police later, but as you wish.'

Lady Farrington laughed without humour. 'Don't be ridiculous! People like us don't speak to the police. They wouldn't dare come near us.'

'Oh, but I think they might when they find out that you insisted your staff lie about your cook's guilt over Mr Aris' death?'

Lady Farrington stiffened. Her hand strayed to her perfect finger waves. 'Give me a moment to make sure Alexander is occupied. But then I'll speak with you for ten minutes only.'

Her heels clicked away across the marble foyer.

So far, so good, Ellie.

It seemed Lord Farrington couldn't have been far away as his wife returned quickly. She motioned for Eleanor to sit down, checked down the hallway and then closed the door. She eyed her visitor coolly as she took a seat. 'What I may or may not have discussed with my staff is no one else's business. I hope you don't imagine I shall trot dutifully to court and say I asked them to do something inappropriate? Because I shan't even entertain the idea and, as a lady, I thought you would know that the point of staff is that they do as they are bidden.' She crossed one ankle over the other. 'So, was there anything else, or did you just wish to enlighten me that some of my staff tattled to your butler when you feigned a breakdown of your car?'

'Actually,' Eleanor leaned forward, 'I rather thought you might like to enlighten me over a few things. The police really are rather trying if you get them involved, I usually find.'

'Tsk, it appears I gave you undue credit for knowing how such matters work, Lady Swift. Alexander is the Earl of Winslow. Even if he had killed Mr Aris, which he didn't, incidentally, and in front of a witness, he could only be tried in the House of Lords. Which would be a paper exercise, a farce conducted purely for the records.'

'True. But I am not concerned with your husband. Although, I realise suddenly I should be speaking to him. He is clearly unaware of the actual situation.' She stood up.

'Sit!' Lady Farrington snapped. 'Alright, yes, I told the staff to lie.'

Okay, Ellie, you've got her where you want her. Now don't blow it! She sat back down. 'Thank you for being honest with me, Lady Farrington. You must see that your actions make no sense to me. Unless, that is, you know more about Mr Aris' death than you are letting on?'

Lady Farrington stared at her coolly without speaking.

Eleanor shrugged. 'Lady Farrington, I put it to you that you told your staff to lie to make sure suspicion was thrown on your cook for Mr Aris' death, which you want to be seen as an accident, not murder.'

It was Lady Farrington's turn to shrug. 'I already told you I did not want any scandal around Aris' death. That is why I agreed to cooperate with you. I knew from your reputation that once you started investigating, you wouldn't stop so I decided it was better to be on the same side as it were. So, yes, I wanted it to be seen as the accident it was.'

Eleanor pursed her lips. What Lady Farrington meant was she was pretending to help Eleanor investigate Aris' murder so Eleanor would trust her and tell her what she found out. And so she could feed Eleanor misinformation to make sure the investigation came to the conclusion she wanted. *The thing is, Ellie, someone tried to play us for a fool not so long ago and it's not going to work again.* She leaned forward. 'No, Lady Farrington. You told your staff to lie and blamed your cook for Mr Aris' death because you knew it wasn't an accident. In fact, you knew it was murder!'

Lady Farrington's eyes flickered momentarily. Other than that, her face remained expressionless. 'I think, my dear Lady Swift, you have an overactive imagination.'

Eleanor leaned back. 'Really? Then I might as well over-imagine some more. I believe you know not only that Mr Aris was murdered, but you also know who murdered him.' She leaned forward again. 'What did you see the night of Mr Aris' death, Lady Farrington? Did you see one of your guests switch Aris' fudge? Or,' she held the other woman's gaze, 'did you or your husband kill him?'

Lady Farrington rose and walked over to the fireplace and stood with her back to Eleanor. 'We are not responsible for Aris' death.'

Eleanor kept her eyes on her. 'And why should I believe that?'

Lady Farrington turned around. For the first time she looked strained. 'Oh, what's the difference now? It would only be a matter of a day or two, I'm sure, before you uncovered the fact that my husband has…' She scooped up a paper from the table and fanned her face.

Eleanor waited.

'Alexander has overstretched himself on investments and therefore also our finances. Neither of us wanted Aris dead because, unbecoming though it is to admit, the Farrington Estate is in a perilous position if the housing deal doesn't go through. Aris was our security. So, you see, we had nothing to gain and everything,' she swept her arm around the room, 'everything to lose if he was killed.'

'Then I take it that Aris' recent extra prosperity was provided by your husband?'

'Yes, a sort of down payment to secure the deal, as it were. It's all perfectly above board.'

Eleanor shook her head. 'None of that explains why you forced the staff to lie and threw suspicion on Mrs Pitkin.' She thought back to the tears the Farringtons' cook had cried in the kitchen at Henley Hall and her calm evaporated. 'Do you realise you have ruined that woman's life?'

Lady Farrington returned to her seat. 'I never really imagined the police would charge her with manslaughter.'

'Then do something about it! Use your husband's influence that you mentioned so clearly only a moment ago to get those charges dismissed.'

Lady Farrington smiled coldly. 'I can't. The deceased's wife asked the police to bring charges, not us.'

Eleanor's anger boiled over. *Is everyone out to destroy one blameless woman's life?* Her eyes bored into Lady Farrington. 'Let's stop playing games. You know who murdered Aris. Who are you protecting? And why?'

Silence hung round the room. Eventually, Lady Farrington spoke: 'I believe this meeting is over.'

CHAPTER 32

'Gosh, Clifford, have you seen the crowds? Most of the town must be here.' Eleanor fiddled with the buttons on her green brocade jacket as she stared at the heaving throng. A sea of light coats and felt hats filled the pavement, the crowd clearly grateful for the lack of rain October all too often threw their way. 'I had no idea so many people would turn up for the final debate.'

'A most eager audience, my lady.'

'Look!' Eleanor slapped his arm. 'Isn't that Lancelot?'

Clifford searched the crowd: 'Where should I be looking?'

'There!' She jabbed at the windscreen. 'The last thing I need is him messing about whilst I'm trying to deliver my speech.'

Clifford stopped the Rolls alongside Lancelot as he spotted them and did a cartwheel on the pavement. Eleanor hopped out of the car: 'What on earth are you doing here?' She noticed Miss Mann standing on the Town Hall steps, looking officious with a clipboard and talking to a policeman, whilst watching Lancelot's antics.

Just what I need, Ellie!

'I say, what kind of a welcome is that? We've come to cheer you on throughout the show.'

'Cheer me on? Show? This is a debate, not a round of gladiator games. I need to… to… Oh, dash it, Lancelot, I have to be professional and I can't do that with…'

Lancelot doubled up with laughter.

'What?'

'Professional! Sherlock? You are nothing short of hilarious. Darling fruit, promise me you'll never change.'

'Promise me *you* will!' she muttered.

'Eh?'

She scanned his face. 'Lancelot, you really don't get it, do you? I'm standing for election here.'

'I know, old thing, dashed good wheeze, what? That's why we're here, silly.'

'It's not a wheeze. I really want…' Eleanor stared at him in horror. 'We?'

He grinned and tucked a stray curl behind her ear. 'We what, feisty MP of my dreams?'

She slapped his hand away. 'Who is "we"?'

'Oh yah, brought the gang along for the jolly.' He waved an arm at five Bright Young Things, taking turns to swig from a bottle of champagne.

Eleanor groaned. 'No, no, no! Please leave and take your cronies with you.'

'Cronies? Steady on old thing, you haven't met them yet! Come and say hi, they're dying to meet you. There's Jules, Maitland and the very naughty Claude, he's an absolute hoot. And the two minxes dripping in sparkly bits are Lavinia and Flavia. We've got some hysterical surprises planned for when the other candidates are droning on, just wait and see.'

Eleanor shook her head. 'Just go, Lancelot. Frankly, I don't care where, just as long as it's far away from here!'

She turned to leave, but he caught her arm. 'But, Sherlock, I came to support you.'

'No, you didn't!' At his hurt look, she softened. 'Well, I know you did in your own way, but you also came to have fun and this is not the time. Can't you see this means the world to me? I want to be elected so I can do something to genuinely help these people have a better chance in life.'

'The only genuine thing you can do to help these people is to run along with this band of frivolous time-wasters.' The voice that spoke was not Lancelot's, but Blewitt's. He stood in front of her and Lancelot. 'Playtime is over. This is a stage for the big boys now, not rank amateurs playing at being politicians.'

Eleanor scowled. 'We'll see who's an amateur at the debate, shall we?'

He grinned. 'No need, dear girl. You've just shown the electorate your true colours by arguing with your boyfriend here in full view of everyone.'

Eleanor spun round to find what seemed like most of Chipstone staring at her.

She glared at Blewitt. 'If you'll excuse me, I need to take my place at the debate!'

Blewitt grabbed her elbow: 'The only thing you have any hope of wiping the floor with is a mop, Lady Swift!' She shook him off and folded her arms as he continued: 'Can't you see you've brought nothing but shame to everyone in this town? You've made yourself a laughing stock. You are nothing more than a jumped-up, interfering, self-centred—'

'You total cad!' Lancelot's blow was well-aimed. Blewitt lurched backwards, clutching his nose. The Bright Young Things whooped and cheered as Blewitt sat down heavily on the pavement, cupping his bleeding nose in both hands.

The Town Hall clock struck 3 p.m. Clifford materialised at her side: 'My lady, I can hear the ringing of the ten-minute bell heralding the imminent start of proceedings. You need to be at your place on the stage, if you intend to continue standing. Good luck.' He gave a deferential half-bow and vanished as magically as he had come.

Lancelot grinned. 'Go get 'em, darling fruit! I'll be cheering you on from the front row. We can celebrate at that fancy new restaurant they've opened on the river afterwards. It's open till midnight.'

She shook her head. 'I can't. We still haven't found Mrs Pitkin.'

Lancelot stared at her: 'Who the devil is Mrs Pitkin when she's at home?'

'She's the cook at Farrington Manor. Or was.'

He frowned. 'The one who put the peanuts in old Aris' pie?'

'Fudge… It was fudge. And it wasn't Mrs Pitkin.'

He shrugged. 'You know I've said it before, you are most deliciously peculiar! Why on earth do you have to find some old woman rather than whooping it up with me and my friends?'

Eleanor held his shoulders. 'Because she's been accused of manslaughter and is facing jail, or if she's lucky, the workhouse, for the rest of her life. Which might not be very much longer if we don't find her soon.'

Impulsively kissing him on the cheek, she set off for the Town Hall, leaving Blewitt mumbling on the pavement.

Through the open doors, Eleanor heard the bell ring again. Was that still the ten-minute bell or the five-minute one? Investigating Aris, and now Carlton's murder, coupled with organising the search for Mrs Pitkin, had left her little time to prepare for the final, all-important debate.

Before dashing out of her bedroom to jump in the Rolls, she'd remembered the Women's League leaflets she'd failed to return to Miss Mann. *They'll help, Ellie. After all, you may not be supported by them any more, but you still believe in their cause.* Opening the drawer of her dressing table, she'd grabbed them and run.

Now inside the Town Hall, she slowed as the master-at-arms' voice echoed down the long corridor towards her: 'Candidates, please take your seat as your name is called. Mr Stanley Morris…' A short, polite ripple of applause followed.

She hurried on down the corridor, pulling the first leaflet out of her pocket. As she opened it to scan the first paragraph, a small paper note slid out and floated to the floor. 'Mr Oswald Greaves,' called the master-at-arms. More clapping and a few foot stampings greeted this.

Despite herself, her feet slowed. *Come on, Ellie, for goodness' sake! Leave it. You need to get in there and win this thing.*

Her feet came to a stop. Something about the writing on the note reminded her of... what? She bent down and picked it up. On it, handwritten in neat but spiky strokes was a recipe for... chocolate and peanut butter fudge.

Eleanor stood frozen to the spot, her mind racing. *Why?* It didn't make any sense. Then everything fell into place.

She spun round and collided with the woman standing in front of her.

CHAPTER 33

For a moment neither spoke, then Eleanor's mouth fell open: 'Mrs Pitkin!'

Eleanor hadn't recognised her at first, for she wore an old black shawl that covered her head and shoulders.

The woman opened her mouth to speak, but before she could, Eleanor had flung her arms round her. 'Oh, I'm so glad you're safe! I… I thought. Oh…' She stepped away. 'I'm sorry, Mrs Pitkin. I was just so worr—'

The woman shook her head. 'Ain't right you apologising to me, after all the trouble I've put you, and Mrs Trotman through.' She hesitated and then looked into Eleanor's eyes and smiled. 'And that's about the nicest greeting anyone's ever given me, let alone a lady like yourself.' Suddenly her face clouded over. 'But there's no time. There's another needs help, even more than I do, and that's saying something.' She looked back up at Eleanor. 'I couldn't think of anyone else to come to.'

The final bell rang out. Eleanor shook her head: 'I'm afraid I'm not that good at helping anyone. Maybe if I'm elected I could—'

Mrs Pitkin grabbed both her hands in hers. 'You don't need a fancy title to help folk. You've already proved that with me, Lady Swift. But now, there's another what needs your help, title or not.'

Suddenly Eleanor understood: 'Where is she?'

With her chest burning, she ran on, leaving the older woman to shuffle a fair way behind. *Please, please let this be the right choice, Ellie!*

Finally, the gates of St Peter's Church appeared. She stumbled on through the graveyard and into the church itself. In the interior, lit only by a few flickering candles, the smell of wax and incense hit her. There was no sound except her own harsh breathing. She hurried up the long nave and searched behind the altar.

'Nothing!' She dashed back to the other end where, in the corner, four stone steps led up to a wooden door. *That must be it, Ellie!* She shouldered her way through and scrambled up the steep, narrow stairs as they spiralled up the bell tower. Gasping at the top, she jerked to a stop.

'You shouldn't have come.' The woman's voice was low and dispassionate.

'Yes... yes, I should.' Eleanor tried to catch her breath. 'It doesn't have to end like this.'

'What would you know?' Miss Dorothy Mann swayed on the narrow ledge that ran around the tower's edge. As her hand clutched one of the stone angels adorning the spire, her face was sickly white, her eyes drained of colour.

Eleanor peered down the shaft, past the ring of bells, and swallowed at the giddy distance to the flagstone floor below: 'I know you didn't mean to kill Aris. Or Carlton.'

'It... it was a mistake,' Miss Mann whispered. 'They both were.'

Eleanor's voice wavered. 'Please. Come down.'

'What's the point?' Miss Mann spat. Then her voice softened again. 'We can't change our destiny. I tried so hard, I really did. But that woman... I never meant for her... When the policeman told me they were searching for her to arrest her for what I...' She broke into low sobs.

Eleanor tried to keep Miss Mann talking. 'Listen, it was Mrs Pitkin who told me where you were. Who told me you needed help.'

Miss Mann looked round. 'I... I don't believe you. Why should she?'

'Because she recognised another woman who needed help.' As she spoke, Eleanor edged forward.

'Stop!' Eleanor froze. Miss Mann 's voice quivered. 'If only I hadn't been such a fool. It could have worked out with Arnold, but I had to ruin it, didn't I? If only I hadn't thrown away my one chance of happiness. If only I hadn't been so pitifully naïve! He… he said he loved me. And I believed him.'

Eleanor tried to keep her voice calm. 'Ari—, Arnold told you he loved you? But he's a married man!'

'It was before he married, but no, not Arnold… it was Ernest told me he… he loved me. I'd never felt anything but plain, useless and invisible. Arnold was always so busy, he was never very attentive. I believed… oh, it doesn't matter now.'

Eleanor took a step closer to Miss Mann, trying to keep away from the yawning shaft that dropped to the floor, forty feet or more below. 'Yes, it does. Ernest lied to you, didn't he?'

'He told me Arnold didn't really love me and had been bragging about a woman he was carrying on with. One who would be a suitable wife for a politician. I believed him. I… I left Arnold.'

Eleanor took another step. 'But then you realised Ernest was lying to you, didn't you? You realised that he was just a womaniser.'

Miss Mann picked up a loose piece of stone edging and hurled it out over the side. 'Just thinking about him makes my blood boil, and my flesh crawl. He used me and… and…'

Eleanor caught her breath. 'Oh, my goodness, you were…?'

Miss Mann nodded. 'Pregnant, yes. But I knew the baby wasn't Ernest's, it was Arnold's.'

'You must have felt so alone.'

'I dreamed of ending it right there and then. But I couldn't take the life of my baby.' She clung to the stone angel as she sobbed.

Even though she had crept nearer, Eleanor was still too far to reach out and grab her – she had to keep her talking: 'So, you returned to Arnold?'

Miss Mann's voice was a whisper. 'Yes. But he wouldn't have me back. What sane man would? Soiled goods and the shame of being with child out of wedlock.' Miss Mann shook her head. 'He said I'd betrayed him with his friend. But Ernest had never been his friend. He lured me away on purpose just to get at Arnold. Even knowing that, Arnold wouldn't help me, even though it was his child I was carrying. His words that day have eaten me up for sixteen long years.'

Eleanor inched forward. 'So, you stayed here in the town all the time you were with—'

'With child? No, I was sent away by an organisation I contacted that helped women in my... my situation. Whilst I was away, I heard that Arnold had married. And after a suitable period, I was brought back and everyone was told I had had consumption. But I wish it had been consumption. I wish it had taken me then, right after the baby was born, because I wasn't allowed to hold it. I never got to cuddle it or kiss its little face. To stroke its cheeks. And that's what's eaten me up all these years. That's why I wanted Arnold to suffer. If he had only helped me and my... his... child. This election would have been his fourth landslide win. It was rumoured he might have been offered a post in the Cabinet. I... I wanted to deny him that by making him too ill to stand. I didn't mean to kill him, I swear on my life.'

Eleanor wanted to rush up and hug her, but she dared not move any closer. 'It's not your fault. Arnold never told anyone except a few people how severe his allergy was. You weren't to know it would kill him. But Ernest found out about you poisoning Arnold, didn't he?'

Miss Mann nodded slowly: 'Ernest said he'd seen me switching Arnold's fudge for the one I'd made. I thought he'd been too distracted to notice. Then he told me he had evidence I'd killed Arnold. When I went to his house, he showed me a piece of the fudge left over. He said it would show that the other fudge didn't have peanuts in it and someone must have added them just to his piece.'

Eleanor slid her hand along the back of the angel Miss Mann was leaning against. 'And he said he'd tell the police it was you? Did he threaten you?'

'Worse! He said if I didn't become his mistress again, he would go straight to the police and make sure I hanged for Arnold's death. I had no idea what to do. I tried to reason with him, but he flew into a rage. I was terrified. And… and then… he was lying on the floor and I was holding that trophy with his blood dripping off onto the rug beside him. I… I… don't remember doing it, but I must have, mustn't I?'

A shout from below made Miss Mann and Eleanor peer over the ledge. A crowd was forming. More people ran in through the gates, pointing up at the tower. Miss Mann looked down and her grip on the statue loosened.

Now, Ellie! Eleanor took a deep breath and took one more step. She was now only a few inches from Miss Mann. She reached out and gently entwined her fingers with Miss Mann's: 'I can help you, I promise.'

Miss Mann cleared her throat. 'All I've ever dreamed of is a man to love me, for me.' She laughed hysterically. 'And now it's too late.'

The crowd gasped below as the figure on the ledge seemed to lean out and let go… Someone screamed.

At the top of the tower, Eleanor held Miss Mann's hand in a vice-like grip. She might have let an election slip through her fingers, but there was no way in hell she was going to let Miss Mann suffer the same fate.

CHAPTER 34

'Oh, dash it, Mater!' Lancelot stared across the dining table. 'Surely Eleanor is allowed to finish telling how she was so unspeakably clever as to realise who the murderer was? She's not known as Sherlock for nothing!'

It was three days since Eleanor had held onto Miss Mann for dear life as the other woman's weight had threatened to drag them both off the tower. Just when Eleanor thought she could hold on no longer, there had been the sound of hurried footsteps, cursing, and then strong arms had pulled her, and Miss Mann, back inside.

As two police constables wrapped the distraught Miss Mann in blankets and led her out, Eleanor had found herself looking into the concerned eyes of the owner of those strong arms.

She came to and realised Lady Langham was talking. 'And how did that Inspector Seldon know you were up the tower with Miss Mann?'

Lord Langham snorted. 'I imagine someone alerted him to the fact that some woman was about to throw herself off a tower, Augusta!'

Lady Langham rolled her eyes. 'I mean, what was he doing there? I thought he was based in Oxford?'

Eleanor nodded. 'He is, but the organisers of the debate at Chipstone Town Hall were so worried about Mrs Brody's women's group starting a riot, they asked for help from Oxford.'

'And a damned good thing they did too,' Lord Langham said. 'But none of that explains how you worked out Miss Mann was the guilty party. It's been eating me up.'

Lady Langham looked up from her plate: 'No, dear, that will be your gout!'

'Aha!' He pointed at Eleanor. 'Not any more, not with the wonderful Mrs Pitkin now safely ensconced in our kitchen.'

Eleanor turned to Lady Langham: 'And is your magnificent, but slightly precious French chef, Manet, really happy with you taking Mrs Pitkin on as second chef?'

'My dear, he is positively over the moon! It has been nothing but rounds of unintelligible tantrums and huffy fits every time I asked for a lighter menu to save Harold's gout from flaring up. Chef Manet now has free rein for dinner and when we are entertaining, and Mrs Pitkin cooks lunch when we aren't.'

Her husband nodded enthusiastically. 'She's quite the whizz at conjuring up delicious English fare without all that rich whatnot that makes the toes and knees burn like billy-oh.'

Eleanor laughed. 'Well, I'm so pleased it's turned out well for you and Mrs Pitkin. She told Mrs Trotman that she loves it here. At Farrington Manor, she had to make all sorts of continental dishes, whereas what she really excels at is good old-fashioned English cooking.'

Mrs Pitkin had also confided in Eleanor that she was thrilled not to be in charge of the cooking when her employers were entertaining. All seemed well below stairs.

Lancelot yawned. 'Can we stop going on about the food and finally let our guest tell us how she found out how Miss Mann killed Aris and Carlton?'

Lady Langham dabbed her napkin at the corners of her mouth. 'Yes, Eleanor, dear. Do tell! I fear luncheon etiquette must bow to my own avid curiosity as well.'

Eleanor took a deep breath. 'Well, Clifford and I always believed that whoever murdered Aris must have known in advance that Mrs Pitkin would make chocolate and peanut butter fudge, but obviously without the peanuts. So, once I saw the recipe fall out of the Women's League leaflet, everything fell into place. That spiky handwriting was just too distinctive. And I remember the second time Dorothy Mann visited, she mentioned how much she loved baking, so she would have had no trouble making the fudge.'

Lancelot waved his fork. 'But what about Ernest Carlton? How did you link it to her as well?'

'Well, we'd discovered that Carlton had taken the fudge that hadn't been eaten and hidden it in his house. We assumed it was to blackmail Aris' killer. Clifford had also found out whilst we were campaigning in Chipstone that Aris and Carlton had fallen out over a woman. And if Aris' killer was at the table the night he died, and was a woman, there were only two choices: Miss Mann or Lady Farrington. Lady Farrington was also the only person at the table who would have known that Mrs Pitkin was going to make fudge.'

Lancelot whistled. Lady Langham looked shocked. 'Lancelot, you can't be imagining that Lady Farrington would have been a suspect of Eleanor's!'

Eleanor cleared her throat: 'Of course not.' *Fibber, Ellie!* 'Anyway, Lady Farrington confirmed that Miss Mann had called two days before the dinner about some hall the Farringtons own that she wanted to hire for a Women's League event. Lady Farrington is fairly certain now that Mrs Pitkin had given her the menu for the dinner earlier that day and it was on the coffee table, where Miss Mann could have seen it.'

'So, what's going to happen to her?' Lancelot said.

'Well, her legal help has put in pleas of manslaughter for Aris and self-defence for Carlton. The poor woman is clearly not of sound mind.'

Lady Langham gestured to the footman to serve dessert. 'But, my dear girl, how on earth did she ever find a barrister of criminal law in her position?'

Eleanor smiled. 'I was delighted to be able to recommend Mr Vernon Peel. Clifford checked back through his cases and made some, erm, discreet enquiries with a contact at Lincoln's Inn and Mr Peel came out with glowing colours. He really was overshadowed by Aris for all those years.'

Lancelot leaned his elbows on the table. 'But how on earth will Miss Mann afford his fees?'

'Lancelot!' Lady Langham tutted. 'Decorum does not allow discussion of a woman's financial situation.'

Eleanor nodded in agreement, relieved not to be pressed on the matter. In fact, Lady Farrington had rung her the day after Miss Mann had been arrested and said she would pay for legal representation, so long as Eleanor told no one. She confessed that when Miss Mann was at Farrington Manor one day drumming up support for the Women's League, they found out there was one thing they shared in common: Ernest Carlton. Lady Farrington had also been seduced by the womaniser, which is why, when she'd seen Miss Mann switch Aris' fudge, she'd covered for her by getting the servants to lie and throw suspicion onto the cook.

She'd feared if Miss Mann appeared in court, Carlton would have to take the stand. And if that happened, her affair might come to light and her marriage would be over. As she said to Eleanor, 'If it comes to it, I can survive losing part of the estate, but I cannot survive losing my husband.' Lady Farrington had even asked what she could do for Mrs Pitkin, which had surprised Eleanor. It seemed she wasn't quite the ice queen she'd imagined.

She became aware that the table was waiting for her to answer: 'Sorry?'

'I said,' Lancelot spoke slowly as if she was a child, 'how did Miss Mann even know that they were having the pudding thing and make one to switch? It can't have been luck.'

'No, although it is a Farrington tradition on special occasions, I've been told. We found out afterwards that Miss Mann had caught sight of the menu for the fundraising dinner whilst visiting Lady Farrington to confirm the details for the hire of the hall. In fact, she confessed that was what gave her the idea.'

Lord Langham snorted into his wine glass. 'Lady Farrington and the Women's League! That's not a pairing of bedfellows I had ever envisaged.'

Lady Langham glared at him: 'Harold, dear, really!'

'He's right, actually,' Eleanor replied. 'Mr Aris suggested it, and Lady Farrington went along with it purely as a favour to him.'

'I think we need a special toast for our intrepid sleuth,' Harold said.

Lancelot jumped up and raised his glass aloft: 'To the most deliciously peculiar female Sherlock Holmes this side of the Cotswolds!'

'Lancelot!'

On the way back to Henley Hall, Eleanor fiddled about with her emerald green silk dress to keep a lid on her emotions. The last few days had taken their toll on her.

Clifford pressed the button on the glovebox in front of her. It opened to reveal a very welcome brandy miniature and a glass. She took a grateful sip and felt her shoulders relax.

'I really am appalling at this stiff upper lip thing, Clifford.'

'Thank goodness for that, my lady! And at the risk of prompting the need for another drink before we reach our destination, may I confide something to you?'

'Gracious! Erm... yes, of course.'

'It concerns Miss Mann.'

'Oh dear, Clifford! I'm not sure I'm recovered enough to take any more drama, but go on.' She leaned back in her seat and closed her eyes.

He cleared his throat. 'When Miss Mann became pregnant, she was helped by a women's association that sent her away to another town during her confinement. After the baby was born, it was adopted by a kindly couple who raised it as their own. For many reasons, the association doesn't let the mother know any details about the adoption.'

Eleanor opened her eyes and nodded. 'I understand why they do it, but it's hard on the mother.'

Clifford nodded. 'True. Unfortunately, in this case, after the war the husband was in ill health and the couple couldn't afford to keep the children, their own or the adopted child. They found places in service in a large country house for the two sisters, but no one would take the adopted child.'

Eleanor sat upright. 'What happened to it?'

'In the end, the desperate couple contacted the original women's organisation where it had come from. The organisation's director knew your uncle and—'

'Clifford! You're not telling me—'

'Yes, my lady. I believe Polly is Miss Mann's child.'

Eleanor was flabbergasted. 'Did my uncle know whose child it was?'

'He may have guessed, my lady, but being a gentleman, he never pursued the matter.'

She rubbed her eyes. 'Gosh, well, I think we all agree that it is best Polly doesn't learn about this. Her mother will likely end up in prison or an institution, and if her father…' She shuddered. 'Polly is part of our family now and always will be. One day she may need to be told, but that's not today.' She shook her head. 'Gracious, that does require another drink, but it will have to wait until we get back to the Hall. There's something I need to do in Little Buckford first.'

As the shop bell dinged, the small throng of ladies at the counter turned towards the door. On seeing Eleanor, all conversation stopped.

She smiled at them: 'Good morning.'

'Good morning, Lady Swift,' they chorused.

One of the ladies stepped forward. It was Mrs Luscombe, owner of the linens and haberdashery shop in Chipstone, where she'd tried to buy a matching shawl for her scarf.

'Forgive me, Lady Swift, but I, we, just want to say well done for saving that young woman's life.'

Eleanor held up her hands. 'Thank you, but any of you would have done the same.'

Mrs Luscombe nodded. 'Maybe, but it was you who did.' She glanced behind her. 'I hope the other ladies don't mind me being their unofficial spokeswoman, but I'd be proud to have you as our Member of Parliament.'

A wave of consent ran around the shop. Eleanor smiled, but shook her head.

'That is very kind of you to say, but as you know because I was otherwise occupied and missed the last debate, I was barred from standing.'

'Will you stand again in the next election?' a voice at the back asked.

Eleanor sighed. 'I'm really not sure, hopefully that will be quite a few years away. Let's hope no more MPs drop dead in suspicious circumstances.' She glanced at Mr Brenchley. 'However, I've learned you don't need a fancy title or the backing of an organisation to help someone in need.' She looked down at the rolled-up paper. 'And I hope you won't be disappointed, but I'm not going to be making any more speeches.' She approached the counter: 'Mr Brenchley, I wonder if you would mind furthering your already superb services to our wonderful community by displaying this poster? If you approve, of course.'

The shop fell silent. Brenchley coughed nervously and unrolled the poster. As he read it to himself, his face split into a wide smile: 'I'd be happy, no, honoured, to display this, Lady Swift.'

'Excellent! I've got more here for Chipstone, I'm hoping I can persuade some shopkeepers in the town to display them.'

Brenchley held his hand out. 'Then why don't you leave them with me and I'll pass them around tonight at the Chipstone and District shopkeepers' meeting? I'll make sure everyone takes one.'

'Really? That would be frightfully kind of you.'

As she passed Mrs Luscombe on her way out, the woman called out to her: 'If you're in Chipstone next week, Lady Swift, do call by and pick up the shawl to go with that lovely scarf you're wearing. It will be waiting.'

Eleanor thanked her and made her escape. Standing outside the shop, she could hear Brenchley inside, reading out the poster to the curious ladies crowded around the counter:

'Do you or anyone in your family need to see a doctor? Are you having difficulty in affording the doctor's fee? If so, Lady Swift of Henley Hall will pay the seven shillings for each and every appointment. If you are also struggling to pay for the medicines prescribed, Lady Swift will pay the cost of these until the treatment has run its course. Please call in person at Henley Hall or telephone Little Buckford 342 and…'

Back at the Hall, Eleanor was recounting the drama up the tower yet again to an eager audience: 'Yes, it was so lucky Mrs Pitkin was hiding out in the very church where Miss Mann tried to…' She blanched at finishing the sentence.

Mrs Butters patted her arm. 'Don't you think about that, my lady, it's all over now.'

Eleanor nodded. 'I'm still in the dark as to how Mrs Pitkin found out the police were going to arrest her. DCI Seldon was furious that someone leaked the news. However, it meant that she was there and saw Miss Mann climb the tower. She tried to find someone, but everyone was in the Town Hall for the debate, so in the end she went there and literally bumped into me.'

'It was so selfless of Mrs Pitkin to come out of hiding to make sure help arrived in time,' Mrs Butters said.

Mrs Trotman wiped her flour-covered hands on her apron. 'She's a good sort, for certain, my lady. I can never repay you for all that you've done for her.'

'Gracious!' Eleanor blushed. 'I only wish I could have done more sooner.'

Mrs Butters smiled at her: 'One thing I've learned, my lady, is one person's need is another person's good deed.'

Eleanor thought back to the last few days and how Mrs Pitkin had risked being arrested to help Miss Mann. How Lady Farrington had agreed to secretly pay for Miss Mann's legal costs. Not just because she feared her affair with Carlton being exposed, but also because she felt compassion for her, having been tricked by the same man. How Mrs Aris, on learning of Miss Mann's story, had told DCI Seldon that she was dropping all charges of manslaughter against her. *And how you, Ellie, played your own small role in all of this.*

Mrs Butters caught her eye and patted her arm again: 'Your parents would have been proud, my lady.'

The lump in Eleanor's throat stopped her replying. She simply smiled back and wondered yet again how her staff always seemed to know what she was thinking.

The kitchen door opened, and Clifford appeared, bearing five flutes and a bottle of champagne. He placed it on the table and half-bowed to Eleanor.

'I believe, my lady, you never had that second drink?'

As he uncorked the champagne, Eleanor looked around the kitchen: 'Where's Polly, Mrs Butters?'

The young girl appeared, red-faced and out of breath, from round the range. 'Sorry, your ladyship, I was just trying to wrestle your favourite slippers off Master Gladstone again. He won't give them up.'

Eleanor laughed as the bulldog appeared behind her, her slipper firmly in his jaws: 'I think, Polly, they're Gladstone's slippers now.'

Clifford waited until Mrs Butters had filled Polly's glass with elderflower cordial and then cleared his throat: 'If you will allow me to propose a toast, my lady?'

She nodded and everyone raised their glasses.

'To the best Member of Parliament Little Buckford never had!'

A LETTER FROM VERITY BRIGHT

Thanks so much for choosing to read *A Witness to Murder*. I hope you enjoyed reading it as much as I did writing it. If you'd like to follow more of Ellie and Clifford's adventures – and maybe find out if Ellie and Lancelot's romance blossoms – then just sign up at the following link. As a thank you, you'll receive the first chapters of Ellie's brand-new adventure and be the first to know when the next book in the Lady Swift series will be available. Your email address will never be shared and you can unsubscribe at any time:

www.bookouture.com/verity-bright

And I'd be very grateful if you could write a review. Reviews help others discover and enjoy the Lady Swift mysteries, as well as providing me with helpful feedback so the next book is even better.

Thank you,
Verity Bright

🐦 @BrightVerity
📘 veritybrightauthor
🖥 veritybright.com

ACKNOWLEDGEMENTS

Thanks to our indefatigable Maisie for her ever-insightful editing and Lauren and her team for their eagle-eyed proofreading (and much more). Thanks also to the rest of the Bookouture Team for their part in keeping Ellie and Clifford in cognac and confit and Master Gladstone in sausages and slippers.

Mrs Pitkin's Double-Layered Chocolate Fudge

If you liked the sound of Mrs Pitkin's chocolate fudge, we hope you'll make your own! Her recipe is based on an Edwardian one. Send us a picture on social media if you make it.

If you want to make your fudge look fancy, put your decorations on the top layer once it has cooled a little, but before it has set. You could use crystallised angelica or ginger or piped icing.

Ingredients
379g tin of sweetened condensed milk
25g unsalted butter and extra for greasing
175g dark cooking chocolate, broken into squares
175g peanut butter – smooth or crunchy**

**If, like poor Mr Aris, you suffer from a peanut allergy, you can substitute a nut butter (as peanuts are a legume, not actually a nut), or try Nutella.

Method
1) Line a shallow baking tray with greaseproof paper and grease thoroughly with butter.
2) Mix the half the condensed milk and butter together – use a double boiler or place a bowl on top of a pan of boiling water – until the butter has melted. Add the chocolate and stir until melted. Pour into the baking tray, allow to cool and place in the fridge until the mixture sets, usually an hour or two

3) Mix the rest of condensed milk with the peanut butter as you did for the condensed milk and chocolate in Step 2. Stir continuously until the peanut butter has melted and mixed with the condensed milk. Remove the baking tray from the fridge and pour the peanut butter mixture on top of the first layer. Allow to cool, then place back in the fridge until set hard, usually another hour or two

4) Remove the fudge from the fridge, slice into pieces. Will keep for a day or two in the fridge, but best enjoyed fresh!

Made in the USA
Middletown, DE
24 February 2021

34370406R00158